THE NICE GUY

ABI SABINA

DEDICATION

♥ ♥ ♥

Nice guys don't always finish last. This one is for the good guys in our lives that make us believe in love.

1

♥ ♥ ♥

IVAN

I CHECK THE TIME on my watch and run a hand down my face. The line at the coffee shop is longer than usual, and I'm about to leave before I'm late to my appointment. As much as I need some coffee, I can't risk being late to work.

I look behind me, and my eyes catch on the woman standing there with round, green eyes. She's unfamiliar, which is rare in my small town. Nothing is a secret in Sunshine Falls—not even a new person, so I wonder how I haven't heard of her before.

Her long auburn hair falls in waves around her heart-shaped face, and she has an air about her that seems misplaced here. My eyes catch on the light freckles across the bridge of her nose before taking in her professional attire.

"Do I have something on my face?" Her brows lift when I don't stop staring at her.

"What? No. Of course not." I turn around, facing the front of the line and cursing myself for gawking at her. I couldn't help it, though. She's beautiful.

It's not every day that I see a woman like her.

I feel a tap on my shoulder and look back at her.

1

"I was kidding." She smiles, and dimples pop up on her cheeks. My weakness.

"Oh, good." I nod, smiling back.

"And if I did have something on my face, I'd appreciate the head's up. There's nothing worse than walking around with food smeared on you." She scrunches up her nose.

"I agree." I chuckle. "If I ever see you with something like that, I'll make sure to tell you." I wink before looking back at the line.

Old Joe has been at the front for five minutes, ordering the entire coffee shop. I should have known hitting snooze would put me behind him in line on Lion's Club meeting day.

I step out of line and look at the beautiful stranger. "You can have my spot."

If I stay here, I won't make it to see my client on time, and an animal's well-being is more important than coffee. I can always grab a cup at work after my appointment.

"You're leaving?" She tilts her head.

"Yup. Duty calls. It was nice to meet you."

"You, too."

I glance at her once more before walking out of the coffee shop and racing to my car to drive to the ranch where I have to check on my client's horse.

Being a vet has always been my dream job, and becoming a partner at Healing Hands six months ago maximized that dream. Now I don't only work the job I want, I have the role I've worked hard for.

Driving out of town, I think back to the auburn beauty. I wonder where she's from. Based on her dress pants and silky top, she's probably here for work or something.

Unfortunately, women like her aren't abundant in town, making the dating scene very difficult. It doesn't help when you're not exactly a flirt who easily approaches women.

I pull into the ranch and drive down the long dirt road. Vast land lies before me with a house to the right and a large barn behind it with another smaller one next to it. I park near the smaller barn, and Roger, the rancher, walks out of it to meet up with me. A smile lifts my lips as I grab my bag and get out of my vehicle.

"Ivan, mi amigo," Roger says.

"Hey, what's going on?" I shake his hand. He's one of my favorite clients. Coming out here always gives me a sense of peace.

"It's Buddy." I recognize the name as one of his horses. "He's had some yellow discharge from his nose and his breathing is labored. I thought it was a cold, but I'm starting to sense it's something more." We walk into the barn, and Buddy is peeking out of a stall, looking nothing like his usual self. His eyes are downcast, and I spot the yellow discharge Roger mentioned right away.

"Hey, Buddy." I smile at the horse, opening the stall door.

My movements are tentative and soft so he doesn't get spooked. Reaching out, I run a hand down the side of his face.

"I hear you're not doing too great," I tell the horse. "I'm going to help you feel better, all right?"

I begin assessing him, running my hands carefully down his neck before I examine the area by pressing down a bit more. Buddy flinches and flares his nostrils when I touch a gland too firmly.

"Whoa, sorry about that." I pat him softly.

"What's going on?" Roger asks from the outside of the stall.

"He's got a sensitive gland." I continue examining Buddy, checking his eyes, listening to his heartbeat with my stethoscope, and gently touching the area around the inflamed gland.

"I'm going to need your help to do a nasal swab," I tell Roger. "Hold the bridle in case he moves."

Buddy acts like a champ as I swab his nose, but then he sneezes all over me afterward. I wipe my face with my shirt as Roger guffaws. Regardless, I praise him with a carrot. Whoever said my job didn't have some hazards? It could be worse than horse snot stains.

"Good boy." I pet his back before we step out of the stall.

I look at Roger after packing my equipment.

"I'm pretty sure it's equine influenza, but I'll have confirmation for you as soon as I get the results from the swab. I'll have to examine your other horses to make sure none of them have it since it's contagious. Keep Buddy isolated for two weeks, but he'll need complete rest for six weeks to avoid long-term consequences. Keep him somewhere that's well-ventilated and free of dust. Make sure he eats and has plenty of water."

"Just what I need." Roger sighs. "He's my best horse."

"I know, but he'll be back to new soon. We don't want to risk complications." I clap his shoulder.

"Thanks, Ivan."

"You're welcome." I smile sympathetically. "I'm going to check the others quickly, and I'll be out of your hair."

"You're always welcome here. I'm lucky to have you on my team. I can't think of anyone better."

"Thanks." I smile. It's always nice to hear clients say that my role matters. I live for helping animals and easing their owner's worries.

After I check the rest of the horses, who seem to be symptom-free, I get ready to leave.

"Call me if Buddy worsens or any other horses show signs of infection, and I'll immediately come over. If Buddy's fever goes above one-hundred-and-four, I'll administer non-steroidal anti-inflammatory medication. For now, give him lots of fluids and keep him isolated." I shake his hand.

"You're a good man, Ivan." Roger nods.

"Just doing my job." I get in my car and head to the clinic with a feeling of accomplishment.

I love the work I do, and every time I finish with a patient, this sense of fulfillment consumes me. I'm doing exactly what I was meant to.

When I arrive, James is by the receptionist area. He looks up and smiles. James has been my mentor for years. Instead of going away for college, I stayed local so I could work for him and learn everything about the business and veterinarian field. Getting hired after college was a given in my mind, which would've been really awkward if he hadn't given me the vet position.

"Ivan, I'm glad you're here. We need to talk." His voice booms with joy, so that must mean it's a positive conversation.

He walks out from behind the reception counter and meets me at the opening that leads down the hall to our offices.

"How was Buddy?" he asks as we walk to his office.

"I have a nasal swab to test, but I'm pretty sure he's got equine influenza."

He looks me up and down. "Ah. Horse snot. That's not good for a rancher."

"Nope, but the other horses seemed clear."

"Great." He claps my back. "Anyway, I want to talk to you about some changes."

"Changes?" I inch my head and turn to look at him.

"Don't look at me like that." He laughs. "It's all for the best."

I open my mouth to speak, but my words are cut off when the woman from the coffee shop walks out of James's office and halts, staring at me with furrowed brows.

"You." I point at her and look at James. "What's going on?"

"Ivan, meet my niece, Madison."

"Niece?" I choke on the word.

Just my luck that I see a beautiful woman and she ends up being his niece.

"Yes." He chuckles.

Madison seems to be frozen in place, too, until she snaps out of it and steps forward, reaching her hand out.

"It's nice to officially meet you, Ivan."

"Yeah, nice to meet you, too." I shake her hand and glance at James.

"Did you already know each other?" James looks between us.

"We spoke briefly at the coffee shop this morning," Madison explains.

"Well, great. Let's go into my office and talk." He opens the door for us to enter, and I wonder what his niece has to do with this meeting.

Madison smiles tightly, likely aware of what James will say. This can't be good. When I saw her at the coffee shop, I was hoping for a different interaction with her, maybe one where I could ask her out.

We sit in James's office. Madison is on the edge of the chair, her knee bouncing. My eyes move to James, who's sitting back in his seat with a grin.

"You two look like quite the pair." James extends his hands toward us and nods in approval. I furrow my eyebrows, glancing at Madison.

"Uncles James," she says through clenched teeth.

"What? Let me look at the newest partners for Healing Hands together." His fingers create a rectangle as if he were framing us.

"Partners?" I croak. "I don't understand."

"I'm retiring." He slaps his desk and smiles as if he just told me that the Dallas Cowboys scored a touchdown.

"Excuse me?" I lean forward, staring at him. I must've misunderstood him because James told me he still had a few years before he thought about retirement despite being in the age range.

"Susan has been on my case about it. She wants to travel. When Madison called me to ask if I had a job opening, I knew it was the perfect moment to step away and hand over the reins." He smiles at his niece with adoration. "Take my advice, Ivan, happy wife, happy life." He laughs boastfully.

I admire James and enjoy his quirky sense of humor. I do not, however, enjoy this surprise announcement he's sprung on me. Although, being managing partner, James can choose someone to replace his job without consulting me.

"How have I never heard of Madison before?" I lift my brows.

"I've spoken to you about her." He nods, sure about this, but I'd remember if he ever mentioned another potential partner.

"I'm from Dallas," Madison says. "I am a veterinarian and have worked for a clinic in Dallas since I graduated. I have years of experience and understand how the business works."

"Madison is an excellent vet, and I think you two will be great together." James nods proudly. "I've wanted her to come work here for years, but Madison is stubborn."

"Uncle James," she says tightly.

"It's the truth, sweetheart, but you're here now, and I couldn't be happier. I know she'll run it the same as I have all these years." He looks at me. "I'll help merge this partnership, but I'm confident you won't need me."

I look from James to Madison with a tight smile. Thoughts race through my mind. I don't like change, and this is a huge one. If I hadn't secured my partnership, I'd be afraid of losing my job.

"Why don't you two get to know each other better and talk about your roles in the clinic?" He smiles at us.

"I thought you said we'd run it the same way we always have." I lift a brow.

"Absolutely, but it's always important to incorporate your own ideas. Soon, I'll be off to a sandy beach for two weeks, and you'll be here working together." He chuckles, but I'm struggling to find the humor in this.

The woman I thought was attractive is now my new partner at work.

You still think she's attractive.

I'm not about to date a woman I work with and jeopardize my career. I've worked too hard to get here and refuse for my hard-earned college degree to get flushed down the drain because I can't control myself around a beautiful woman.

"Why don't you give me a run-down of our clients?" Madison looks at me.

"Sure. I need to run the tests on the nasal swab to get back to Roger. You can help me with that." I look at Madison, standing from my seat. "Then, we can talk in my office."

"You go on about your day as if I weren't here." He leans back, looking way too happy about his impending retirement.

"Come on." I nod toward the door.

We walk out in silence, tension rolling between us in the short walk to my office. I'm unsure about the ideas Madison has, but Healing Hands isn't the type of clinic you find in a big city. The state of my shirt is proof of that.

I yank it over my head, grateful I have a spare in my office. Madison trips, and I reach out to grab her.

"Are you okay?"

"Uh-huh." She looks down at the floor, taking a deep breath.

2

♥ ♥ ♥

MADISON

STARING AROUND MY NEW office, I think of ways to make it feel more personal. Adding in some pictures or cute desk decor would make it feel cozier. I wonder if Ivan would approve. When I saw him at the coffee shop, I didn't think he'd be so serious.

Our first meeting didn't go as smoothly as I hoped. Before meeting Ivan, Uncle James had assured me he'd be okay with the transition, but the look on his face wasn't convincing.

It also doesn't help that we unofficially met at the coffee shop, and I thought he was cute. Okay, more than cute—hot. And seeing him shirtless earlier when he changed shirts was enough to solidify that fact. Almost tripping was embarrassing enough. I didn't want to have to admit I was distracted by his defined chest on top of that. But that doesn't matter. Ivan is a co-worker, and I have strict personal rules about dating someone I work with.

It's a new rule.

From personal experience.

Not that I'm looking to date anyone. My heart's taken all the beatings it can bear. I shouldn't have even flirted with Ivan at the coffee shop. I need to start getting settled in my new job, not make waves in the small-town dating scene after my failed relationship.

Calling what I did *flirting* is pushing it. We spoke for a total of one minute before he left. Now, I know he ran off because he had a client to see, and I admire anyone who puts his responsibility and loyalty to work above coffee.

I just hope we can work well together. Doubts swirl in my mind after seeing his reaction to Uncle James's news, but I'll convince him I'm apt to take Uncle James's place. My uncle's practically been training me since I decided to become a vet. I followed in his footsteps but wasn't ready to leave the city until now. Dallas is my home and where I built my life, but it was time for a change.

Moving to small-town Texas was the best option. Sunshine Falls is my fresh start away from the drama I left behind. And I have no desire to create any drama here.

My chest rises with a deep breath, and I forget about heartbreaking men and traitorous women. Standing, I stretch my arms over my head and a wide yawn takes over. It's time for a break from going over the files Ivan lent me so I can become familiar with our patients and their individual cases.

I walk out of the office and toward the staffroom in search of coffee before my eyes droop closed, and Ivan walks in to see me napping on my first day. That's not the impression I want to make.

When I walk into the staffroom, Ivan is laughing with a young woman who is waving him off. They both look toward me and their expressions drop, reeling in their laughter.

"Hi." I smile at them, breaking the tension that's filled the room. They should feel comfortable having me around.

Ivan and I are equals. If employees can laugh with him, then they can certainly laugh with me as well.

"Hello," the young woman says.

"Madison, this is Kate. Kate, Madison is James's niece. We'll do a formal introduction after lunch today." Ivan's eyes are on me, so I nod.

"It's nice to meet you," I tell the woman.

"Likewise. I was just...getting coffee." She holds up her mug. "I'll be right back to work."

"If this is your break time, please take it." I assure her with a nod. "I need some coffee myself."

Kate nods and takes a sip of her coffee, the silence in the room deafening. To keep myself busy instead of standing awkwardly in the middle of the room, I grab a mug I from the cupboard Uncle James showed me this morning and place a pod in the coffee maker. While I wait for it to brew, I wrack my brain for something to say, but they both dropped their conversation so fast, that it feels awkward even speaking.

Instead, my eyes scan the room, and a cork board catches my attention. It has some messages for the week, schedules, and a joke section. I read it to myself.

Where did the flock of sheep go on vacation? On a cruise sheep.

Chuckling, I shake my head and look at Ivan and Kate.

"That's funny." I point to the paper. "Is there a schedule to take turns adding a joke?"

Kate opens her mouth, but Ivan cuts her off.

"No, it's anonymous."

I tilt my head and stare at him. "You're telling me that in this small clinic you have no idea who places the jokes here?"

"It's crazy, right? Whoever it is seems to be a real ninja." He shrugs, sliding a hand into his pockets.

Kate bites her lips as she looks between us. I have a feeling they know exactly who tells the jokes and are keeping it a secret. But why?

"Okay." I'll figure it out. "Hat's off to the author." I grab the creamer from the fridge and add a splash into my mug before placing it back in the cold.

"Well, I'm going to go back to work," Kate announces.

She leaves Ivan and me alone, and I get ready to speak but then he asks, "How are the reports looking?"

"Good, good."

"Okay."

I step forward and pause, looking at him while I take a deep breath.

"I know we got started on an awkward foot, but I hope we can set that aside in order to continue running the clinic the way it has."

"Of course. My priority is keeping Healing Hands as successful as it's been up to now, following James's footsteps." Despite his words, there's a hint in his eyes that makes him seem weary about this situation. So much for the handsome and nice guy I saw at the coffee shop.

"I agree."

"Well, I've got an appointment now."

"Right." I'm half-tempted to ask him if I can assist but hold back. Uncle James will take me in his appointments once he returns from a house call, which is something I am not used to.

Hopefully he returns soon so I can get some hands-on work.

♥ ♥ ♥

Be careful what you wish for.

After going into two appointments with Uncle James and hearing his clients question my role, abilities to treat their pets, and sense their hesitation, I wish I were back in Dallas, working at Pet Care with my clients. They believed in me.

You wouldn't be happy there anymore.

"Don't worry, Maddy. This is a small town, and people are accustomed to me, but soon they'll get to know and love you just the same." Uncle James places his hand on my shoulder and squeezes gently.

"I'm not sure if this was the best idea." I shake my head, frowning.

"Nonsense. Give yourself time to adjust, and give our clients time to get to know you. I can't think of anyone better than you to replace me." His eyes are intent on mine. "Besides, you did right leaving that place." His jaw clenches. "That man is a..." He holds back from what I'm sure would be a colorful word choice.

"I know." I place my hand on his arm.

"Why don't I introduce you to the next client and let you handle this appointment?" His smile is hopeful.

"If they're okay with it, then sure." Considering my track record, I might be oh-for-three.

"Great, let's go." He leads us toward an examination room and opens the door with a wide smile.

THE NICE GUY

A man with a...parrot...is sitting on a chair. I've treated birds before, but a parrot here is a surprise.

"Greg, hello," James says boastfully. "This is my niece, Madison." He introduces us, and I shake Greg's hand.

"Hello," I say.

"She'll be working with us, and I thought it'd be great to have her treat Cookie here." Uncle James reaches out and pets Cookie's head.

"Wonderful." Greg smiles, and I feel like my luck is changing.

"Hi, Cookie." I smile at the bird. "I'm excited to help you today."

"No, Cookie. No," the bird yells, and I hop back in surprise.

"It's okay." My words are soothing.

"He gets a bit nervous when he sees the white coat," Greg comments.

I look at Uncle James, who nods encouragingly.

"Tell me what I can do for you today." I look at Greg.

"We just need a nail clipping." His use of *we* is a bit strange, but I nod.

I grab a small towel and slip on a pair of gloves, then wrap Cookie in the towel, keeping her head exposed.

"Crazy bird. Poop. Hello." Cookie goes crazy spewing random words. Ignoring her as much as I can so I remain calm, I open the towel by her feet and place my finger so she can rest her claw around it.

Holding the clippers with my right hand, I lift her nail and cut off the tip. Cookie goes crazy and lets out a curse word that makes me choke-cough. My guard is down, and the bird bends and nips my finger before flying off.

"No!" The word flies out of my mouth louder than intended, eyes wide. Greg tries to grab the bird, flapping

15

his arms around, which only makes Cookie more nervous.

I look at Uncle James with a frown and shake my head. This was supposed to be a routine procedure. It's not my first time clipping nails.

I remove my white coat in hopes that will help Cookie come to me without fear. She must've had some terrible experiences with vets before. Remaining still, my gaze follows Cookie while I mentally talk to her as if that would make her trust me.

Then, Cookie makes the loudest fart noise, and we all freeze. Greg's eyes widen in shock. Uncle James lets out a boisterous laugh, holding his stomach.

Cookie laughs as well and settles on Uncle James's shoulder as if he were a pirate.

"Hold her," I whisper, and he does so, keeping her wings down.

I step closely, petting her down her chest, and then I let her wrap her nails around my finger again. Uncle James talks to Cookie in a soothing voice, and I accomplish the nail clipping.

By the time we're finished, sweat is dripping down my back as if I were standing out in the Texas sun. Greg thanks us and apologizes for Cookie's odd behavior. I have a feeling this is her regular behavior because as he walks out of the examination room, she's yelling, "Bad girl. Hide the body! Don't talk." I really hope that she got that from a TV show and not Greg.

My back slumps against the wall once they leave, and I rub my face.

"I feel like I failed." I shake my head and glance up at Uncle James.

The entire clinic must've heard that parrot and imagined how terrible the appointment was going.

"You didn't. You're a new face, and Cookie wasn't familiar with you. Besides, I'm pretty sure Greg spoils her, and then we deal with the consequences.

I stare at him and push off the wall, squaring my shoulders and putting my white coat back on. I'm trained for this. I'm better than the woman who feels sorry for herself. My ex-boyfriend really did a number on my self-esteem, but it's time I take my life back in my own hands, and that begins with believing in myself again.

"Let's have lunch." He gives me a side hug.

3

♥ ♥ ♥

IVAN

"Mom." I sigh into the phone, trying to get her to stop talking as I park my car in my apartment complex.

"She's single from what I hear. And she sounds beautiful. Is her red hair natural?" She's going on and on about Madison, and it's driving me crazy.

My mistake was answering her phone call on the way out of work. I should've known the rumors had already spread, and my mom would be on top of it,. She and my aunt own the Cuban bakery in town that always lures in the gossips.

I love her, but the way Cuban mothers insert themselves into their kids' lives is unmatchable.

"I'll finally be able to plan a wedding."

"Whoa, whoa, whoa. What are you talking about?" My voice booms as I step out of the car and walk to my apartment.

"Ivan, mijo, don't yell." Says the woman who's permanent volume is always at one-hundred.

"Mami." I try to hide my exasperation and speak as calmly as possible. "There will be no wedding. Madison is my new co-worker. That's it." My speech is slow in hopes that it gets through her stubborn brain.

"Bueno, you never know." She inserts her Spanglish at all times.

"We just met today. Where did you get the idea that we'd even be together?"

"Mary saw you at the coffee shop laughing together," she says as if it were obvious.

I could kill Mary. I take a deep breath and unlock my apartment door.

"Being nice isn't a marriage proposal."

I hook my keys on the hanger by the door and pet Charlie's head when he greets me. Then, I go straight to my room. I'm glad my cousin isn't home yet. No one else needs to bear witness to this conversation. Although, Luna and I both tend to stay under our family's radar. However, being the oldest puts the spotlight on our relationship status. As in, our moms don't understand why we still haven't made them grandmothers.

Luna is like a sister. We're only a few hours apart, so we have different birthdays, but we practically grew up like twins from different mothers.

"Ivan, if you want to give me grandchildren someday, you better start thinking about finding a nice woman. When I was your age, I already had you and your sister."

Here we go with the same speech. What she fails to add is that my dad and her were sweethearts from a young age. When her family moved to the US, he found a way to leave Cuba, parting with his family, so they could be together.

"You know, my sister is already at the age you were when you had me. How about you bother her about this?"

"Bother?" she asks incredulously.

"That's not what I meant." I close my eyes, knowing I messed up with my word choice.

"I only want what's best for you."

"I know, Mom. I just have a lot on my mind." I'm still processing Madison's new role at the clinic, and my mom is trying to marry me off to her.

"Okay. We'll talk later then. If you want to, come over for dinner; I'd love if you did."

"Thanks, but I'll go this weekend. I'm going to work out and then go to bed early."

I hang up the call and change into shorts and a T-shirt before grabbing Charlie's leash. He perks up as soon as he sees me holding it, and his butt shakes in excitement. I chuckle and rub the top of his head before linking the hook to his collar.

"Let's go for a walk, buddy."

I fill my lungs with air once I step outside. My mind's been a mess all day, and I need to sort out my thoughts now that I'm out of the clinic.

A part of me was hopeful that when the time came for James to retire, I'd buy out his part of the clinic and become the sole owner. Little did I know he had a secret family member hiding in the shadows.

It's nothing against Madison personally, but my career is sacred, and anything that can rattle the years of sacrifice I've put into my work feels like a threat. Even if she's a beautiful redhead with dimples.

I pause when Charlie starts sniffing the grass and let him go about his business, cleaning up after him. It's the small joys of being a pet owner. After picking up dog poop with a bag, I'm ready to change diapers.

No. Those are two very different things. Fatherhood and pet ownership don't go together like guacamole and tortilla chips. Besides, he's technically Luna's dog.

I shake my head to release the random thoughts and focus on walking Charlie a bit more before heading back into my apartment.

Once Charlie has fresh water, I go into my room and start my workout routine. Hopefully, Luna will want to go for a run when she gets home.

With my mat rolled out, I start doing push-ups. My arms burn with each movement. After my set, I move on to squats, holding the hand weight. Each breath helps me forget about my job situation and focus solely on the way my body moves and flexes. The burning sensation in my muscles is welcomed. Sweat trickles down my face as my feet hit the floor each time I do a burpee. This is what I needed to release my stress.

A message comes in from my best friend, but I ignore it for now.

"Rough day?"

I startle and look up to see Luna standing by my bedroom door.

"You scared me." My focus was on my movements I didn't hear the door open.

"Sorry." She laughs.

"It's okay. I was waiting for you to get home. Want to go for a run?"

"Only if you tell me if the reason you're overworking your body has to do with James's niece." She smiles widely.

"Not you, too." I sigh, shaking my head and then look at her. "Yes, it does. I was caught by surprise, and you know how much I hate that."

21

"Yup." She pops the P and crosses her arms. "You need to loosen up, Iv. Let me get changed and take Charlie out, and then we'll go for a run."

"Sounds good." I finish up my set of burpees while she gets ready.

I'm ready to go when Luna returns with Charlie, and soon we're stretching outside before starting off in a jog around our neighborhood.

"Tell me your worries," Luna says in a teasing tone after a few quiet minutes.

"It's what you already know. James's niece, Madison, will become my new partner when he retires."

"That's not so bad." She glances at me as her ponytail sways from side to side.

"She couldn't clip Greg's parrot's nails properly. The bird went crazy." The entire clinic heard what was going on in that exam room when Madison was in there.

"Cut her some slack. It was her first day, and parrots are not the easiest animals to deal with." Luna scrunches up her face. "Remember that time I tried to catch one to have as a pet and it bit me?"

"It didn't bite you. It pecked you. You practically suffocated the thing with your pillowcase."

"Bite, peck. Same thing in bird language. And my pillowcase was like a net."

I laugh and shake my head, focusing on the road before me.

"I'm not sure if she'll have the same ideals James does." I go back to the topic at hand. "She comes from Dallas, and you know things in a city are run differently than in a small town."

"How would you know? You've never lived anywhere else."

"My brows furrow with agitation. "I just know."

"No you don't. Why not give her a chance to prove herself?"

"I will. I'm not going to condemn her for no reason. It'll just take me some time to get over this surprise. James has always been the face of Healing Hands. He's been my mentor."

"Now it's time for you to step up to that role and be someone else's mentor."

"It doesn't seem like Madison needs me to mentor her. According to her, she's worked as a vet for some years now." My feet pound against the ground as I breathe deeply. Talking while running isn't the best idea.

"Not Madison. Maybe someone else. One day, you'll have a young man or woman come to you for advice like you did with James. Maybe your fear stems from not feeling adequate to take on that role yet, but you're ready, Ivan." Luna smiles softly.

I simply nod. Does she have a point? Am I afraid of not being enough to run the clinic without James's support? A part of me always saw Healing Hands with James there.

"Besides"—Luna says after some quiet moments—"you've got the whole bad joke of the day thing going."

"They're not bad jokes. Everyone laughs."

"Pity laughs." She shrugs.

"You're just jealous of my joke-telling skills."

"Right. Your comedic genius is a trait I wish I acquired," she says dryly.

"Jerk," I jokingly tease her, and she sticks her tongue out.

"Race you to that tree over there." Luna takes off in a sprint, and I gruff, running after her, but my pace is slower due to my previous workout.

Luna waits for me by the tree, bouncing on her toes.

"You're getting old, Ivan."

"We're literally the same age."

"Not true. You're six hours older than me." Her eyes twinkle with mockery.

"Older and wiser, then." I bump my shoulder against hers.

"Pretty sure I'm the one that gave you sage advice." She rubs my hair and then screws her face. "Nasty sweat." She tries to clean her palm on my T-shirt, but I leap away.

Laughter takes over as she cleans her hand on her leggings. If there's anyone who can make me feel better, it's Luna. She's not just my twin-cousin, like we often joke, but my best friend.

"Come on. I'm tired and want tacos." She takes off in a jog back toward our apartment.

♥ ♥ ♥

Feeling calmer after my workout and shower, I grab my phone and see messages from my family group chat. Opening the app, I head to the kitchen where the smell of hot sauce and grilled chicken makes my stomach growl.

My face falls when I read the first message from Mia, Luna's sister.

THE NICE GUY

Mia: Hey, Ivan, how's your new co-worker? *waggles eyebrows*

Sara: My mom says she's pretty...

Mia: Maybe your brother will give your mom grandbabies lol.

Sara: She wishes.

Luna: I don't think Ivan's thinking about kids.

Mia: You're right. He needs to get to know his new co-worker first.

Sara: Ew, he's my brother. Let's not go there.

Mia: I meant like date. Get your head out of the gutter, Sara.

Sara: Whatever. We should go out this weekend, and Ivan can invite her so we get official introductions.

Mia: Good idea!

Luna: Can't. I work.

Mia: So we'll go after...

Me: I'm not having children, dating my co-worker, or inviting her out so you two can gang up and ask her a ton of questions.

Sara: We're three in here not two.

Me: Luna knows how to behave.

THE NICE GUY

Mia: We do, too!

Luna: Remember when you told his high school crush that he liked her?

Mia: What's in the past is done with.

Me: I struggled to look her in the face for the rest of the year, and we were lab partners.

Sara: I mean, we did you a favor. Man up and ask out the girl you like.

Me: I'm going to exit this chat one day.

Mia: NEVERRRR!!!

Sara: Lol he thinks he could get rid of us.

Me: Luna, do you know where to hide a body?

Luna: I think I have something at the bookshop that gives suggestions on how to become a murderer.

Mia: Ha-ha. You two couldn't live without the funner younger sisters.

Me: More fun, not funner.

Sara: Okay Grammar King.

I look up at Luna who's laughing at our messages.

"Sometimes I can't deal with them," I tell her.

"They're the obnoxious little sisters, but they mean well."

"Right." I grab plates and finish helping her with dinner so we can eat.

All I want to do is go to bed and start fresh tomorrow. Madison isn't going to disappear, and that's okay, but now that my mind is clear from exhausting my body, I can handle it.

I hope.

4

♥ ♥ ♥
MADISON

AFTER RECEIVING THE FIFTH message this morning, I shut my phone off and throw it in my desk drawer, slamming it shut a few times to release my frustration. It's been a week since I've been in Sunshine Falls, and Ben hasn't stopped contacting me. No matter how many times I block him, he finds new numbers to get through to me again.

"Um." Wide brown eyes stare at me. "Everything okay?"

Ivan stands in my doorway with crossed arms. My eyes move to his defined biceps, accentuated by the fitted sleeves on his Polo shirt. He's the kind of man who steals women's attention with his wavy brown hair, round eyes, and full lips.

"Madison?" He breaks through my thoughts.

"Yeah, great." I plaster on a smile. "What can I do for you?"

"Well, if you don't beat me like you beat your drawer, I was hoping to discuss a few things."

"Oh, sure." I nod, lifting my hands. "No beatings, promise." I sit up taller and point to the chair across from my desk. "Sit."

"Thanks." His eyes roam to the wall behind my desk where I hung my diploma before meeting mine.

"What's going on?"

"Have you finished going over the files I lent you yesterday?"

"Yeah." I pat the stack off to the side of my desk.

"Great. Any questions about them? Usually, James and I have our separate patients but we work together outside of the exam room, and sometimes one of us has to cover for the other."

"It's all pretty straightforward. I do know how to do this job, Ivan." I assure him because my gut tells me he isn't confident about my role here.

"I'm sure you do." He nods. "However, working at any new office is a change."

"Of course." My smile is forced, hoping we can get to the point where we aren't awkwardly interacting and can act like true partners. This job needs to go well. I have nowhere else to go.

Staying in Dallas was too painful, despite my parents asking me to find a different job in the city. I needed to get away. Those streets hold too many memories.

Ivan opens his mouth to speak, but his phone rings. He sneaks his hand into his pocket and ignores it, looking at me again.

"Anyway..." He takes a deep breath, keeping his expression professional and impassive but his phone rings again.

"Do you want to take that?" I point toward him.

Sighing, he holds his phone up and frowns.

"Sorry, it'll be a minute." He touches his phone screen and then puts it to his ear. "Hello?"

I hear a woman's voice on the other side and look down at my papers, busying myself.

"Mom, I'm at work." Ivan closes his eyes, scrubbing a hand down his face. "Can we—"

He stops talking, so she must've interrupted him. I can't help but smile at the way he sheepishly sits back in his seat. If I thought he was attractive already, seeing him give into his mom's demands is adorable.

No, Madison. He isn't adorable or handsome or hot. He's your co-worker. That makes him off-limits.

"Mom, I gotta go. Yes. No..." He rolls his eyes, and I bite back a chuckle.

Suddenly, his eyes widen and he glances away from me, saying something in Spanish. He hangs up and frowns.

"Sorry about that."

"You speak Spanish." Way to go. That was *so* not smooth.

"Uh, yeah." He nods slowly. "My family's Cuban."

"Oh. I didn't know that. Not that it matters." I shake my head.

"Okay." He presses the side button on his phone and looks at it, leaping to his feet. "I gotta go to my next appointment. I'll pick up the reports afterwards." He pushes the chair in before rushing out of my office.

It seems the conversation with his mom rattled him, or maybe it's the fact he had to answer the call in front of me. I sit back in my chair and grab my phone, turning it back on. A scowl takes over my face when new messages pop up from my ex-boyfriend and go into my settings to block the new number he's using to contact me.

The man doesn't understand what *we're over* means. Maybe I should send him one of those singing telegrams so he gets the message.

Once you cheat on me, you're dead to me. There's no forgiving that. And he cheated with a client who was a friend.

♥ ♥ ♥

I finish up with a patient and walk them out of the exam room toward the receptionist. An older woman with a panicked expression paces back and forth in the waiting room. When she sees me, her eyes round with hope, and she hobbles toward me.

"Doctor, I need your help." She clasps her hands together in front of her chest. "My dog got into a fight and is injured."

I nod, looking at the receptionist who smiles weakly.

"Do you have an appointment?" I grab the clipboard with the list of patients.

"No." The woman shakes her head. "Poodles is injured, though. She's bleeding." She turns to look at her Golden Retriever, who is laying on the ground with pained eyes.

"Let me take a quick look, and if she doesn't have any major issues, then we can tend to her after our scheduled appointments."

I crouch beside Poodles and run a hand down her back. I check for any breaks or deep cuts and come back clean. She has a few scratches on her front legs, but they aren't life threatening.

"Good news. She'll survive." I smile. "If you give us a bit, we can clean out the scratches and bandage her."

"What's going on?" Ivan comes to the front desk. "Is everything okay, Mrs. Stoll?"

"No." Mrs. Stoll's eyes water. "Poodles is hurt. She got in a fight with a cat and didn't fare too well." Her lip quivers. It's hard when your pet is injured.

"I just looked her over, and she's okay. Thankfully, the wounds are superficial."

"Can she walk?" Before she even responds, Ivan walks over to Poodles and picks her up.

His eyes scan the room, and he smiles. "Teresa, do you mind waiting a bit?"

"Not at all." The woman sitting with a cat on her lap nods.

I stare at Ivan, lips pursed, and watch him take the dog back with him. Frustration rolls through me at the way he disregarded my authority.

Caring for animals is my priority, but I assured that Poodles didn't have any critical injuries before asking Mrs. Stoll for wait a bit.

I shake off my annoyance and smile before checking on the rabbit my client brought in.

When we have a moment to breathe, I knock on Ivan's office door to talk to him about what happened earlier. He sits at his desk, looking at his computer, his finger brushing along his lower lip. His gaze lifts to mine, and the man is wearing tortoise-shell rimmed glasses.

Goodness. Focus on him and not the way those glasses make him look hotter than usual.

"Can we talk?" I focus on the reason I'm here.

"Of course." He leans back on his chair, resting his crossed hands on his desk.

"What happened earlier can't be a regular occurrence."

"And what was that?" He lifts his brows.

"Allowing a walk-in to take another person's appointment. We have to stick to our schedule and respect each person's time slot."

"Excuse me?" He leans forward, his chair squeaking with his movements. Leaning on his elbows now, he steadies me with his gaze. "We had an emergency. There are exceptions to rules."

"That was hardly an emergency, and you know it. Regardless, I gave Poodles a quick glance to be certain. She would've gotten the care she needed when we finished with our appointments." I lean forward as well, not backing down.

"If someone comes in needing help, we take them in, Madison." The way he says my name like he's chastising me makes my blood boil.

"Ivan, we owe it to our patients and clients to treat them with respect. A walk-in can't take priority when we have a waiting room full of people and packed schedule."

"Teresa didn't mind. She said as much when I apologized afterwards. We're a community in this town." He arches a brow.

"That's not the point. We need to have structure, if not this will become a zoo, no pun intended." I cross my arms.

"We run well, even when we have the occasional walk-in. Is there anything else you don't agree with?" Sarcasm drips from his words. He pushes back on his chair, grabbing a pen and tapping it on the surface.

"House calls. It breaks up our routine and is financially hurting us. Gas prices have increased. Our clients should call for appointments and come to us."

"You're kidding." He huffs out a humorless laugh.

"I'm not. House calls take longer than seeing a patient here, and that will keep us from seeing more patients in a day."

"Are you one of those people who believes our appointments with patients should be on a time-constraint? Five minutes, in and out." He shakes his head.

"I believe in being efficient and structured."

"You're wrong."

"Excuse me?" I lean back with flared nostrils.

"You're. Wrong," he says slowly. "We need structure in life, sure, but this clinic isn't about being a money-making machine. Our patients deserve the attention they need, and we're who their owners trust in times of need. I know you're from a city, but things are different in a small town. Maybe your first lesson in training should be learning how a community works. Not everything is learned in a veterinarian textbook. You need to learn to be flexible."

"I am flexible. If I'm with a patient that needs more time, I won't just stop treating them, but we can't have clients running this place or we'll lose sight of who's in charge." It's common business practice. I don't understand what he doesn't see about this.

"Are you in this for the money or your love for animals?"

I can't even believe he's questioning me. Who does he think he is to ask about my ethics?

"We both know no one would do this job for the money alone. I take my career seriously, and I did not decide to become a vet with the idea of making a quick buck. It's an exhausting job, emotionally draining some days, and a huge responsibility."

Ivan simply stares at me impassively. When he doesn't say anything to my comment, I shake my head and push my chair back.

"Don't undermine my authority in front of a client or *our* employees again. If we need to discuss something, we do it behind closed doors." I'm seething. Turning around, I walk out of his office before I say something regretful.

Working together is like a marriage. You need to learn to communicate and handle situations together. It's teamwork, but I'm not sure how this team is going to go. We're both set in our ways. Unfortunately, both of our beliefs don't run down the same path.

It was so easy back in Dallas. I knew everyone for years, and we all just clicked. We had the same ideas and mindset when it came to work.

I exhale deeply and head to my office, sitting down and dropping my head in my hands. If only Uncle James were here. Actually, it might be good that he isn't.

For someone who blames his earlier-than-planned retirement on his wife, he sure is taking advantage of my presence to have a more laid-back schedule. Hopefully he's back tomorrow as promised.

Thankfully, I'm living with Uncle James and Aunt Susan while I get settled in town and my new role at the clinic, so I can talk to him at home tonight. While I am taking over his clients, he's still a part of our clinic and the one who gets the final word. Surely, he'd understand where I'm coming from.

5
♥ ♥ ♥
MADISON

"WHAT?" I BLINK AT Uncle James, positive I misheard him.

"Your aunt and I are going on vacation. You've met most of my patients already, and Ivan will be there to help you with anything."

Ivan, right. He's been a great help.

"Isn't it a bit soon?" I frown.

"Nonsense. You know what you're doing. I trust you, Maddy." His smile brightens his face.

He looks so happy. I don't have the heart to beg him to stay and train me a little longer. I know how to do my job and run a clinic, but something about Uncle James being present makes me feel safer.

"Where are you going?" I ask.

Aunt Susan walks into the dining room at that moment, beaming with happiness.

"We're going to Aruba for two weeks. I found a great deal with a travel agent. I've always heard it's beautiful—sandy beaches, clear ocean water, and uninterrupted relaxation." She sighs dreamily, as if she were already laying on the sand in Aruba.

"Wow," I breathe out.

"So what was it that you wanted to talk about?" Uncle James asks.

"Nothing." I wave him off.

I can handle Ivan and work. If Uncle James trusts me, then it's for a reason. He's handed off the right to implement changes and bring up different ideas.

I won't allow his vacation to be ruined because of me. He deserves to take a break, and that's why I moved here.

Also, to escape facing your ex every day and heal your heart.

Thoughts of Ben enter my mind at the worst times.

"Are you sure? Is everything okay at the clinic?" His brows furrow as if he can read my thoughts.

"Absolutely." I plaster on a smile and pray Ivan doesn't reach out to tell him about our argument.

If there's something I've always aimed for, it's to make my uncle proud when it comes to my career. He's my inspiration.

"I'm glad to hear you're adapting well, sweetheart," Aunt Susan says.

"Yeah." I sigh, looking down at the wooden table. What's a little white lie while I get used to living and working here? It's harmless if it gives them peace of mind.

"I know this has been a hard time for you, but we're so happy you're here." Her hand lands on mine and she squeezes gently.

"Me too." I look up at her, blinking back tears.

As tough as I make myself seem on the outside, Ben's betrayal still weighs heavily on my heart. I thought we had a future together despite our age difference, and you don't move on from that just by moving out of town. It takes more than a few weeks to overcome it.

The heart has memories etched on it that are difficult to cover up. Like tattoos on skin, I'd need a huge laser beam to undo those memories, and even then the scars will still be there.

"Let's have dinner and then you can help me pack." She excitedly claps her hands. "I could use a modern woman to help me dress." She winks.

Chuckling, I agree to help her and stand to set the table while Aunt Susan adds the finishing touches to dinner. Few things compare to Aunt Susan's biscuits and roast beef, but I'd never tell my mom that. If I told her my aunt's cooking was better than hers, she'd disown me.

♥ ♥ ♥

Ivan stares at me unhappily after Uncle James has told him he'll be away for two weeks. He must dislike not having a buffer around, but that's too bad for him because I don't plan on leaving anytime soon.

Of course, he's wearing his glasses again so it's difficult to ignore that hot professor vibe he's giving off.

"When do you leave?" Ivan asks Uncle James.

"On Wednesday, so I'll be around for a few more days, but you two are in charge now. You're a team, so this will be the perfect time for you to look at each other as partners without me meddling." He looks between us with a raised brow.

I wonder if someone told him about the situation with Mrs. Stoll.

"Of course," I speak up.

"Good." Seeming pleased, Uncle James grabs a folder from his desk and looks up at us. "Madison, I'll be with

42

you in a few appointments today, but besides that, I'll be out of your hair."

"Great." Ivan's voice holds a hint of sarcasm. "I need to get to a client." He stands and walks out of the office.

Uncle James watches Ivan walk away, his signature bushy eyebrows raised slightly. "How are things really going? I'm sensing some tension between you and Ivan. Are you sure this is what you want?"

"Of course." I assure him, not wanting to raise any flags.

"I know your ideal life wouldn't have led you here to Sunshine Falls, but you can find happiness here. We're a great community." He smiles genuinely.

"You say that like this is my last resort. I chose to move and work here. I've always wanted to be like you when I grow up." I grin.

"You're grown, Maddy. It's time to fly." Uncle James sniffles and looks down at the folder in front of him. "Let's get to work."

He tells me more details about some of his other clients and their expectations before going to our next appointment.

By the time I get a break, I head to the staffroom for some coffee and check out today's joke. Reading it is my mental break each day.

Why did the kangaroo fail its driver's test? Because it couldn't reverse.

I laugh and snort, covering my mouth and nose with my hand before looking around to make sure no one was around to hear me.

This is the best one yet. I serve myself some coffee and read it again, chuckling. The door to the staffroom opens, and Ivan walks in. My smile instantly drops, and my guard goes up. We still haven't had much of a conversation, and eventually one of us is going to have to give in and be the bigger person.

"Coffee break?" he asks, lifting his chin toward my cup.

I could be sarcastic and state the obvious, but I nod instead. Look at me, keeping the peace.

"At least it's Friday," Ivan adds.

"Yup."

"Are you still upset about yesterday?" He glances at me with raised brows.

"Upset? No. I do think we have a lot of work ahead of us if we're going to work together."

Ivan sighs, looking up at the ceiling. "Look, I didn't mean to undermine your authority, but I am always going to put an injured animal first."

"While I agree that an emergency should be a priority, Poodles injuries didn't fall under that category."

"You need to be more open-minded." He moves around the kitchen, grabbing a mug and placing it on the drip tray on the coffee maker before adding a pod and choosing the setting he likes.

I snort at that because he's the kettle calling the pot black. "Look who's talking."

"James has been running this clinic the same way for years. I've witnessed it for over ten years myself. It works. We may not make what a vet does in a big city, but it's plenty to live comfortably *and* keep our clients and patients happy and healthy."

"Do you think I'm some money hungry woman?" It's the second time he points out the financial aspect.

"You wear designer brands." He shrugs.

"How do you know?" I look down at my trousers and flats.

"I have sisters," is all he says.

"Right. Well, sorry to break it to you, I'm not only focused on my salary, but I do think it'll be smart to make some changes in order to keep order and effectiveness in the clinic." I cross my arms, my coffee forgotten on the counter.

"Don't you think our clients would be taken by surprise and find the changes abrupt and inconvenient, resulting in damaging our reputation and risking losing them?" His eyes bore into mine.

"There are no other vets in town. What risk do we have? We're convenient for them regardless."

He shakes his head. "Just because we're the only clinic in town doesn't mean we're going to take advantage of our clients or make things harder for them so it's easier for us."

I take a deep breath, exhaling frustration. He's clearly not understanding me. "Ivan, I'm not saying these things to be difficult, but some of our current services are out of our way. This is a small town, if we can make a house call, they can come to the clinic. And walk-ins shouldn't take priority when we have other people waiting to be taken care of. I'm trying to be fair." My eyes round, and I hope he sees that I'm not the bad guy here.

"We're already experiencing a big transition with James retiring. I vote for keeping things the way they are. Let's get to know each other first and mesh our styles of working." He grabs his mug once the coffee maker has brewed the pod.

"That's what I'm trying to do, but you're not allowing me to be me here." It's like he doesn't want me to be happy here. Wait a minute...

I narrow my eyes at Ivan.

"Do you want me to hate working here so I leave and you can buy James's part of the clinic?" He seems to want to run this place alone.

"What? No." The way he scowls makes him look guilty, as if I caught him in the act.

"I think you do. Bad news for you, Dr. Romero, I'm not going anywhere." I arch a brow.

"Good." He takes a drink of is coffee and has the audacity to smirk.

He's infuriating, and it doesn't help that he's so darn hot, too. That taunting smile makes him look like major trouble that I shouldn't get caught up in.

"I'm heading back to work." I grab my coffee cup and walk out of the staffroom.

Whether Ivan's just stubborn or he really wants to get rid of me, he's got another thing coming because I don't give up easily.

When I walk into my office, I hear my phone ringing. Forcefully grabbing it from my desk, I'm about to shut it off when my best friend calls. I exhale, leaning against my desk.

"Hello?" I answer the call.

"Hey, sugar." Lily's voice is music to my ears. I miss her.

"Hi." I sigh, blinking back tears, and take a seat at my desk.

"What's going on?" Her tone changes to concern. "If that jerk is bothering you, I'll kill him myself."

I chuckle and shake my head, scrubbing a hand down my face. "You don't even like to kill spiders."

"Spiders make webs that trap bugs. That's important work. Besides, I'd make an exception." Lily is too sweet to hurt anyone.

"I appreciate it, but you won't have to."

"Then tell me what's wrong, sugar bun."

"I'm just stressed." I close my eyes. "Ivan is a challenge to work with. I've offered ideas and given my opinion on a few things just for him to shut me down. As if I don't know how to run a clinic."

"Why did he shut you down?"

"He says this isn't a big city. We have a different way of doing things, but they don't make our jobs easier." I tell her all about my argument with Ivan yesterday.

"Oh, friend. I'm sorry you're going through that. You're amazing at your job, and I know how much you care for animals." Her words of support make me smile.

"Thanks, Lily. How are things over there?" I haven't had much time to talk to her, and I miss her a ton.

"Great. Josh got a promotion."

"That's amazing. Congrats to him!" Lily and Josh have been married since college. They're the perfect couple and such an inspiration.

"Thanks. We're stoked and the raise is much appreciated. Darn, I gotta go. My client just walked in." She hangs up before I can even say goodbye and I laugh. That's just like Lily to lose track of time. Where I'm a perfectionist, she's a bit messy and free-spirited. I love that about her. We balance each other out.

Putting my phone away, I stare at my computer screen before grabbing a notepad and jotting down some thoughts. Maybe if I organize my ideas, Ivan will understand where I'm coming from. Clearly, my form of expression hasn't been successful with him.

I'm focused on my task when a high-pitched scream echoes around the clinic. Jumping from my seat, I rush out in search of the panicked yelling. I open the door to an exam room to find one of our clients with fear in her eyes and Ivan with tense shoulders.

The room is destroyed with tools thrown around the floor and a small bowl of water tipped over on the exam table. I lift my gaze to see a cat caught in one of the ceiling pipes. Its body is pressed between the ceiling and pipe, wiggling to get free, claws out.

It hisses at Ivan, and his wide eyes flash over to me in panic. If I weren't so concerned, I'd gloat about his abilities to treat a cat, but we need to get it down from there safely.

"I'll help," I offer.

"Thanks. I'll climb up and try to grab him. Can you grab the towel to hold him in once I get him?" He points to a white towel on the counter.

"Sure." I nod, holding it open and reassuring our client that her cat will be okay.

When Ivan gets close, the cat's hisses grow louder. He stiffens and so does the cat.

"It's okay, Tiger, I'm only going to help you." Ivan's voice is soft, but it doesn't do anything to calm the cat. Instead, he tries to reach out his claws in an attempt to attack Ivan, but in the position he's in, he doesn't reach.

Ivan flinches and lowers his arms. He takes a deep breath, looks at me, and nods. "Ready?"

"Yeah."

I have no idea how he's going to grab the cat without getting attacked, but he reaches up and works to slide him out of the tight spot, which causes the cat to lift its back and make it difficult. Claws fly back and forth, scratching Ivan, who groans but remains as calm as possible.

After a few minutes of fighting, the cat slips down and lands on its feet instead of my arms. Seeing the red lines on Ivan's arms, I'm grateful it went for an independent landing.

"Tiger!" the woman cries, bending down and grabbing her pet, squeezing him tightly. The cat purrs softly, giving us the stink eye. Cats are in a category of their own.

"We'll give him a minute to calm down," Ivan says.

"Let's postpone for another day when he's not so shaken up." The woman looks between us with a frown.

"Whatever you'd like. We can reschedule your appointment at the front desk." Ivan keeps his tone professional, avoiding my eyes.

He walks her out and tells Rose to book another appointment. Then, he goes into another exam room. I follow behind him, worried about the scratches on his arms. Blood prickles on his skin.

"Are you okay?"

Ivan's back is to me as he reaches for cotton and hydrogen peroxide.

"Yup." His voice is tight, hissing in pain.

"Here. Let me help you." I grab a clean cotton ball and some more hydrogen peroxide, carefully cleaning the injuries on his arms and palm.

He takes a deep breath, and I look up into his eyes. He shivers as I softly rub the cotton against his arms, muscles flexing against my hands.

"I take it he isn't the purr-fect patient?" I attempt to joke in order to break the tension.

Ivan's shoulders shake. "Nope."

"What were you trying to do? Kill him?"

"Har, har. Not funny, Madison. I needed to trim his nails." His lips press together.

"Ah." I nod. "I'm familiar with stubborn animals and nail trimmings."

"Yeah." He sighs. "I guess this evens the score." He shakes his head.

"I'll make sure to add it to our scoreboard." I smile.

Ivan rolls his eyes and throws away the cotton he used to clean up his injuries. "I'm not competing against you, Madison." His body is tight, and if I have to guess, Ivan hates not being able to complete a job.

The feeling is mutual. Anytime I've failed at helping a patient, it feels like my world has shattered. Leaving him to stew, I walk out of the exam room and check if my next patient has arrived.

6
♥ ♥ ♥
IVAN

THIS HAS BEEN THE longest Friday of my life. Between James telling me he's going on vacation and the nail trimming disaster with Tiger, I'm ready to go home. Unfortunately, James is intent on getting Madison and I together for happy hour. He won't take no for an answer, and I can't really use a sick family member as an excuse when I live in a small town. Everyone knows everything.

Scrubbing a hand down my face, the Band-Aid there scrapes my face. It reminds me of the moment Madison grabbed my hands and took over cleaning out my injuries. Her touch was gentle and welcoming. No woman—aside from family—has ever taken care of me in that way, and I liked it.

I grab my wallet and phone from my desk drawer as James appears at my door.

"Ready to go?" He smiles brightly, way too cheery. Probably because he's leaving for Aruba in a few days. I'd be stoked about that, too.

"Yup." I walk out of my office.

James claps my shoulder as we head down the hallway.

"I know things are a bit shaky now as you get used to these changes, but I trust both you and Madison to navigate my ship together. This place means the world to me, and I can't think of two people better suited to continue my legacy than you."

I take a deep breath, processing his words. James has been the best mentor, and it's important to me to keep Healing Hands running the way he intended. As for his niece, she has other ideas in mind.

"Of course." I nod because I'm not about to tattletale on Madison.

We're adults and have to learn to work together. I can't have James questioning my capabilities.

"Hey," Madison says when we reach the waiting area.

James grabs her hand and then mine, holding them together as if uniting us in some kind of *Power Rangers* move. I lift my brows and look at him as if he were crazy. Madison has a similar expression, wide eyes staring at her uncle and then at me.

"You two are going to make this place thrive." He looks between us, still clutching our hands. "I believe in you."

I swallow and stare at Madison, who's unable to hold my gaze. She looks like she's fighting back from laughing.

"Now, let's go." He releases our hands and wraps an arm around Madison's shoulders.

I have no idea what in the world just happened, so I follow them out of the clinic and get in my car to drive the short distance to the restaurant.

A yawn takes over when I pull into the parking lot of Roy's Tavern, a bar and grill in town. I wish I were home on the couch, watching TV after the week I've had. Here goes nothing, though. Maybe I can have a beer and leave.

Madison and James are already waiting for me by the door. I hold the open door so they can walk in and then enter behind them.

Roy's Tavern is a staple in Sunshine Falls, though you wouldn't guess it based on the interior. It's simple with square tables, a wooden ceiling, and a long bar with shelves on the wall behind it housing different bottles.

It wouldn't win an award for interior design, but we come here for the camaraderie and Roy's hospitality. Coming here is like being at a friend's house.

"James, Ivan!" Roy's voice booms from behind the bar.

I smile at the older man with the round belly.

"Hi, Roy," I call out as James walks over to him and shakes his hand.

"We're here for happy hour. Can we take a seat at any table?" James asks him.

"Of course. Who's the pretty lady?" Roy smiles at Madison. "Is she your new..." He waves between us, and I cut him off.

"No," I say abruptly. "I mean, this is Madison, James's niece and the newest addition to Healing Hands."

Roy whistles and looks at James. "Did the missus finally convince you to retire?"

"She did." James nods. "The clinic is in good hand with these two."

"Happy to hear it. Go on and take a seat, and I'll send a waitress over to take your order."

We sit at a table not too far from the bar as silence settles over the table. James smiles as he looks around, his hands clutched on the table.

"Is this where everyone hangs out?" Madison breaks the silence.

I nod. "Yeah, depends what you're looking for. Roy's is the place to come to when you want to relax and be with friends."

"Cool. I had a place like that in Dallas." A wistful expression takes over her face. It's hard to ignore how beautiful she is. I look down at the Band-Aids on my arms and smile to myself as the ghost of her touch still lingers.

"Now, you have a friend you can spend time with," James tells Madison. "Ivan and his family are great. You'd get along with Luna, his cousin. She's one of our clients as well."

Madison stiffens. "I'm sure."

I tilt my head, wondering what that reaction's about. Is my family not good enough for her city ways? Narrowing my eyes, I try to get a read on her, but she looks away, pretending to observe the bar.

"I don't want her to feel lonely while Susan and I are away," James leans in and whispers.

"I won't be lonely." Madison sighs, shaking her head.

"She's a stubborn one." James chuckles. "I just want to make sure you're okay." He squeezes her arm and smiles at her.

I may have never heard of Madison before, but it's clear that her and James have a strong bond.

"Hey, y'all," Hannah, our waitress, says.

We went to school together, and I used to have a crush on her but never did anything about it. Sara's words in our group chat the other day ring loud. Despite being surrounded by girls in my family, I'm not smooth when it comes to women. I was always kind of shy growing up. The glasses didn't help when it came to being picked on.

"Hey." I smile at her.

She looks around the table, and her eyes land on Madison. "You're new." She points her pen at her.

"I'm Madison, James's niece." Madison smiles awkwardly. She must not be used to people pointing things out like that to her face.

"Nice to meet you." Hannah looks at me. "Do you work with Ivan?"

"I do."

"Cool." Hannah smiles. "So what can I get you?"

"I'll have a glass of Chardonnay," Madison orders.

"I'll have a beer," I tell Hannah.

"Make that two beers," James says, lifting two fingers.

"Great. I'll be right back with your drinks." Hannah walks away.

She returns quickly with our drinks, and James holds his glass up. Madison and I follow suit, looking at him.

"I'm so proud of you two. Ivan, you're not my family, but I've known you since you were a boy. You've worked hard to get where you are, sacrificing a lot for your career. There's no one else outside of my family that I trust with my business." His eyes shine with pride before cutting to Madison.

"Maddy girl, I know you're going to do amazing things. The past has led you here, where you belong."

Madison's shoulders sag, and I wonder what the double meaning behind James's words is.

"You've already made me proud, and I know you'll treat Healing Hands like your own baby. I've been waiting for this day since you told me you were going to veterinarian school." Tears fill his eyes.

No pressure. James is just handing over his entire life and passion and dreams. Madison and I will need to talk and make sure we don't fail him. Letting him down is not an option. We'll put our differences aside and find a middle ground. It can't be that hard.

He moves his glass forward, prompting us to toast.

"To new chapters in life and continued success." His smile is blinding.

Madison and I look at each other, and I press my lips together. We definitely need to make sure we make him proud.

After James's speech, I lean back in my seat and begin to relax as I take a sip of my beer. James talks nonstop about the itinerary they have for Aruba.

"Your aunt wants to go scuba diving, but I told her we're too old for that. I may be a vet, but I'm not looking to have a closeup with any sharks." James's eyes widen in fear.

I laugh and shake my head. "I don't think you'll have to worry about sharks, James."

"Have you been to Aruba? I bet those waters are infested with dangerous animals." He shakes his head, dead serious. "And what if I run out of oxygen in my tank?"

"You'll have a guide. It's not like they'll drop you off in the middle of the ocean and leave," Madison says, looking at me as she bites back her laugh.

"Ivan, mijo!" Roy's wife, Sasha, interrupts us.

I stand and give our family friend a hug.

"How are you?" I ask.

"Great. Roy told me you're here with your new lady, so I had to meet her." I choke and widen my eyes, shaking my head.

"Not my lady." I hit my chest, and James laughs.

"Sasha, this is Madison, my niece and the new partner at the clinic." He thankfully corrects her.

"Partner? Ohhh..." Sasha nods slowly. "I misunderstood." She smiles at me and waggles her eyebrows. Leaning into me, she whispers, "Es bonita."

I cough again, grateful she spoke in Spanish because the last thing I need is Madison thinking that I think she's pretty. She *is* totally gorgeous, but she's my co-worker. I have strict personal rules that include not getting involved with anyone at work.

"What did she say?" James looks between us.

"Nothing." I wave him off. "You know Sasha." I smile at her and wrap my arm around her shoulder.

"Nice to meet you, Madison. I apologize for the confusion."

"It's okay," Madison says with a smile. "It's nice to meet you, too."

"Well, I'm going to get to work before Roy fires me. Ivan, tell your mom to return my call. I want to place an order for dessert next week and catch up."

"I'll let her know. You know she's not well-versed with technology and doesn't realize she has missed calls."

"You need to give her a course on using a smart phone." She points at me.

"No. Next thing I know she'll open an Instagram account and do anything to go viral," I joke.

Everyone laughs, and Sasha heads to work while I sit back down. James leads most of the conversation while Madison and I interact when necessary. Thankfully, he's a talkative person. If it were up to me, I'd just look at the table wondering what to talk to Madison about.

Besides our argument, I haven't gotten to know her enough, and I'm not great at small talk. Maybe I should make an effort to get to know her better if we're going to run the clinic together. It's the best option. I love my job and would hate to grow to resent it because of my own stubbornness.

All I know is that she worked at a clinic in Dallas. I don't even know her specialty, her favorite part of the job, or anything. It's time I change that so we can flow seamlessly at work the way James and I do. It's for the best.

"What have you liked so far about working at Healing Hands?" I ask to break the ice.

Madison tilts her head, doubt clouding her eyes. I don't blame her. We didn't get off on the right foot.

"Uncle James has done a great job of creating a place where people feel like family. It's a true community."

"Even walk-ins?" I arch a brow, teasing her, but she doesn't get it because her face drops into a scowl.

Madison doesn't respond, so I wrack my brain for something else to say.

"Our clinic is a community," James says. "It's what I've always strived for."

Madison nods, taking a sip of her wine. Her eyes narrow at me, and I feel like a jerk. So much for trying to make amends and get to know each other better. I try to mentally apologize or explain, but she looks away, taking a deep breath. I wish I knew what was going through her mind, though I have a pretty good idea it's plotting my death. Or at the very least, my resignation.

Note to self: Not everyone understands your humor. Think twice before making a joke that could distance people instead of break the ice.

7

♥ ♥ ♥
IVAN

"Hi," I CALL OUT as I walk into my parents' house.

"Ivan, bring in the pack of water bottles I left outside please." My mom's voice rings through the house.

I look behind me before closing the door, and sure enough a pack of twenty-four water bottles sits by the front door. I lift them and close the front door with my foot before entering into the house and dropping the bottles on the counter.

"You invite me over for dinner for my muscles, right?" I joke, flexing my arms.

Sara screws her face and rolls her eyes. "Put those away." She waves her hand.

"Careful with the knife, Sara," my mom chastises. After an unfortunate incident with a lime, mom reminds her often to be careful. Sara hates it which makes me laugh.

I smirk and move around the peninsula to give my mom a kiss on the cheek.

"You didn't bring the girl. I asked you to grab the bottles so she could see what a strong man you are."

I lean back and stare at my mom while Sara tries to hide her chuckle.

"What girl?" I pretend I have no idea what she's talking about.

"No seas tonto." She slaps my arm.

"I'm not acting a fool." I lift my arms to defend myself. "I told you I'm not dating anyone." I step away from her.

"Why not?" My mom puts her hands on her hips, and Sara smiles, enjoying the show.

"Because she's my co-worker not my girlfriend. Do you think I'm hiding this from you? We haven't even gone out together for any rumors to spread."

"You went out to Roy's yesterday."

"With James," I clarify. "If I go on a date with someone, I do not want their uncle to be the third wheel."

I wish I could say this is unusual behavior for my mom, but she's always been like this. It's why I never told her who I liked when I was growing up—she wouldn't hesitate to tell the girl all the reasons she should date me and I'd die of embarrassment.

"Sasha said you were together at the bar so I thought..." She trails off, not needing to say anything else. I bet Sasha called her nonstop until she answered and told her enough for my mom to take it the wrong way.

"If I have a girlfriend, I'll tell you right away." It's a half-truth because it'd be worse if she found out through town gossip, but she'd also take over the relationship with her excitement.

"You can't even properly flirt with a woman. If you're counting on your skills, you're going to be single forever," Sara teases me.

"Says the person who spilled her drink all over herself when the guy she liked asked her where the bathroom was." My brows raise.

"Whatever. Someone bumped into me. The timing was coincidental." Sara crosses her arms.

"Right. Your hand was shaking from the timing."

"You're obnoxious," Sara says, sticking her tongue out at me.

"And yet, I'm your favorite brother."

"The only one I have."

"Hey," Ana, my youngest sister, says. "What are you guys doing?"

"The hard labor that the youngest gets away with not doing," Sara says, sighing as if she's been working manual labor all evening.

"Hard labor?" Ana looks from her to the tomato on the cutting board. "Let me go file a complaint with human resources." She shakes her head.

"Being the youngest makes people think they're the smartest." Sara playfully rolls her eyes.

"Not the smartest, but definitely the most loved." Ana smiles wickedly.

"Actually, the oldest is the most loved. I fulfilled their dream of being a parent. The rest of the kids are just extra."

"He's so obnoxious," Sara mock-whispers to Ana.

"The most."

"I'm the best big brother." I reach out and ruffle both of their hair.

"Hey! I'm going out after. Do you know how long it takes to straighten this frizz?" Sara pats her hair down, running her fingers through it.

"I love you all the same, but if you get hair on the salad, I will be angry," my mom says, pointing her finger at Sara.

Ana and I laugh. She's unbothered by the messy hair. It was already in a bun anyway.

"How's school?" I ask her as I settle on the stool. Ana is a senior in high school, and then she's off to college.

"Good. I had a killer exam yesterday, but I hope I passed."

"Of course you did," my mom tells her.

"I'm great, too," Sara speaks up, back to preparing the salad. "The middle child syndrome—everyone forgets about me." She shakes her head, feigning annoyance.

"Even if we wanted to, you'd make yourself known. It's impossible to get rid of you," I tease.

"Ha, ha. *Sooooo* funny. Don't think I forgot that you tried to throw me in the trash when I was a newborn." Sara glares at me with pursed lips.

"In my defense, you cried way too much and that's what Dad did with my toy that made too much noise."

"What did I do?" My dad walks into the kitchen right at that moment.

"Throw away my toy piano when I was three." I lift my brow.

"That thing would give me headaches." He shakes his head, grabbing a knife from a drawer.

"So did Sara when she was a baby."

A wet splat lands on my cheek and there's a tomato chunk on the counter in front of me. I look up at my sister. "You're going to pay for that."

She laughs and shrugs.

"You didn't bring your girlfriend?" My dad looks around the kitchen.

I sigh, dropping my head back and praying for patience.

"I don't have a girlfriend," I say slowly.

I'm going to write a sign and staple it to my shirt so no one else embarrasses me. The last thing I need is someone to ask about this in front of Madison. It'd be my luck that one of my mom's friends comes into the clinic and sees us working together and shows her excitement about us "dating," calling us some power couple or something.

I do not need Madison thinking I'm telling people we're together. I've already messed up by using my misunderstood humor on her.

Come Monday, I'll clear the air and let her know that I was joking.

"Ivan, come out and help me with the barbecue." My dad claps my shoulder, so I stand and follow him outside.

Instantly, the smokiness from the grill hits me, and it feels like home. Growing up, we barbecued a lot. My dad loves it.

Roger always gifts us a few steaks from his cattle throughout the year, and my dad saves them like his prized possession.

"How's work?" He gives me a pointed look.

"It's good. I'm getting used to working with someone else that isn't James. Day by day, right?"

"That's my boy. Always looking at the bright side. Changes happen to teach us a lesson. Look at your mom and me. We had to come from Cuba with nothing, and it made us stronger. This will make you a better professional."

I nod, smiling at my dad. My parents never miss a chance to remind us of the challenges they overcame, but it's taught us how to be resilient through change. Although my sisters and I were born here, our family history is a part of us. Through our parents and grandparents, we've learned what it means to struggle and find your place. It's what has allowed me to pave my own path and fight for my career.

As soon as the meat is cooked, I help my dad take the food inside, and we sit at the dining table. Nothing beats my mom's rice and beans, so I serve myself a hearty plate.

"Hungry much?" Ana lifts her brows.

"You get to eat mom's cooking every day. Let me savor this."

"That's because you moved out." She shrugs, taking a bite of food.

"I'll remember this when you come visit during the holidays next year and you're craving mom's cooking."

"She's going to send me care packages." Ana smiles smugly.

"Ha. Black beans won't survive the shipping."

"She can freeze them. Right, Mami?" Ana gives my mom her best pout, and I roll my eyes.

"Of course, mi amor." My mom smiles affectionately.

As much as I tease my sisters and complain about my mom being all up in my business, I wouldn't trade my family for anything.

♥ ♥ ♥

"Do you want to go out?" Sara sidles up to me as I'm putting the plates in the dishwasher.

"Where?" I eye her.

"Mia and I are going to go to The Copper Cellar to listen to live music. She asked Luna if she wanted to go but hasn't heard back."

"Really?" I check the time on my watch. Luna should be home already.

"Yeah." Sara shrugs and moves to help my mom clean up the kitchen.

I finish filling the dishwasher and send Luna a text message to make sure she's okay.

My phone buzzes in my pocket as I'm drying my hands. I fish it out and check my messages.

Luna: Hey, I'm home. My phone ran out of battery. What's up?

Me: Just checking in. Sara said you hadn't responded to Mia's messages.

Luna: I'm ignoring her lol.

Me: Why?

Luna: I don't feel like going out but ran out of excuses.

Me: I'll go too and we can leave early. It'll be cool to listen to live music and relax.

Luna: But I'm in the best part of my current read.

Me: You can read it all day tomorrow. I'll even cook lunch.

Luna: Ok. I'll go. You twisted my arm with your promise of cooking.

Me: Lol thanks. If not our sisters will gang up on me.

Luna: They do that anyway.

Me: Whatever. Meet you there in a few.

Luna: Ok!

Luna is my partner-in-crime. I'd much rather she go out with us than go alone with Mia and Sara. They'd use me to babysit their purses while they go socialize.

I'll never admit it to them, but there are times I wish I was more outgoing like them. It's hard to find your place when you grew up being teased. It conditioned me to be more reserved, and I prefer being in the comfort of my safe space than putting myself out there.

Sara and I say goodbye to our parents and drive out to The Copper Cellar. I warned her that I may leave before she'd want to go home, but she assured me Mia would drop her off back home.

"Now that we're alone. Is there really nothing going on between you and Madison?" She looks over at me, crossing her leg under her and stretching out the seatbelt.

"No." I glance at her quickly. "We work together, and I met her like a week ago." My words come out defensive.

"Okay." She lifts her hands in surrender. "Just asking, geez."

I pull up to the bar parking lot and find a spot pretty quickly. Sara squeezes my arm and squeals excitedly.

"I love the nights they do live music."

"It is cool." We head toward the entrance and spot Mia already by the door.

"If it isn't my favorite cousins." She beams, hooking her arm in Sara's.

"Hey." I smile at her.

They talk rapidly about the performance as we walk into the packed place. Whenever The Copper Cellar brings an artist to sing, no matter how unknown they may be, it gets extra crowded. People love bragging that they saw a star sing in a small bar before they were famous.

That and there's not much else to do in Sunshine Falls on a Saturday night.

I say hi to a few people as we pass by, and background music pumps from the speakers before the live show begins. The lighting is dim with copper beer barrels illuminated behind a glass wall across from the bar and people dance and talk as they have their drinks.

Sara and Mia push along until they spot an open high-top by the bar. Taking a seat, I look around while tapping the top of the table.

"Hey." Mark, a friend, stops by.

"Hey, what's up?" I clap his hand and smile.

"Not much. Came out to listen to some music tonight. Hey, ladies."

"Hi, Mark," Sara says.

"Hey," Mia responds, barely looking at him as she stares down at her phone.

He looks at me with raised brows, and I shrug.

"How's work going? Heard James is retiring."

"Yeah. It's going well." I catch up with him a few minutes before he gets called away by someone else.

My phone buzzes, and I look at the screen, seeing a message from Luna.

Luna: Hey, where are you?

Me: By the bar at a high top.

Luna: Ok, heading over.

"Luna's here," I mention to Sara and Mia.

"Reed is here, too," Mia says, looking around the bar. Reed is her best friend. She swears there are no romantic feelings from either of them, but I'm not too sure.

I wave my hand in the air when I see Luna a few feet away and she smiles gratefully.

"Hi." She reaches our table.

"You've been ignoring me," Mia accuses, pointing a finger at her.

"My phone ran out of battery." Luna shrugs, unbothered by her sister's attitude, and I fight back a chuckle. She may have run out of battery, but she disregarded Mia's messages.

"What's up?" I lift my chin.

"I'm tired but ready to mingle." She shimmies and then grimaces.

"You're such a liar."

"I know. I can't mingle even if I wanted to. Like how does one just spark conversation with another person? Unless they're reading a book I've read or have a dog, I'd likely not know what to talk to them about. Like, man, it's really hot and humid today, huh? And the person would respond with, 'Well, we live in Texas,' so yeah." She's rambling and all over the place.

"Take a deep breath, Lu." I pat her shoulder.

"Yeah. So when does the show start?"

"At nine. Do you want something to drink?"

"I'll have a glass of wine. Here." She reaches for her purse, but I stop her.

"This round is on me." After gathering Sara and Mia's orders, I head to grab our drinks. While I wait for my turn, I spot a redhead sitting at the end of the bar, spinning a cup around on the countertop. When her eyes lift in my direction, they widen in surprise.

I smile and nod at Madison. She seems awkward sitting there alone. I could go talk to her, invite her to sit with us like James mentioned, but that would be pushing it. And my sister would give her the third degree as if Madison were my girlfriend.

I'll pass.

8

♥ ♥ ♥

MADISON

THE RELIEF I FEEL from seeing a familiar face makes me breathe easier, even if it is Ivan. When Aunt Susan and Uncle James insisted I come out tonight, I had to. Not only because it's good to get out and make a life for myself here, but also because I'm living in their home and maybe they wanted some alone time.

Sure, they're going to Aruba in a couple of days, but I'm breaking up their routine by being there. Hopefully, I'll be able to get my own apartment in town soon.

They may try to convince me not to, but I need my own place and I want to give them back theirs.

I do a half-wave at Ivan, but his attention turns to the bartender. I don't blame him. I'd hate to miss the window of opportunity to make a drink order. I didn't expect this place to be so packed.

If I had friends in town, this is where we'd get together. The bar is cute and inviting with the wood and brick combination.

I need to figure out how to make friends here first. At work I'm assertive and confident. My social life is a different story. Besides, I now have some trust issues that make it harder to open up to people.

Not to mention, everyone here is likely wondering why *James's niece* moved to town. That makes it harder to just spark conversation.

A woman goes up to Ivan and whispers something, making my heart stop. I'm not sure why. It's not like I have a thing for Ivan. I don't. Sure, he's handsome but that's all.

Maybe it's because he's the only person I know here, a crutch in a sea of strangers, and if he has a girlfriend, then I don't even have him as that.

I should leave. In moments like this, I miss Lily and my home in Dallas. I never felt alone there.

The woman talking to Ivan catches my eyes, and her eyebrows lift. Great, Ivan probably told her who I am. She slaps his shoulder and nods her head in my direction. He stares at her with wide eyes and a tight jaw, a warning look if I ever saw one. Instead of shying away from him, she laughs and looks at me with a smile.

This is strange. Maybe he didn't talk badly about me, and his girlfriend wants to get to know me better. It would make our work situation easier.

I look away from them and down at my glass of Coke. The last thing I need is to be called out for being nosy. That title belongs to the people in town who have already given me the third degree, including their intense curiosity about why I decided to move here at this point in my life, a question I've dodged for now.

No need to get my love life circulating on the gossip mill.

When I glance back up, they're no longer standing by the bar. I breathe out and listen to the song playing over the speakers. There's nothing better than sitting somewhere and allowing the music to take you away, especially if it's Kenny Chesney.

I forget all about Ivan, his girlfriend, and work problems and zone into the lyrics about life on a beach somewhere.

"Hey." A voice interrupts my daydream, and I stare at the woman who was talking to Ivan, accompanied by another one.

"Hi." I tilt my head and look at them.

"You're Madison, right? You work with Ivan," the new woman says.

"Yes." I nod slowly when the two women smile at each other with mischief.

"I'm Sara, his sister. This is Mia, our cousin."

His cousin.

Something about that lightens my insides. It shouldn't. I shouldn't give a dog's tail about Ivan's personal life. My only concern should be having a peaceful work relationship so we can succeed together at Healing Hands.

"Nice to meet you."

"Are you here alone?" Mia asks.

"Yeah." I shift in my stool.

"Mia, Sara." A rough growl sounds above the music.

Goodness, it's like a male's mating call. That sound should not be sexy.

"Yeah?" Sara turns around with a wide smile. "We're meeting Madison since you didn't want to introduce us."

Ivan takes a deep breath, running a hand through his hair. His eyes squeeze shut for a few beats before he looks up at me.

"I apologize for these two scheming girls. Let's go." His jaw ticks.

"It's okay." I smile awkwardly, not wanting to be in the middle of a family discussion.

"Ignore him." Sara looks at me. "Come sit with us. We can't leave you here alone. And we can get to know each other better."

"I'll take your drink," Mia offers, reaching for my glass.

My eyes meet Ivan's, not wanting to ruin his night. We already had to interact yesterday, and I haven't forgotten how he tried to throw me under the bus in front of Uncle James with his comment about walk-ins.

Holding on to that annoyance, I shake my head.

"It's okay. I'm going to finish this and leave."

Mia and Sara look at each other and back at me. They look comical, like cartoon characters whipping their heads around.

"I know my brother can be a total pain sometimes, but the rest of us are nice." Sara bats her eyelashes at Ivan in that obnoxious way siblings do, and laughter bubbles out of me.

Just for the fun of seeing these women torture Ivan, I stand.

"If you insist." I give him my best smile and walk past him, following the two women. Ivan groans behind me but doesn't speak a word.

"Luna, this is Madison."

"You both fought about who was going to go talk to her. I know who she is." Luna smiles at me. "I apologize in advance for these two." She points at Sara and Mia.

I open my mouth, but Mia speaks up before I can get a word out.

"Ignore her. She's as grumpy as Ivan is. It's the older sibling syndrome. Do you have any siblings?"

"I have an older brother."

"So you know what it's like." Sara leans in and whispers conspiratorially while Mia grabs a stool. She ignores the man telling her it's taken and tells me to sit.

"I do." I nod at Sara and then look at Luna and Ivan.

I can already tell what their family dynamic is like. Ivan probably gets hazed a ton.

"You shouldn't listen to anything they say. They like to stick their noses where they don't belong." He looks at me with pleading eyes.

This is fun.

"I don't know. I think it'd be great to talk to them so I can get to know my co-worker better." I smirk and turn my attention back to Sara. "Older brothers are annoying, but mine is seven years older, so we didn't spend a lot of time together growing up."

"That's no excuse." Sara shakes her head. "I'm four years younger than Ivan, and look at me, living the younger sister dream." She widens her arms, proud of her interference in his personal life.

"I'm going to leave," Ivan grumbles.

"How are you liking Sunshine Falls so far?" Luna asks.

"It's a nice town. Definitely different than Dallas."

"I can imagine. I've only been to Dallas once, but it was such a contrast to life here. Not to mention, I got lost and my phone ran out of battery so I had to ask people how to get back to my hotel room. It was a mess." She shakes her head, laughing to herself.

"It is a big city," I tell her.

"Yeah. And work is good?" She looks at me with a meaningful expression.

"Uh, huh." My eyes cut toward Ivan and back to Luna.

"But tell us how Ivan really is at work. Is he all serious and stern?" Mia asks, pressing her lips together, imitating the expression.

I lean forward conspiratorially, just to make Ivan sweat a bit. "He's quite rigid."

"I'm not." Ivan throws his hands in the air. "I'm the opposite of rigid. I'm not the one implementing rules that are strict." He lifts a brow and stares at me.

I glare at him, taking a deep breath.

"Well, that escalated quickly," Sara says. "Don't take him too seriously. His career is his whole life. He's very protective of it." She rolls her eyes, giving him a warning look.

Someone taps on a microphone, breaking the tension. I look toward the stage and ignore the man to my right. My comment was meant as a joke the way his family was teasing him, but it seems he doesn't have a sense of humor.

"Good evening, everyone," the MC says. "Are you ready for some great music?"

The bar erupts in cheers and howls. Some people whistle loudly. I lean back in my seat and release an exhale. It seems that even outside of work Ivan and I are destined to not get along.

I wish it were different, but maybe our personalities just don't match up. Our ideas are too different, but our stubbornness is too alike for this to balance out and work.

A young guy wearing a ball cap approaches us with a smile as the band gets ready to perform.

"Hey, guys."

"Dude, where were you? You texted like twenty minutes ago that you were here," Mia tells the guy.

"I got caught up talking to Damien and Greg." He wraps his arm around her shoulder and tousles her hair with his other hand.

Mia fights him off and pats her hair down.

"You're so annoying." She shoves his shoulder.

"But you love my anyways."

"Ugh. Having a best friend like you is hard work. Anyway, this is Madison, Ivan's new co-worker. This is my obnoxious best friend, Reed." She introduces us.

"Hi." I smile.

"James's niece. I've heard about you."

"It seems like the entire town has," I deadpan.

They all laugh, except Ivan.

"Welcome to small-town Texas." Mia shrugs.

"I've become quite accustomed to it the last couple of weeks."

Music starts playing, quieting the conversation as everyone gets enraptured by the live performance. Going to concerts is one of my favorite past times, so this is an unexpected treat in a small town.

My head bobs to the music, and the singer belts out the first verse of the song, waving his arm to hype up the crowd. People start breaking into groups and dancing. The song is catchy while keeping the twang that's true to country music.

"He's really good," Sara says.

"Yeah." Mia nods, moving along to the song.

"Let's go dance." Sara pulls Mia's arm, dragging her away.

I laugh quietly at their antics and focus on the song.

"They're a mess," Luna says, leaning in.

"They're funny." I lean back on the stool, my heart thumping as silence settles over the table.

Ivan's body is stiff while he sits between Luna and me, his eyes glued on the performance. Reed tells him something I can't hear, and Ivan nods in response.

"Do you like country music?" Luna asks.

"I do. I grew up listening to it."

"I love it. We grew up listening to Spanish music at home, dancing salsa, but country music is my favorite."

"That's cool. I'm not great at dancing, less so to music like salsa."

Luna giggles. "It's not that hard."

"I have two left feet." I laugh. "Is the band local?" I ask, changing subjects.

"I don't think so." She shrugs. "I didn't even realize there was live music today until Ivan told me. I'm here in solidarity." She lifts her closed fist, and I laugh.

"Why?"

"We made a pact years ago that we wouldn't leave each other alone in social situations with our sisters. It's like they live to embarrass us, even when they don't mean to."

"Really?" I scrunch up my nose.

"Yeah. They have no filter and think they act on good intention, but they don't realize those so-called good intentions are terrible." She rolls her eyes.

"Oh, man."

"Yeah. One time they slipped my number to a barista they thought I liked. I was mortified when he called and explained he had a girlfriend in college."

My eyes widen. "No, they didn't."

"Yes," she hisses. "I didn't even like the guy. I was friendly because he was nice."

"I would die."

"Keep your distance," she warns, then chuckles. "I'm kidding about keeping the distance, but yeah, they've got their own ideas and run with them without consulting anyone."

"I can see that with how they approached me. I take it they were curious about me."

Luna nods. "And they like to torture Ivan."

I look at the man in question, but he's deep in conversation with Reed. He looks more relaxed now; it's a side of him that I haven't seen at the clinic. He's laughing softly, his eyes crinkling.

Crushing on the hot vet I'm partners with doesn't fall under my plans to move to Sunshine Falls, so I ignore the way his body shakes and forearms tighten as he grips his glass. Looking back at the stage, I remind myself the disaster that comes from having even a tiny inkling of a crush on a co-worker.

I already had a one-way ticket to Heartbreakville. I'm not planning on going through that again.

Sighing, I shake off thoughts of Ben. I don't even care about him anymore. It's what we could've had that prickles. The dream of a family, a house full of laughter, and unconditional love. Someone who cheats doesn't fit that mold.

Neither does another man you work with.

9

♥ ♥ ♥

IVAN

I REMOVE THE *Joke of the Day* from Friday and grab the flashcard with today's joke to pin on the cork board. The door opens, so I look over my outstretched arms and drop them instantly when I see Madison.

"You're the jokester?" Her eyebrows lift in surprise.

"Yes." I sigh. The last thing I need is for her to take this from me. Although, I hope that after our limited interaction this weekend, she'll let me have this.

The jokes are my thing, what I added to this office.

"What did the dog tell his son about his first crush? It's puppy love." Madison reads it aloud and snorts. "Puppy love. I get it." She shakes her head, smiling.

I remain quiet, hating that I got caught by her.

"I didn't peg you for the person putting these jokes up, and yet it doesn't surprise me. They're funny."

Relief floods me upon hearing her comment. "Thanks. It lightens the mood a bit when someone walks in here. Except for Harold," I whisper. "He scoffs at every single one to my face." I shake my head.

"Well, he has been a vet tech for about four-hundred years. He's probably dreaming of the day he can retire. Does he know it's you that puts them up?"

"Yeah, he doesn't care." I shrug, grabbing my mug. "Anyway, I think we should meet today to discuss a few things."

Her eyes widen. "Oh. Yeah. Sounds good." Her response is stilted.

"James and I had Monday meetings to discuss the upcoming week. Since we're practically strangers, I think it'd be good to keep that routine," I explain.

"I agree. We had something similar at the clinic in Dallas."

"Great. Is there a specific time you prefer?"

"We can meet now." She makes a cup of coffee and adds a splash of creamer.

"That works for me. My first appointment is at ten."

"Your office or mine?" She takes a sip of coffee.

I swallow thickly. Why does that sound like a proposition? It's clearly not. We're two people who work together, although I can't deny that seeing her outside of this environment, with a sundress on and her long hair in loose waves made my heart jump. She looked as uncomfortable as I felt, and a part of me felt solidarity with her.

"Mine is fine." I nod and walk toward the door, opening it for her.

She smiles tightly and walks out of the staffroom. We're silent as we make our way down the short hallway to the offices and enter mine.

Once we're seated, I ask Madison about her schedule this week. I hope that from here we can discuss the issues we're both at odds with.

"I have a pretty packed schedule. I've got patients throughout the day. It seems everyone needs to see a vet this week. I'm actually surprised at how busy we are for a small town." Her eyebrows lift as she talks.

"We have a lot of clients. The farm animals make up a significant portion of our days, too. We also serve people from other towns," I explain. "You'd be even more surprised how many of our patients aren't from Sunshine Falls. James has made a name for himself." I take the opportunity to bring up what I really want to talk to her about.

"I can see that. He's always lived to serve others and help animals." She smiles fondly.

"I agree, and now it's up to us to continue his legacy."

Madison nods, taking a deep breath. "He did give us a big speech, right? Handing his entire life over to us."

"He did, and I'd hate to disappoint him. James has been my mentor and idol for as long as I can remember." I give her a meaningful look.

"As well as mine." She arches her brow.

"So you can understand why we can't just change everything he's built. I understand you have different ideas about how to run a clinic, but I think we should stick to the way Healing Hands has always run."

"I don't want to change the entire way you run things here, but I do think it's important to take advice from someone on the outside to make the clinic run better. Walk-ins throw the entire schedule out of whack."

"Don't you understand that we're our clients' saving grace? These pets aren't just animals to them, they're part of the family. In some cases, part of their livelihood." I lift my hands in exasperation.

"I do, Ivan. Honestly, I care about these people and their pets, but I also believe in being effective. What happens when a client complains that their appointment got pushed back because of a walk-in? We could potentially have a bigger issue that will ruin our reputation if someone says we disregarded their time." She shakes her head.

"Everyone here is the type of person who's willing to take the shirt off their back for someone."

"What about when we have someone unfamiliar with the clinic?" she argues.

I can understand what she's saying. To prove it, I'm going to extend an olive branch.

"Then let's negotiate. We accept walk-ins, but unless an utter emergency, they have to wait." I cross my hands and look at her expectantly.

"What if we don't finish until closing time because we have a packed schedule like today?" She tilts her head, challenging me.

"I'll stay past closing time." I don't even hesitate. I'd do anything to help someone.

Madison sags in her chair and furrows her brows. She probably thinks I'm being stubborn or playing the hero card. It's neither of those things. I don't mind working late if it means helping an animal.

"People will say I don't care." She gives me a vulnerable look.

"They won't." I shake my head.

"How do you know?" She crosses her arms, a protective shield coming up.

"Because if you really do care, you'll work hard to prove it to them with your actions each and every day."

She tilts her head and opens her mouth and then closes it. She knows I'm right. No one expects us to work after hours, and this is a hypothetical situation where we might have to extend our work hour. It's not something we'll experience every day or every week.

"Okay." She sighs, giving in. "Walk-ins allowed, but they have to wait until everyone with an appointment has been seen."

"Unless it's an emergency," I add.

"Yes, Ivan." She says this slowly, as if pacifying a child. "About house calls."

"We're not getting rid of those. Some people don't drive and live in the outskirts of town. It's hard for them to make it to us. Not to mention, the ranchers and farmers."

"Do we have a lot of clients that are ranchers?" Her eyes widen.

"Quite a few. We are in rural Texas."

"Right." She nods. "Those are exceptions, obviously. I don't expect someone to come in with their horse."

"Someone tried." I chuckle.

"Really?" Her eyes widen. "What'd you do?"

"At that moment, I told them to come out back, and I was able to assess the horse. Then, I told the man to call us if he needs us, and I'd drive out there. Everyone's face when the man opened the door and pulled in a reluctant horse was pure gold. I wish I had video evidence of that day to replay on a stressful day."

Madison cracks a smirk, quickly dismissing it and putting her professional mask back on. "Then we add an extra charge to house calls." She stares at me in challenge. "Gas prices are up. Our time is valuable as well." It's the same argument she gave me not so long ago.

"Fine, we add a surcharge, except for the ranchers and farmers. Their situation is different and we already charge them a fair price."

"That works for me." She nods.

"Look at us, working as a team," I joke.

Madison looks at me unamused.

"Oh, come on. You can smile, you know?" I push.

"I know." She smiles, but it's purposefully forced. It's a shame, she's beautiful when she allows herself to grin freely.

Great, my family's talk about Madison is getting to me. I should not be noticing any of these things.

Shaking my thoughts away, I focus on the conversation.

"So we agree on these things? Do we need a contract to sign?" It's meant as a joke.

"I think we're good." She glares at me, but a ghost of a smile lines her lips. "Although, I do have another idea to maximize our income."

"What?" I lean back, afraid of what she might bring up, but if I expect her to be flexible, then I need to be as well.

"Pet boarding service. We can offer to care for pets when people are on vacation." She smiles as if it were the best idea.

"No." I shake my head.

"What?" Her brows crinkle. "Why not? It's a great idea, and it's another way to generate income without much work."

"Without much work? It's a huge liability. We may not need a night staff, but we'll need to be alert to the cameras in case there's an emergency or something goes wrong. We also risk a client accusing us of maltreatment or not feeding their pet the right food, not taking them out enough times, the list is endless. Boarding animals is on a whole other level, and while we are the experts when it comes to caring for animals, it's not the same as keeping them overnight or for an extended period of time."

"You realize how silly that sounds, right? You just said it, we are the best people to care for animals. It's our job." She leans forward and stares at me as if I've lost my mind.

"It's a risk."

"Look, I've seen our financial reports. While the clinic is doing great for a small-town veterinary, we could scale up. This is the perfect way to do so."

"It's not all about money," I argue again.

Madison takes a deep breath and closes her eyes for a moment. When she blinks them open, determination shines in her gaze.

"It's not, but we need to keep this place flourishing the way James has all these years. Each year, there are more expenses and prices increase. It's life." She softens her gaze, trying to convince me.

"I'm not sure it's the best option." Something about it doesn't sit well with me.

"Let me create a plan for it and present it to you." She leans forward, resting her elbows on my desk.

Her eyes shine with golden hues. It's like she's casting a spell on me, pulling me in to agree with her. If I'm not careful, I'd give in.

Scrubbing a hand along my chin, I nod. "Fine, but I make no promises."

"Thanks." She sits back with a triumphant smile.

I may regret this, but I need to give her this if I expect her to work with my ideas. That's the whole point of a partnership, right?

A knock sounds on the door, and we both look at it.

"Come in," I call out.

"Dr. Romero, sorry to interrupt, but we have a situation out in the waiting room." Rose's face screws up.

"What happened?" I push my chair back and stand.

"You should both come. A woman found a coyote and wants to get it checked out."

"A coyote?" Madison's face pales.

"She thinks it's a dog."

"How in the world does she confuse the two?" I ask.

"The problem is that she's fighting to keep it as a pet. I tried to explain the laws, but she's not having it." Rose frowns.

"We'll go." I look at Madison with raised brows. "No time like the present to work together."

We head out and see a young woman hugging the coyote. I grimace and walk carefully, not wanting to scare the animal.

"Doctor." She looks up at us. "I'm so glad you can see me. He's got a hurt leg. I found him on the side of the road, limping, so I picked him up." The young woman's voice shakes.

Madison and I look at each other before approaching the woman. I bend down and look at the calm animal. It's clear that this is a coyote, but the woman seems oblivious.

"What's your name?" I ask her.

"Mary."

"I'm Dr. Romero, Mary. And this is Dr. Grover. It seems you found a coyote." I reach out carefully, allowing the animal to sniff my hand.

"This is a pup. I know the difference between a coyote and a dog." She glares at me with narrowed eyes.

"I am sure this is a shock, but why don't you come with us to an examination room and we can discuss this?"

"You're going to try to take him away from me." Mary raises her voice, getting agitated.

"Of course not," Madison speaks up. "We just want privacy to examine him." She smiles.

Mary looks between us with wide eyes and nods.

"So much for not taking walk-ins, huh?" I whisper to Madison, who shakes her head. She might be in shock, likely her first experience with a wild animal and all.

Once in the examination room, I bring out a book about animal anatomy and find the information on coyotes. Showing Mary the book, I begin to tell her the similarities.

"As you can see based on the photos, your buddy here is a coyote. Although part of the canine family, they are wild animals and should be treated as such."

"No," Mary says forcefully. "He's mine. You can't take him away from me." Her eyes are wide and wild, making the coyote nervous.

The animal curves his back and stares at us. Having him feel threatened isn't ideal.

"Mary," I warn. "You're scaring the animal." This is one of those situations where I wish I were better trained with wild animals.

Madison looks at me with wide eyes, squatting down. "It's okay, buddy," she says softly.

"Don't talk to him!" Mary yells.

"Mary, it's a risk having this animal. We can call wildlife rehabilitation so the coyote receives the help he needs and return home. Otherwise, you're risking it living a short lifespan. You don't want that, right?" I look in Mary's eyes.

"No." She shakes her head. "But I can keep him safe."

"Unfortunately, coyotes can be dangerous if they feel threatened. If they injure someone, they have to be put down. We don't want anyone suffering because of this. Not the animal or a person," Madison says.

Suddenly, the coyote jumps out of Mary's arms, growling, and I crouch. Apparently his injured leg is forgotten when instinct kicks in. My heart pounds, and I look around to make sure Madison and Mary are okay.

Baring its teeth, the coyote inches back. Mary's face pales, staring at the animal, and screams.

I take a deep breath and grab my phone, calling wildlife before figuring out how to get out of this situation.

"Hey, Steve, we have a situation. Can you come down to the clinic to collect a coyote?" I speak into my phone, letting the local wildlife rehabilitator know what's going on.

"Be right there." He hangs up, and I pocket my phone.

My eyes remain on the coyote as I try to protect Madison and Mary.

"Be careful," Madison says tightly.

"Of course. Cover Mary. I'm going to try to calm this animal down."

I clap my hands loudly, remembering the tips taught to me if I ever come in contact with a coyote. Who knew I'd need to do this in my own clinic instead of out in the wild? The animal moves back as I stand tall, keeping eye contact. I hear the squeak of the door opening, and see Mary leave the room out of the corner of my eye.

"Allow walk-ins and get potentially attacked by a wild animal," Madison says under her breath.

"It's this or let that woman take the animal to her home and have a bigger issue." I keep my eyes trained on the coyote.

"How about next time someone comes with a wild animal, we call wildlife right away?"

"I'll take that into consideration when I'm not having a stare-off with a coyote."

"I'll accept that," Madison says, and there's an undertone of humor in her voice.

When someone knocks on the door, the coyote perks up.

"It's me, Ivan." I recognize Steve's voice and nod to Madison. She opens the door to let him in. I step back and let him do his thing, staying in the room in case he needs help.

Once he's gotten the animal under control and sedated, I thank him.

"No problem. This is what happens when wild animals cross humans." He shakes his head. "They don't think about the repercussions to everyone involved and the harm it can be to the animal."

"In Mary's defense, she really thought it was a dog, but her reaction to learning it's a coyote was uncalled for," I tell him.

"Well, it's not my first rodeo with Mary." He shakes his head. "She brings animals in all the time and begs me to let her keep them. It's probably why she came here this time."

"No kidding." I laugh.

"I'll talk to her. Hopefully she listens to me this time. If I give her an update on the coyote's care, it might help her move on."

"Sounds like a good plan. Thanks again, man." I walk him out of the clinic.

He finds Mary after putting the animal in his truck, and she tries to hide from him by looking down at her phone.

"Mary, let's have a chat." Steve sighs, sitting beside her.

"Well, that's one way to start the week." Madison stands beside me, her hands in her pockets.

"Definitely got my blood pumping." I release a deep breath and let go of the tension in my shoulders.

"I prefer starting the day with Zumba," she quips.

I look at her and laugh. "That would be a safer option."

"You've clearly never seen me dance. Zumba may be more dangerous to my well-being, but it beats facing a coyote." She shakes her head, walking away.

Now, all I can envision is the image of her hips shaking while she dances Zumba, even if uncoordinated. That is a risk to *my* well-being.

10

♥ ♥ ♥

MADISON

I TAKE A DEEP breath at my desk to calm down after the stressful morning. When I walked into the clinic today, I did not expect to face a coyote. Coyote attack isn't on my Bingo card for this new chapter of my life.

This is why we need to be more careful about walk-ins. If they aren't vetted, we could have a potential problem on our hands. I don't care if it's my best friend. If she brings a wolf, I'm sending her to Wildlife Rescue. The only wolves I like are the Jacob Black kind from *Twilight*.

At least Ivan is being more open to my ideas, even if I have to give in a little to his. It's part of the compromise in a partnership. Slowly, we'll find the middle ground to run this place the way it suits us both. I'm not a stranger to running a clinic, therefore, I'm just as apt as Ivan to offer suggestions and make changes. I'll always have the best interest of Healing Hands at heart. I saw how my uncle built this place and turned it into what it is today, even if I was living in Dallas.

Buzzing comes from my drawer, and I reach into it to grab my phone. My brows furrow when a text message from an unknown number stares back at me, making my heart race with frustration.

> Unknown number: Maddy, come on. Don't do this to us and what we had. We were a great team. I miss you like crazy. Give me a chance. Let me prove that I regret it. You're all I want. The person I love. I need you.

I take a deep breath, closing my eyes. My attempt to relax my clenched jaw is pointless as anger pulses through me. If I could punch a wall and not break my fingers, I would. Right now would be the time to have the strength actors do in movies to take out their frustrations. Or a punching bag. That would work, too.

I moved, left Dallas in order to start a new life. I don't need Ben to pop up everywhere.

Okay, not everywhere but his messages are getting beyond annoying. I'd rather be one of Taylor Swift's exes and get blasted in her songs than have to deal with this man.

My fingers hover over the screen, and I decide to end this once and for all.

> Me: Ben, we're through. Done. Finito. There is no us. You made sure to ruin it. Leave me alone. I've moved and moved on, and we both know you already did way before we ever ended. Goodbye.

I release an exhale and block this number as well. At this point my list of blocked numbers that belong to Ben are longer than a child's Christmas list.

Checking the time on the phone, I jump to my feet and race out of my office, late for my next patient.

Great, here I am preaching about punctuality and time-efficiency, and I'm running behind.

Forgetting all about cheating ex-boyfriends, I walk to the exam room and find Tom, one of our vet techs, outside with a clipboard. He's working with me on this patient.

"Hey, what's going on with Milo?" I ask before walking in to see him.

"He's been in pain and struggling to stand when he's sitting or lying down. He's got a bit of a limp, too. I suspect arthritis." He frowns.

"Okay, thanks. Let's go in."

I smile before opening the door.

"Hello, Mrs. Davis, how are you?" I squat in front of her and look at Milo, curled on her lap. I softly pet him before looking up at his owner. "Tom explained Milo here's in pain and not moving like his usual self."

"He's not." She shakes her head with sadness, her hand running along his back. "He's usually so active, but in the last few weeks he won't even give his lady friend her treat."

"Lady friend? Do you have another dog?"

Tom clears his throat as Mrs. Davis places her on her chest. "Oh, goodness, no. I can't handle two of these." She laughs, patting Milo's head. "Watch this," she whispers, placing Milo on the floor.

He looks up at her with round eyes as his back legs shake. Mrs. Davis grabs a treat from a bag in her purse and places it in front of Milo. He stares at it then looks to the side. That's when I notice a plush dog.

"You see?" She raises her brows, but I'm not sure what I'm supposed to see. "Delilah is his special friend, and he always gives her treats, but he won't even move for that."

"Delilah? The toy?"

"Shhhh..." Mrs. Davis quiets me. "Don't let him hear you. To Milo, Delilah is real. The love of his life. Tom has witnessed their love before, right?" She nods at Tom standing beside me.

"Yup." He struggles to keep from laughing.

Just then, Milo slowly pushes the treat with his snout toward Delilah and leaves it in front of her. Of course, she doesn't eat it. That would be weirder than this situation.

When I think it can't get worse, Milo walks toward Delilah and licks her, making me feel like I'm spying on a love affair. A dog in love with a plush toy. I've seen it all.

"Ah, there's my boy. That's true love, sacrificing your favorite treat for your partner."

Okay, never mind. The weirdest part is that Mrs. Davis encourages it as if Delilah could return feelings toward Milo. I'm not going to break the news to her. If it makes her happy, then we'll leave it as is.

Mrs. Davis sniffs, grabbing a tissue from her purse. Is she crying? Oh no. I've dealt with broken-hearted patients when they've lost their beloved pets, but I'm not sure what's going on here.

"My Harry was like that. He'd give up his favorite dessert so I could have two. Now he's gone. I don't want Delilah to go through that pain if there's something wrong with Milo. She'd be devastated." Mrs. Davis cries into her tissue.

Ah, this I could work with.

Delilah must be a metaphor for Mrs. Davis, and she can't process what it'll mean to lose Milo.

"I'm going to examine Milo to see what's going on so I can help to heal him in the best way possible." I smile, looking at the real dog and the plush toy cuddling together.

Shaking my head, I carefully reach for Milo to place him on the table, but he snaps at me. I jump back, making sure he doesn't take my fingers as his treat, and Mrs. Davis giggles.

"He's protective of his Delilah."

I look at her over my shoulder with a forced smile. "Right, well, I just need to check on him." I look back at the dog. "Here, Milo, Milo. Come get the treat." I pull one out of the pocket of my scrubs and hold it out.

Milo tilts his head, looking intrigued.

"That's right. You know you want this." I wave it a bit, but he doesn't move.

"If Delilah is on the table with him, he'll feel better. Having the support of your love does that."

"You're serious." I look at Mrs. Davis again.

"Of course, dear. Have you never been in love?" Her eyes widen as if I've lost my mind.

"Yup." I nod, hating to admit that. "We'll try that." I look at Tom with wide eyes.

However, when I go to grab Delilah, Milo growls like a protective alpha. Pugs are supposed to be peaceful dogs. It's why everyone loves them.

"Milo, take Delilah to the table," Mrs. Davis says in a harsh tone.

Surprised by the way she took authority after all her lovey dovey words, I stand and widen my eyes when

Milo gently grabs Delilah with his teeth and limps to my feet. Just like a dog moving its pups.

"Wow," I breathe out.

Finally, he lets me carry him and Delilah, placing them both on the exam table.

"All this, and I'm not even wearing my white coat," I joke to Mrs. Davis.

She chuckles and waves her hand. "He's just a special kind."

"No doubt."

I check his joints and muscles. Poor Milo whimpers and curls into Delilah when I assess his back legs.

"It's okay, buddy," I whisper. "We're going to do an X-ray and some blood tests."

"Come on, buddy." Tom reaches for Milo, who yaps while Tom carries him.

"We'll be back shortly," I tell Mrs. Davis over Milo's barking.

"I should go with you to make sure he feels comfortable."

"I promise you he's in good hands. It's normal for him to feel scared, but we'll take great care of him." I smile, and we take him out of the exam room, and Delilah stays behind—much to Milo's chagrin.

"What is up with this love affair?" My eyes widen toward Tom, who laughs as we walk to the X-ray room.

"Every time Mrs. Davis comes in, she shows all of us that trick no matter how many times we've seen it."

"Except she thinks it's adorable and real love."

"She does." Tom nods. "Since she lost her husband, she's kind of held on to this strange love affair between her dog and a toy. She once left Delilah behind at the clinic, and she went hysterical."

"Poor woman. I think she's holding on to the grief of losing her husband by using this situation."

"I agree." Tom sighs. "Let's get this dog checked out." He opens the door to the room where we do X-rays and helps me settle Milo on the table.

Tom holds the wriggling dog while I run the X-rays. It's clear to see once I have the images that there's cartilage loss and bone-to-bone contact.

"We've got our answer." I hold up the X-ray.

Then, I do some bloodwork. Milo is not a fan of needles, and Tom struggles to keep him calm while I find his vein. Thankfully, it's done quickly.

After going back to talk to Mrs. Davis and prescribing the proper medication, I move on to my next client. I'm running behind after taking longer than necessary with Milo. I'm usually more punctual than this, and a part of me hates that I'm late.

Back in Dallas, there were more than two vets in the clinic, allowing us to see more clients as a whole while balancing the workload so we'd have more time in between appointments to stick to our timetable.

When something like X-rays and stubborn animals prolong an appointment, then it pushes back all the rest. It's not how I like to run things, but I don't see a solution. We can't exactly cut back the amount of appointments we set each day if we want to keep generating the same amount of money each month.

By the end of the day, I'm exhausted and ready to go home and take a long shower. I walk to my office to grab my things and run into Ivan in the hallway. With his glasses on. My goodness, it should be illegal for him to wear those. They're not good for my heart.

"I hear you met Milo and Delilah." He chuckles.

"That was interesting."

"You mean, you don't think it's normal to share food with the love of your life?" Ivan's eyes twinkle.

"If they're both living, it's perfectly normal."

He laughs openly, and it's a sight for sore eyes. When he pushes the glasses up the bridge of his nose, I smile. It's not a sexy move at all, but watching him do it is endearing. It makes him seem more boyish and less stern professional.

"Yeah." He shakes his head. "By the way, good work today. I heard our clients were happy with you."

"Are you complimenting me?" I feign surprise, placing my hand on my chest.

"Don't get used to it." Ivan fights a smile, adjusting his glasses again.

"Well, I much prefer to be told the truth." I bat my eyelashes. "Tell me how our clients said I was a competent vet."

He tosses his head back and stares at the ceiling, mumbling unintelligibly. When he looks at me again, he arches a brow.

"I never said you were incompetent. I just don't agree with the rat-race, money focused mentality."

"Oh! I've got a joke! Why was the rat training so hard?" I pause for a beat. "It was getting ready for the rat race!" I slap my thigh and laugh at my joke.

Ivan stares at me as if I'm crazy.

"Oh, come on. That was funny. I should add it to the board."

"No." His voice is forceful, making my laughter catch. "It's the one thing that's mine. That I implemented."

"Surely anyone can add a joke." I cross my arms.

"Everyone knows it's me. It's my way of lightening up the office."

"You're a possessive joke-teller." I shake my head.

"I'm not, but..." He trails off.

"You're ridiculous. Do you think people will like me more if I add a joke?" My eyes widen.

When he remains quiet, I roll my eyes.

"Or do you not want them to get along with me so my adaptation here is harder?" My teeth clench. "So much for talking things out this morning, huh? Practice what you preach, Ivan. Maybe you're not ready to run this place yet." I turn on my heel and walk away.

What difference does it make if the joke is his or mine? When I thought we were making progress, he goes and acts like a jerk. He may look hot in glasses and his muscles might be attractive, but his fluctuating attitude leaves much to be desired.

11

♥ ♥ ♥
MADISON

AFTER A GOOD NIGHT's sleep and asking Uncle James for advice on running the clinic without mentioning Ivan and me clashing, I'm determined to make today a better day. Who cares if Ivan thinks he's the one in charge of the jokes? I can still get to know our employees and build a friendly relationship with them. Starting with donuts this morning. Who doesn't love a treat at work?

I've been eyeing a bakery on my way to work, and this is the perfect excuse to stop in. Baked with Amor is such a cute name, and I am excited to see what they have.

Finding a spot across the street, I pull in and walk toward it. It's still amazing how people in town stare at me for being new here, but I've watched all the small town movies and series. *Sweet Home Alabama, Hart of Dixie, Gilmore Girls.* People are nosy.

Opening the door to the bakery, the smell of pastries, sugar, and a loud gasp instantly hit me. Before I can take in the decor, a woman is rushing to my side.

"You're Madison." She has an accent that doesn't quite fit Texas, and her smile is bright and welcoming.

"Um, yes." I nod slowly, eyes wide when everyone stops talking and stares at me.

"I'm Ivan's mom, Clara. It's so nice to meet you. Emma, ven!" she yells, looking back at the counter.

Another woman who looks like Ivan's mom comes out from a back door, wiping her hands on a dish towel.

"I'm making the pastelitos, Clara." The woman stops in her tracks and grins. "Oh."

That *oh* sounds scary. As in, I should slowly back away from this situation before I get cornered.

"Madison, James's niece. Hello." Emma rushes to my other side, wrapping her arm around my shoulder. "How are you? I'm Emma, Clara's sister. We're so happy you're here."

Both women walk me to the counter, using their free arms to open the way for me, making the other customers move out as if they were parting the sea.

"What brings you by?" Clara asks.

"I, uh, wanted to take some donuts to work." Why am I suddenly doubting my decision?

"Donuts? Can you believe she said *donuts*, Emma?" Clara looks at her sister.

"No, no." Emma shakes her head as if her words weren't enough to get the message across. "You can't take donuts. I'd be offended."

"She's right. Take pastelitos. I'll package an assortment and some croquetas."

"Pastelitos?" I am not sure what that is.

"Cuban pastries. Trust us." Clara winks and walks around the counter, grabbing a box. "Tell me about yourself. I've tried to get Ivan to open up, but he's been tight-lipped. That boy of mine." She rolls her eyes. "As if I were going to plan a wedding."

I cough at her words, wondering why she'd say that.

"Don't get her nervous." Emma slaps her arm, causing Clara to almost drop a pastelito she's putting in the box. It'd be a shame to have to throw away that scrumptious looking pastry.

"I'm not. I didn't say anything about her and Ivan getting married. I said he thinks I'm planning a wedding."

Why in the world would he think that? We're not...dating.

"Look at her. She's about to run away." Emma points at me before murmuring something in Spanish.

Great, now they're talking about me so I don't understand. I look around at the other people in here, and they're all talking and giggling.

"I apologize for my sister," Emma says. "She gets ahead of herself."

"Ivan and I work together. That's all." I clarify because clearly something got lost in translation.

"Of course, mija," Clara appeases with a smile. "You're just so beautiful." She looks at Emma. "With her hair color and eyes, and Ivan's complexion, they'd make adorable babies."

Oh, my goodness.

Unsure what to say, I focus on the box piled with pastries and realize how many she's added in. My eyes bug out.

"Oh, that's more than enough," I spit out. "We're just a few employees. Thank you."

Clara's eyes snap up at me. "I know, but one of these per person isn't enough. They're the best pastries. Ivan loves the guayaba ones, so make sure he gets two, okay?" Her brows lift, and I'm suddenly afraid of her Mama Bear persona.

"Of course."

"Gracias." She smiles and closes the stuffed box, grabbing another smaller rectangular one. "The croquetas are here. We don't mix the pastelitos and croquetas. This is our grandmother's recipe. She used to make it for us in Cuba while we were waiting to leave the country."

"Wow." The display has a variety of treats, including the donuts I was originally coming in here for. Honestly, the pastelitos she packed look better.

If it wasn't so awkward coming here, I'd be here every other day. But apparently, Ivan's mom thinks we're getting married and having kids for some reason.

After a long goodbye, where I practically need to rip the boxes from Clara's hands as she goes on and on about how Ivan loves his job, will come around to me working there, and reminding me to give him two—no, three—*pastelitos de guayaba*, I leave the bakery and head to work.

When I walk into the staffroom, a few people are reading the Joke of the Day, so I catch their attention.

"Hey, everyone," I call out. "I brought us something to get through the day after yesterday's stressful events."

"Thanks." Kate smiles at me over her shoulder.

"I love anything Baked with Amor makes." Rose walks away from the cork board and opens the box I placed on the table, licking her lips and eyeing every pastry as if she hasn't eaten in weeks.

"I'm glad. Enjoy." I go for a mug and make myself some coffee.

Once it's brewed and prepared, I read today's joke with a hint of resentment. My attempt to bond with Ivan was ruined when he acted like a jerk.

Taking a sip, I read the joke to myself and spit out the coffee with a sputter. *That little...*

My rat race joke is pinned on the board. He stole my idea.

"Are you okay?" Kate calls out around a mouthful of flaky pastry.

"Yeah." I grab napkins to dry the coffee stains on the rest of the announcements on the cork board.

This is not the way to make a good impression. I pat down the wet marks, but it doesn't remove the darkened spots that came from my mouth.

"Hey, you're all here." Ivan saunters into the room with his hands in his pockets. "What'd you think of today's joke?" He's all smiles and confidence.

"It was a great one," Rose says.

"Made me snort-laugh," Kate adds.

"Definitely a good one," Tom agrees.

I narrow my eyes at Ivan, hoping he gets my silent message of death threats. He's got some nerve. He probably doesn't come up with the jokes himself. He steals them all from others.

"I'm glad you think so." He grins at me as he approaches. "Uh, did you spit here?"

Crossing my arms, I nod. "My shock made me sputter." I arch a brow, lips pinched.

His face falls, like he had a sudden realization. "Oh, man. Wait. I had a plan." He looks from me to the employees eating pastries. "I'm glad y'all liked the joke. It's actually Madison's. She told it to me yesterday, and I thought it'd be nice to involve her." He looks at me with pursed lips, but I'm having a hard time believing him.

"Really? It's great, Madison." Rose smiles.

"I'm going to use that when I train for my next marathon," Tom says.

They all praise my joke, but my focus is on Ivan, trying to get a read on his true intentions. Then again, why would he use my joke knowing I'd speak up.

"I was hoping to be in here before you arrived. I was harsh yesterday and felt guilt afterwards. I thought you'd like to see your joke up there." He tilts his head toward the board.

"You didn't steal it?"

Ivan chuckles. "No way. I have a book of ideas to use for jokes. I don't need to steal yours. It's my flex."

"Dad jokes are your *flex*?" I bite back a smile.

"Yeah." He laughs and nods proudly. "Isn't that what Gen Z uses to say it's something that you're good at?"

"I don't understand Gen Z lingo, and it moves way too fast for me to keep up. I'm more stuck on the fact that you think these dad jokes are your pride and joy."

"Do you laugh when you read them?" He tilts his head, widening his stance.

"Yeaaah." I drag out the word.

"Then my job is done correctly. I flexed, or whatever." He shakes his head, and I can't help but laugh at his confusion on the word, though he might be using it the right way.

"Good job flexing." I pat his arm and his bicep tenses, giving me a different kind of flex. I freeze, removing my hand from his body, and step back, knocking down the box full of sugar packets.

"Madison, you're jumpy today," Kate says, laughing, and rounds the table to help me clean up my mess.

"Yeah." My insides feel rattled.

Ivan is making me jittery. Who needs coffee when my co-worker gives me the spark of energy I need?

"Wait." Ivan looks from Kate to me. "Did you go to Baked with Amor?" His face pales.

"I did. Your mom said to eat three pastelitos of guayaba." I smirk.

He squeezes his eyes shut and groans. "Please tell me you met someone else that really wasn't my mom," he mumbles.

"Oh, it was your mom." I cross my arms. "You and I should talk at some point, though."

He lifts his hands in mock surrender. "I am not responsible for what comes out of that woman's mouth."

"Your mom is great," Rose says. "She makes the best pastries and desserts." She takes a huge bit of another pastry that looks like it might have cream cheese in it. It definitely has coarse sugar on the top.

"Yup, great because she isn't your mom." He won't look me in the eye, which makes him look guilty. It's kind of adorable.

Remember what happened the last time you thought a co-worker was charming.

Oh, right. No fraternizing with the partner. The only partnership Ivan and I will have is a professional one where we often don't agree, and sometimes, like today, feel like a team.

12

♥ ♥ ♥

IVAN

"Ivan..." Madison walks into the room I'm in, her words trailing off. My head turns in her direction, and she's standing with her head tilted and arms crossed. I've been avoiding her ever since she went into my mom and aunt's bakery. I can only imagine what they told her.

"Why do you have a cat on your back?" Her voice rings with humor.

I rest the pen on the report I'm filling out and smile.

"A cat in a hat and a cat on my back. I'm working out new rhymes. Forget Dr. Seuss, Dr. Romero is the new writer in town."

"Wow." Her eyebrows slowly lift on her forehead. "That's..." She trails off.

"Left you speechless?" I smile at her, the kitten walking further up my back until he's holding on to my shoulder.

"Yeah. I have no words. Are you the same guy that makes up those jokes? Because this one was terrible." She shakes her head.

"I thought it was good in a bad-joke kinda way. What's going on? Ow." I jolt when the cat's nails pierce into my skin. Reaching around, I try to grab him, but his nails go deeper into my back.

112

"You little..." I squeak in pain. "Some help here?" I lift my brows.

"Says the man with a cat on his back." She grins.

"Madison," I plead.

"Fine. I'll help the new Dr. Seuss. It was a short-lived career."

I grimace when she grabs the kitten and pulls him off my back while his claws sink further into my skin. His back nails pierce my middle back, causing me to yelp. She finally gets him off and places him on the floor.

My shoulders tense. "Is this payback for using your joke without telling you first?" I stare at her with wide eyes and rub my shoulders.

I lift my shirt and look in a small mirror in the room, trying to see the scratches on my back. The kitty was fine when we were alone.

"Any chance you can help me clean up? Pass me a cotton with hydrogen peroxide, please." I point to the cabinet without waiting for a response.

"Right." Madison nods, moving awkwardly to the cabinet. She pulls one open and moves supplies around with her hand.

"A little faster?" I call out, looking at the scratches turning more red by the second.

"Why do you have a cat in here anyway?" she asks while she searches for what I asked.

"A neighbor found the kitten in the street and brought him in this morning. I examined him before asking the front desk to get the adoption prep ready but got carried away playing with him," I explain.

"He is cute," she comments.

"My back stings." My teeth clench.

"Well, lower your shirt while I look for the hydrogen peroxide."

"No. My skin will stick to the fabric. The hydrogen peroxide is in front of you. Do you need glasses?" I tease.

"No." She glares at me and places the bottle and cotton balls in front of me on the table.

Meanwhile, the kitten is trying to climb my legs. "Wonderful, I'll have scratches there, too. I'm going to look like I was in a cat fight with rebels. *A meowtiny.*"

Not the time to come up with jokes, Ivan.

Madison laughs. "You do know how to clip his nails, right?"

"Of course, but I've been busy. A little help with the cat? Can you grab him, please?" I shake my leg softly.

"You're on your own on this one." She smirks, crossing her arms.

"Thanks for being a supportive partner," I deadpan.

"It's called tough love. This way you learn your lesson."

"I know how cats act, but he's too cute not to give in to his demands." I bend my arm behind me, trying to clean up the scratches but don't quite reach.

Frustration grows as I try to swing my hand up and down to clean the scratches with the hydrogen peroxide but fail to do so. The ones on my middle back are tough to get to, and I look at Madison.

"Any chance you can help here?" I awkwardly wave my hand behind me.

"Um, sure." She steps forward, grabbing the cotton from my hand and starts dabbing the cuts. "Seems as if I'm always the one to heal your cat scratches." She shakes her head. "Between the situation with Tiger and now this, I'm guessing cats aren't your strong suit."

I grimace and jolt.

"Can you hold still?" Madison places her other hand on my shoulder.

"I'm trying." I look at her through the mirror's reflection. Her long hair is in a ponytail, giving me a full view of her face.

Her eyes lift to mine, holding me captive for a second. We stare at each other, tension rolling between us. I swallow thickly and hold my breath. She really is beautiful. Her hand moves the cotton across my skin with slow strokes. The sensation makes me feel tight and tense. Her touch is gentle, and her eyes gaze deeply into mine.

My breath falters, and she steps back.

"Sorry, did I hurt you?"

"No." She did anything but hurt me. I've been hypnotized.

What is going on?

Madison is my co-worker, nothing else. I've already decided not to mix my personal and professional life no matter how much my mom interferes. Of course she called me and told me all about meeting Madison and how pretty she is. She also made a point to clarify that in no way did she mean that Madison and I were getting married and having children. I wanted to snap my fingers and disappear.

I let my shirt fall and smile tightly.

"Thanks." The cat sits on the floor, staring between us.

Right, buddy. You felt that tension too, huh?

Madison shakes her head and crosses her arms. "Anyway, while you're in here acting like a cat's climbing wall, we have an injured owl outside that looks like it wants to kill me."

That snaps me out of this trance.

"I doubt that."

"Have you ever stared into the eyes of an owl? Also, who in the world actually has an owl as a pet?"

"A wizard?" I joke.

"Can you be serious for a sec? What's gotten into you?" She throws her hands in the air, blowing out a frustrated breath.

"I am. Have you never seen *Harry Potter*?" I shrug.

"Oh, my goodness. I think the sugar in your pastelito is affecting you." I love the way she pronounces *pastelito* as if the I is a double E.

Distracted with her pronunciation, I snap back into the conversation to hear her say, "The owl, from a human not a wizard, wants to kill me. Or it seems like it. We'll discuss your interest in *Harry Potter* later." She arches a brow and shakes her head.

"Maggie has the owl, but it's not her pet in the traditional way. She's a foster parent for the rehabilitation center," I explain.

"Oh. Well that doesn't change the fact that he's crazy."

"She. And I'll help you. Not that you were much help here." I bend down and grab the kitty, placing him in a kennel for now. I need Rose to get the adoption prep done, or I'll end up with a cat at home.

"Are you trained to work with owls?"

"I am." I've worked hard to be as knowledgeable as possible in my field. "Somehow, I ended up taking a training on how to work with owls. It was accidental when I was in college, but it turned out to be helpful."

"You surprise me, Ivan." Madison shakes her head. "This patient should've been on your schedule."

"You automatically took over James's clients. We should go over them and make sure we don't need to make any other changes. It doesn't look right in front of the client."

"I agree."

My head snaps back to stare at her. "Excuse me?" I pause. "Did you just agree with me?" I taunt her.

"Don't get used to it," she says evenly.

"Too bad. I kinda liked it." I wink at her and continue walking.

Madison stumbles over her feet, and I reach out for her arm.

"Careful there. Are you okay?"

"Yup." She purses her lips. "I must be nervous about this owl." Her eyes avert mine.

"We got it, team." I hold my fist out to her, and she stares at it, scrunching up her nose. "You're going to leave me hanging?"

"I have no idea what's wrong with you today." Regardless of her words, she fist-pumps me.

"This is me." I open my arms wide. "Charming, nice guy."

"Tone it down a bit." She rolls her eyes.

I laugh and open the door to the exam room where Maggie is waiting for us.

"Good morning, Maggie. How's Spooks?" I put on the protective glove on my hand. "Is she ready for her check-up?" I smile at her.

"She is. I think she's improved a lot, Dr. Romero." Maggie looks from me to Madison.

"Have you met Dr. Grover? She's our new partner and a great addition to our team." We need our clients to feel confident about this change, so we need to make sure they understand Madison's value in our clinic.

"We met earlier. Welcome to Healing Hands," Maggie says with a smile.

"Thank you. I'm happy to be a part of the family."

I glance over at her and grin. It seems she's getting the hang of what we do here. We're more than a money-making machine. If only she'd apply that mentality to all aspects. She's still intent on giving me a full report about the benefits of having a boarding program.

Madison helps while I assess Spooks. She's hesitant to get too close to the bird, but she does a good job of hiding it in front of Maggie.

"She's doing great at home," Maggie updates me while I check the owl's wings.

"I'm glad to hear that. If it weren't for you, who knows what would've happened to her." I lift the left wing.

"I love volunteering. I always wanted to have a ton of animals, and this allows me to do so."

Spooks flaps her wings, and Madison ducks, covering her head.

So much for keeping her cool.

"It's fine," I whisper.

She glares at me, focusing back on the owl. Once we finish, I give Maggie the good news that Spooks is back to optimal health.

"I'm so happy to hear that. Thank you, Dr. Romero. You, too, Dr. Grover." She smiles at us and after a few more minutes of chit-chat, leaves the exam room.

Madison breathes out, leaning against the table. "Even her name is Spooks. Did you see the way she was looking at me? Definitely giving me the stink eye." She shakes her head and moves to the sink to wash her hands after removing her gloves.

I lean against the wall, crossing my foot over the other one, and chuckle at her exaggeration. "I am going to take the kitten to Rose so she can start the adoption process."

"I'll take him." She looks at me over her shoulder as she rinses the soap from her hands.

"Seriously?" I lean my head back.

"Yeah. He's adorable, and any cat that attacks you is a friend of mine." She chuckles playfully.

I push off the wall, pointing at her. "I resent that. He loves me. These are love scratches." I point to my back.

"Right." She nods with furrowed brows. "Love scratches, he says. I'm going to have to teach you the different behaviors of animals."

I chuckle and slip my hands into my pockets. "I'm very aware of animal behavior. I'm a vet, remember?" I pull my scrubs shirt as proof. "That kitty loves me. But if you're serious about adopting him, that'd be great."

"I am." She nods, smiling. "He's adorable, and I already have a name picked out. Boots. Did you notice his feet are a darker shade?" She shifts on her feet, her face glowing. "He's way too cute."

"I can't say no to that." That got resolved quicker than I expected.

"Thanks. I appreciate it. Besides, I think Boots can protect me while I'm alone at home considering he got you good." She laughs when I scowl.

"Funny girl."

"I am. You should pass over the Joke of the Day job to me."

"You're not that funny." I look at her unimpressed.

"I'll prove you wrong."

"I'm sure you will," I say under my breath.

She's definitely taking small actions to show me she's different than I originally judged her to be. I'm not giving up my jokes, though. No matter how beautiful she is or how much she bats her lashes my way.

Liar. If she gives you a wide and honest smile, you might just give her the world.

13

♥ ♥ ♥

MADISON

I GRAB BOOTS AND cuddle the Tabby kitten. As soon as Ivan said that the cat didn't have an owner, I decided to take him. He's too cute to leave behind, and seeing him climb Ivan is an image I will forever thank Boots for.

There's no hotter view than a strong man letting a tiny cat climb on his back while he works. Ivan was just chilling while Boots did his thing, and I had to stop myself from admiring the view.

Then, he had to go and lift his shirt, exposing his defined back with perfect muscles that seem like an artist sculpted them to fit a museum. The first time I saw his bare chest, proving my hypothesis that he works out, but he gives his back the same attention.

I was stuck in place, unable to move or speak as he tried to reach the scratches on his back, making him flex even more. The red marks against his tan skin made his pristine body seem imperfect in a way that made my heart skip a beat.

The image of Ivan's eyes piercing my soul through the mirror earlier is also throwing me off-balance. What in the Hollywood movie scene was that?

If this was a country song, it would've been the slow, croon type that talks about slow-building love that lasts a lifetime.

Unfortunately, life does not play out like a sweet song. Mine has been more like a messy heartbreak song. Those are my favorite, anyway. Who doesn't want to go all Carrie Underwood with a baseball bat when your boyfriend cheats?

At least in my daydream, I reacted that way. It helped direct my anger and hurt toward something, even if I wasn't about to actually act on it.

Instead, I left town. There's a country song about that, too.

Boots claws at my lap, and I smile down at him before lifting him to my face.

"You're adorable," I tell him, squeezing his face. His meows make me chuckle. "Okay, okay. I'll loosen up. Go on and play." I place him on the floor and let him roam around so he gets acquainted with my office.

I grab the paperwork for Spooks's appointment and fill out the report with her progress. It's better than daydreaming about the hot vet I shouldn't like.

Instead, my attention goes to a situation where I felt completely out of my element. I have to wonder how I fit in this clinic. It seems most times I'm not prepared for what happens.

It's a feeling I hate. Nothing is worse than being unprepared and untrained to see a patient.

I arrived at Healing Hands feeling confident. I've been a vet for years, worked with a variety of animals and illnesses, but coyote, owls, and stubborn parrots are not my specialties.

Ivan, however, has experience in all sorts of animals it seems. Insecurity makes me question how good I really am at my job. I thought I was great in Dallas, but it seems a small-town clinic is not easier than a big city practice.

Shaking my head, I lean back in my seat and breathe out slowly. My heart races at the thought of not being up to par to work here, and I know I need to do something. Maybe I can find courses or read books on working with wild animals so I'm more prepared if we have situations like this week. It seems living in a more remote area opens the possibility of treating them.

I grab my laptop and search for a book on treating ranch animals and wildlife. Once I find the two books that seem the most educational, I purchase them. One thing in this career is that you never stop learning and growing.

Working here the last few weeks has been a serving of humble pie. From the relationship the staff has, to the clients being treated with familiarity, it's nothing like I'm used to.

And I want to become a part of it, merge into this community instead of being the outsider observing it.

When I finish the report on Spooks, I continue working on my proposal for boarding services. While it is a big responsibility, we did this in Dallas and it worked well. No one had to stay extra hours, and we took turns being on-call through the security cameras in case something happened.

Adding statistics of profit and expenses, a theoretical situation, minimum of pets necessary to make it work, and our nearby competition, I feel confident about this. Ivan can't say this isn't a good idea. I'm willing to be flexible, and he should be, too.

I stand and stretch, feeling my joints tight with tension. With Boots in hand, I head to Ivan's office to tell him I'd like to meet tomorrow to go over my proposal.

I knock on his office door and walk in. His back is to me, on his phone.

"Okay, I'll head over now." He turns and sees me, eyes widening. He mustn't have heard me knock.

"Sorry," I mouth.

He nods and continues listening to the person on the line.

"Yeah, don't worry. Give me about thirty minutes, and I'll be there." He blows out a breath, and I inch back, feeling like I'm intruding on his conversation.

He lifts his hand to stop me and says goodbye before hanging up.

"Sorry, I didn't realize you were on the phone."

"It's okay. I gotta go, though. That was Roger. I need to go out to the ranch."

"Now?" I ask. It's past closing time.

"Yeah." He crosses his arm, taking a defensive stance.

"Can I go with you?"

He leans back, eyebrows inching up in his forehead. He looks like a cartoon, staring at me with surprise.

"Don't look at me like that." I laugh awkwardly.

"I'm surprised. I thought you'd lecture me about working overtime." He tilts his head.

"No time like the present to see the ranch and the animals." I give him my best smile, not wanting to admit that I want to learn and get hands-on experience because I've never worked with farm animals.

"And what about Boots?" He lifts his chin toward the kitten in my arms.

"I'll take him in a carrier."

"If you want to." Ivan shrugs, grabbing his wallet from the drawer. "Let's go, then."

"I'll follow you," I say before heading to my office to get my purse and then one of the carriers we have here.

Boots fights me when I put him in the carrier, but I finally get him inside with a few scratches of my own on my arms.

"Ready to go, City Girl?" Ivan chuckles.

"Of course." I glare at him.

♥ ♥ ♥

I drive behind Ivan, taking in the vast land that surrounds us as we leave Sunshine Falls behind. The ranch is about twenty minutes away from what Ivan told me, and it's clear that it's a different world out here. It's beautiful as I pass fields with bales of hay and others with horses grazing.

We drive through the gates of a ranch, and my car rocks on the gravel road while Boots purrs. I can't tell if he's calmed by the rocking car or still resentful I put him in the carrier, but I can't exactly drive with him loose in the car or let him roam the ranch. Horses are in a large pen, and cattle roam in the distance, grazing grass.

I park beside Ivan near a large barn and see a man waiting outside for us. His eyes narrow when he sees my car, looking between the two of us.

"Roger, hey." Ivan reaches the man and shakes his hand.

"Hi, Ivan, thanks for coming out here so quickly. Seems I can't catch a break lately." Roger looks at me with curiosity.

"This is Madison," Ivan says before he can ask. "She's James's niece and our new partner at Healing Hands."

"Oh. Nice to meet you." He smiles my way. "I can't complain. My horse is getting double the attention from two professionals. Come into the barn." He guides the way, and I look at Ivan with raised brows in a silent question. I didn't even ask him what was going on here.

"Colic," he whispers.

Nodding, I look around the barn and inhale the unique scent of hay. A couple of horses peek through the stalls, curiously taking in the newcomers. I've always admired the beauty and serenity of horses, even if I never had the chance to interact with them.

"Here we are," Roger says with a deep furrow, looking at a horse that's laying on the ground. "He hasn't been eating or drinking and his bowel movements are almost nonexistent." Roger looks at us with a frown.

"We'll figure it out." Ivan claps his shoulder and opens the stall, looking at me expectantly.

I enter with him, waiting for instructions. Ivan listens to the horse's heartbeat before feeling around the abdomen. The horse flinches and groans. I remain an observer, helping Ivan whenever he asks for something. It's amazing to observe him work, the way his bottom lip tucks between his teeth when he's concentrating.

"I'm going to do a rectal palpation." Ivan tells Roger and then turns to me. "Ready, City Girl?" He smirks.

I roll my eyes and nod. I'll prove to him that a city girl can fit in the country. Just because I haven't worked on a farm doesn't mean that I can't treat a horse.

"We're going to help you, Dash." Ivan whispers, running a hand down his coat. "I need help standing him up." He looks at me.

"Okay."

We work together to get the horse up on his feet and then guide him so he's restrained. Using the stall door, we create a barrier to protect Ivan during the exam.

Ivan grabs a shoulder-length glove and tells me to continue to quietly restrain the horse. I nod and smile at Dash, mentally speaking to him. Our eyes connect, and a sense of peace and empathy hits me. He looks desperate.

I focus solely on the horse, not giving Ivan much attention so to not spook Dash. Ivan moves away after finishing up and looks at Roger.

"He has an intestinal blockage."

I press my lips together and pet Dash's neck.

"I'm going to give him an anti-inflammatory and then administer fluids and electrolytes through a nasogastric tube. We'll be here for a bit."

"Thanks." Roger nods, his shoulders tight with stress. "I'm going to do some work and leave y'all to it."

I smile encouragingly and look back at Dash.

"You'll be okay, boy." I glance at Ivan. "What do you need?"

"I'm going to inject the anti-inflammatory and then we'll get the nasogastric tube in. Mind passing me that bag?" He tilts his head toward the one hanging on the stall.

"You got it, boss," I say jokingly.

Ivan groans but focuses on his task. I hand the bag over to him and prepare the injection so he can administer it. It feels good to work out here. The air has the musky scent of dry grass and animals, and yet it's freeing. For the first time, it feels like Ivan and I work as a real team. No second-guessing, dancing around each other, or misunderstandings.

Ivan begins inserting the tube through Dash's nose, but he's resistant.

"Shhh...careful, boy," he says, removing the tube to start again. "Let's try this again." He looks at me and nods.

"Go for it. I'll keep him calm."

He starts again and prompts Dash to swallow to help with getting the tube down, and Dash is more cooperative this time. Once the tube is placed correctly, Ivan swipes the sleeve of his scrubs across his forehead and takes a deep breath.

Ivan begins administering fluids and electrolytes, which will help Dash immensely. We lean against the stall wall and observe him.

"He's a great horse," I say after a few minutes of silence.

"He is. All of Roger's horses are great. And they're important to his ranch."

"I bet." I put my hands behind me, trapping them against the wall and my back. "Does he have cattle?"

"Yeah, raises them for beef. Best meat around here, in my opinion."

"Wow. How long have you been treating his animals?"

"Since I graduated." Ivan checks on the tube to make sure it's all flowing properly.

"That's cool." I rock back and forth, trying to think of something else to talk about.

"What about you? You've really never worked with farm animals?"

"Unfortunately, I haven't. I never had the opportunity, but this is amazing." I wave a hand around.

"It is."

Silence falls over us again while Ivan checks on Dash, and we wait to administer another round of fluids. Suddenly, I remember about Boots.

Great, I'm already failing at being a cat parent.

"Snap. I should check on Boots. Maybe he needs to use the bathroom."

"Use the bathroom?" Ivan stares at me as if I've lost my mind.

"It's a more polite way to say he needs to pee or poop. He doesn't exactly have a sandbox in the kennel." Sarcasm drips from my voice.

Ivan rolls his eyes. "Yes, yes. I know what that means. Go on. I'll be here."

"Be right back."

"Uh, huh." Ivan focuses his attention back on Dash.

I rush to my car and open the door, smiling at Boots.

"Hey, little guy. Sorry about that. We're running a little behind. Do you need to use the bathroom?" I open the carrier, and he jumps out before I have a chance to react.

I throw my hands in the air. "Come back here!"

Boots runs ahead of me, bouncing around in the tall grass.

"Boots," I warn.

The last thing I need is to make a ridiculous impression on my first visit here. Boots ignores me, running faster. I scrub a hand down my face and go after him without trying to scare him. When he doesn't listen, I bend down and slap my thighs, prompting him to come to me. It might work if he were a dog, but cats are a completely different breed when it comes to cuddling.

My heart starts to race when he runs toward the chicken coop.

Oh, no.

"Boots," I hiss, trying not to call attention to the situation, but he doesn't even hear me.

I take off after him, halting right in front of the coop. Boots is inside, and a chicken is glaring at him, moving its neck ready to peck him. He hisses, arching his back.

This can't be good. I'm either going to lose my pet cat after adopting him a few hours ago or Roger is going to be down a chicken. I don't know which is worse.

"Boots." I grip the coop fence, and he looks at me. "That's it, boy, come to momma." I open my arms.

While he's distracted looking at me, the chicken pecks his back. Boots meows loudly and reaches his claw out to scratch the chicken. I scrub my eyes as they get into a fight. This cannot be happening.

Note to self: clip kitten nails right away.

I search for an opening and find a small square opening near the ground. There has to be another door. Scanning the area, I come up empty, but I'm more distracted in the cat and chicken fight going on. Boots screeches and jumps away, but now more chickens have joined in, protecting their own and ganging up on my poor, albeit rascal, little guy.

I drop to my knees and squeeze through the small opening. The first half of my body makes it in, observing the situation up close and personal. My hands grip the ground, grimacing when my palm lands on chicken droppings, and I pull forward, but my body stays where it is.

"Biscuit on a cracker." I huff to myself.

Nothing happens when I push my body back.

This situation is getting worse. I wiggle my body, crawling my legs back to reverse out of here, but my hips are stuck right by the frame of this door.

Why did I think this was a good idea?

My hands move, and I feel another wet splat. Looking down, I grimace. More chicken poop. *Wonderful.*

"Ow!" A chicken pecks my forehead, and it stings. Spooks the owl has nothing on the angry look this hen is giving me.

She pecks me on the forehead again, and I scream. I wave her away with one hand while maintaining my balance with the other. Poop on my hand is fine. I'm a vet and have dealt with worse, but I do not want to land face first on the ground.

The chicken doesn't let up, probably thinking she's protecting her family from an intruder. I look around for Boots, and the little traitor is up on the fence, looking down at me with what looks like a devious smile.

"What in the world?" A male voice sounds behind me, and I try to crane my head to look out the other side of the fence.

"What happ—?" Ivan's question gets cut off, likely from seeing me. "Madison, what are you doing?" His voice is tight.

"If you wanted to steal some eggs, you could've used the door for humans," the other man says. It doesn't sound like Roger.

"I'm so sorry, man. Madison is my partner at the clinic. I'm sure there's an explanation for this." The accusation in his voice is evident.

"There is!" I call out. "Boots ran from me and ended up in here. He got into a fight with the chickens, and I was trying to get him out. I didn't see the other door," I explain.

I feel something brush along my legs and scream, shaking them.

"Is Boots the cat crawling on your legs?" the other man asks.

I relax when I hear it's Boots and nod. "That would be him. He's not getting any extra treats today."

"We'll help you out," Ivan says, flatly.

I want to die right now. I don't think I'll ever recover from this. My heart is in my throat as the two men pull my legs.

"Maybe we need to butter her," the other one says, laughing.

"Funny," I deadpan, grimacing at the force they use to pull my legs.

"I've heard of kids getting their heads stuck in railings, but never a woman getting her body stuck in a chicken coop." This man doesn't let up.

It'd be great if he'd shut up.

"Hang on, let me take a picture to put it on our joke wall in the break room." Ivan chuckles.

"Don't you dare."

"Didn't you want a chance at the Joke of the Day?" Humor laces his voice.

"Ivan," I warn on a growl. "This is not the moment."

They finally get me out of there, and I sit on the ground, staring up at them. The young man wearing a cowboy hat chuckles while Ivan shakes his head, holding Boots.

"I'm Danny, one of the ranch hands."

"Thanks for saving my life." I stand, brushing my hands against my scrubs. My face flames, but I do my best to stand tall.

"You're welcome. Next time, use the door, and you might want to add some Neosporin on those peck marks." He tips his hat and walks away, laughing to himself.

"Soooo..." I awkwardly shift on my feet, lips pressed together.

"You've earned the nickname City Girl. I don't want to hear any complaints about overtime when this scenario pushes back our schedule."

"My lips are sealed, but you didn't really take any pictures, right?" My eyes round.

"You'll have to wait to find out." He shrugs. "By the way, you're no longer allowed to come to a ranch without adult supervision." He cracks a smile. "Let's finish here so we can leave. You need to clean yourself up." He hands Boots over to me. I grab the mischievous kitty and scowl at him.

Feeling disappointed, I feel the need to apologize. "I am sorry. I was desperate when I saw all the chickens attacking Boots." I reach for Ivan's arm and think better of it since they're still stained with poo.

"There's a sink in the barn. Wash your hands and face there. I have Neosporin in my bag that you can apply."

"Darn poultry." I glare at the coop.

I follow Ivan into the barn, and he shows me to the sink before getting back to Dash. I place Boots on the ground between my feet, wash up, and bite my lip when I splash water on my face. I'm sure to have scars. Attack of the birds. There's a name for a horror film.

After grabbing the Neosporin from Ivan's bag and applying it, I go to my car to put Boots back in the carrier and head to the stall to see what Ivan's up to. I hope he doesn't hold this against me for too long. Although, he's right that I've won the nickname City Girl all on my own.

14

♥ ♥ ♥

IVAN

I DON'T KNOW IF I should laugh or be angry at Madison. Seeing her stuck in the chicken coop through the hen's door would make me laugh in any other situation. Thankfully, Danny was cool about it, and his jokes lightened the mood.

I administer the last round of fluids on Dash and shake my head, chuckling to myself.

"Are you laughing?" Madison walks into the stall.

"I was thinking what an *egg-cellent* point you proved by that move. Clearly, our farm clients will remain as mine." Thankfully, this happened at Roger's farm. He is easygoing and won't take this the wrong way.

"Are you seriously being punny right now?" She crosses her arms.

"I'm a *comedi-hen*." I shrug.

Madison laughs, looking more relieved than she did a few minutes ago.

"You're not that funny." She rolls her eyes.

"Careful or I'll post the picture on the joke wall," I playfully threaten.

"Ivan Romero, I'm your partner. Cut me some slack." She slaps my arm.

"You have chicken peck marks on your forehead and you expect me to be serious?" I laugh. "How did you even think that was a good idea?" I shake my head.

"I didn't. I looked for a different entrance but didn't see it. The last thing we needed was Boots to hurt one of Roger's hens. Then, the chickens ganged up on him, and I was scared he'd get injured."

"What do you call a gang of hens?"

She lifts her hand to stop me. "I get it. You're hilarious. We'll give you a medal at work tomorrow." She rolls her eyes.

I smile at her sarcasm. "We're lucky it happened here and Roger won't complain, but we do need to be more careful." My expression turns serious now.

"I agree. It was a one-off." She rolls her lips between her teeth, her cheeks turning pink.

"Nest time, call for help."

She glares at me, and I lift my arms. "That was the last one, promise." I laugh.

Her smile makes an appearance, and she walks toward Dash to check on him. She looks so much like the woman I met at the coffee shop before we were thrown into this situation. That's a dangerous feeling, and yet a part of me likes it. I've always played it safe, and with Madison I'm tempted to throw caution to the wind and dive in.

But we have a business to run successfully. James has to be proud of us. We can't have people in town talking about how we're ridiculous vets, or questioning why James thought it was a good idea to retire and leave us in charge.

Once I'm done with Dash, I carefully remove the nasogastric tube, and pet him softly.

"Good job, boy."

Washing everything up and putting it away, I call Roger to the barn. Madison stays by Dash's side, running a hand down the center of his face. She seems to have taken a liking to the horse, much better than the chickens.

"Hey," Roger says as he meets us by the stall. "How's my boy?"

"He should be better soon. I recommend you start feeding him good-quality grass every four to six hours once his system is back to functioning properly with bowel movement. Keep him hydrated and his meals small to start with. After twenty-four hours, you can increase the amount he eats given there are no complications. If there are, call me, but I think he's going to be great." I pat Dash's side.

"Thank you, Ivan. Madison." He looks at her and chuckles softly. Her hand goes to her forehead, but she remains quiet.

"You're welcome." I shake his hand.

"It was nice meeting you," Madison tells him.

"Likewise." Roger nods, remaining professional.

I grab my bag and walk out of the barn with Madison beside me. Once we reach our cars, she pauses and looks at me.

"I really am sorry, Ivan. I'm better at my job than this." She shakes her head.

"It's fine." I nod, not wanting her to feel worse than she already does. Despite my jokes, I can tell she feels terrible about this situation.

Her tense shoulders are proof enough that she's stressed. We need to support each other to make this work. I can't help but want to protect her.

"Follow me out."

"Yeah." She nods.

"It's fine, Madison. What's done is done." I smile encouragingly. "It'll make for a funny story someday."

"I still can't believe I did that. I've always prided myself on the work I do, not silly antics like this. It's so out of character, but Boots was outnumbered." She sighs heavily.

"Then you're a superhero to Boots."

"Right. The traitor that left me defenseless."

"I mean, he's a cat. It's pretty normal behavior in my eyes." I try to joke to lighten the mood.

Madison glowers at the cat sitting in his carrier as if he were an angel. I chuckle at the way he looks at her with his angled head.

"He's lucky he's cute," she says.

"Very true." I look at her profile, noting the cuts. "Don't forget to disinfect the scratches on your face."

"Ugh." Her hand reaches up to touch them. "I'm going to need pounds of concealer to hide these at work tomorrow. The last thing I need is our staff thinking I'm not capable of doing my job."

"That won't happen."

She arches her brow, challenging me. "Says the man threatening to post a picture."

"All in good fun. Anyone can have an incident in this industry. I mean, look at me and Boots. He got me good on my back."

Madison chuckles, her face lighting up a bit. It's a beautiful sight. One I shouldn't be admiring, but I can't help it.

"Thanks for being understanding."

"Oh, I wanted to shake you when I saw what happened, but I get it. We're equals, Madison. I'm not going to parent you." I shake my head, running a hand through my hair.

"I appreciate that." She rocks on her feet with her hands in her pockets. Her scrubs are a dirty mess, and it's such a contrasting view of how she normally presents herself.

"I'll see you tomorrow, City Girl."

"I'll no longer fight you on the nickname." She smiles. "Goodnight."

I get into my car and take a deep breath. It's been a stressful afternoon and yet having Madison here felt good. Shaking away that growing feeling in my chest, I pull out of my spot and drive away from the ranch with Madison behind me.

I can't help but look at her through my rearview mirror. She chews on her bottom lip, touches her face, looks to the right, likely at Boots. When her lips start moving and her head rocking, I chuckle to myself. So she likes to sing in the car.

Having uninterrupted time to observe her allows me to see how she truly is, and it's proving that the woman at work who's tough and inflexible isn't her natural state.

At an intersection, she turns right and I continue straight on. Disappointment hits me at no longer being able to watch her. It's ridiculous.

I have to shake this mood or working with Madison is going to be one big complication. I can't exactly have a crush on my co-worker and act normal. My past has proven that. I am not a smooth operator.

♥ ♥ ♥

"Honey, you're home," Luna calls out when I walk into our apartment.

"I am, and I'm tired." I enter the living room to see her curled up on the couch with a book in her hands and Charlie on the floor by the feet of the sofa.

"I don't blame you. How was the horse?"

Dropping my bag on the armchair, I sit on the couch beside her. "He has colic, but he'll be okay. I left him looking better."

"That's great." She bends the corner of the page and closes her book.

"You know bookworms everywhere are gasping at your guilty pleasure, right?" I lift my chin toward her book.

"If a book isn't well-loved and used, then was it really ever enjoyed by a reader? So I dog-ear pages and annotate directly on the page. It's not like I throw the book in a fire. *That* is a sin." Her eyes wide.

Luna straightens her legs and stretches her arms before standing.

"Can we order dinner?" I look at her, massaging my neck.

"Yeah. What do you want?" She reaches for her phone.

"Anything. My brain has shut off for the day. You decide. So long as I don't have to cook, I'll be happy. I'm gonna shower." I walk toward my room, the pressure of the day finally weighing down on my shoulders.

What I need is a hot shower and to watch some TV. Anything to take my mind off the woman who's invading my thoughts.

I check my phone and see a message.

Ezra: Hey buddy, how's work going? I'm going to visit town in the next few weeks, so we'll get together.

Me: Work's okay. Long day, but I'm glad you'll be in town. Let me know when so we can plan something.

Ezra: For sure. How's it going with the new partner?

Me: It's getting better. Although, she got stuck in a chicken coop at work today.

Ezra: How in the world did she manage that?

Me: Long story, but she was trying to save her cat.

Ezra: Lol... Maybe I can meet this woman when I'm in town.

Me: Considering my mom thinks her and I are going to get married, you'd get an invitation to my engagement party.

Ezra: Hahaha. That sounds like your mom.

Me: She's only gotten worse with age, but don't tell her I said that.

Ezra: I won't. I'll let you know the exact date I'll be in town once I'm sure. Maybe I can see Luna, too. It's been far too long.

Me: Good plan. I'll let her know.

After a shower, I meet Luna in the living room.

"Ezra's coming to town in a few weeks, and he wants to get together."

Her gaze lifts from her book, unimpressed. "*Luna-tic* Ezra?" She arches her brow.

"He was like ten when he called you that. He's matured since then."

"I'm sure," she says sarcastically, crossing her legs. "What'd you order?"

"Enchiladas. You look like you could use some comfort food." She lifts her brows.

"Thanks. Definitely a good choice." I sit on the couch next to her and grab the remote. "Do you mind?"

"Nope. Are you okay, though? I sense you're going through some things." She places her book on her lap and turns to me.

"I'm fine." I sigh, tossing my head back on the sofa to help relax my tight muscles.

"Right, and I won most popular girl in high school." She huffs, arching a brow.

"You weren't unpopular." I laugh.

"You know what I mean. I didn't run in Jenna's circle. By the way, I have tea," she singsongs. "I heard Jenna's getting divorced." Luna's eyes widen.

"Really? I thought her and Greg were in love *forever and ever.*" I try to imitate Jenna's high-pitched voice.

Luna laughs, shaking her head. "I guess not. I can't even feel sorry. She was so cruel to us growing up. Not that she's any nicer now." Her nostrils flare.

Jenna hated us. She used to make fun of our background and the food we ate growing up as if beans and rice were so foreign. These are the same people who go to a Mexican restaurant and order a burrito with beans and rice.

Just because we're Cuban doesn't mean we're aliens. We live in Texas, for goodness sake, Hispanics and Latins aren't a foreign concept here.

"Anyway, I thought that would brighten your mood but clearly it didn't." Luna waves her hand. "Tell me what's going on."

"Just a long day. Madison went with me to the ranch and well...she's not very knowledgeable with ranches it seems."

"What does that mean?" She tilts her head.

"We had a rescue kitty brought in today, and after examining it, I was going to put it up for adoption. Madison said she'd keep it."

"That's nice," Luna interjects.

"Of course." I nod. "I think it's great, but the kitty—Boots—was in the car. Since we were taking a while, she went to check on him and let him out a bit. Long story short, he snuck into the chicken coop and got into a fight. Madison tried to crawl through the chicken door to save him and got stuck."

"Oh, no." Luna covers her mouth with her hands, but her shoulders shake with laughter.

"Yup. A ranch hand and I had to pull her out. It was a disaster. We're supposed to be professionals, and there's one of our vets stuck in a chicken coop." I blow out a breath and run a hand along my stubbled jaw.

"That's hilarious, though." Luna slaps her knee.

"It'd do great in *America's Funniest Home Videos*." I chuckle. "She looked ridiculous."

"I can imagine." She shakes her head. "Are you guys getting along better?"

"We are. This situation annoyed me, but if it were Charlie in that coop with chickens attacking him, I might have been desperate enough to do the same thing." I reach down and pet him.

He looks up at me, his butt waggling, and turns over on his back so I can tickle his belly.

"Spoiled guy." I rub his stomach.

"He is spoiled. Sometimes I think he's more human than canine." She smiles at me. "Don't let one situation ruin the progress you've made with Madison. You two are stuck working together for the long haul unless one of you decides to back out of the business, and I don't see that happening." She pats my arm.

I nod, knowing she's right.

"And," Luna continues, "you could be a bit more flexible. I know you're understanding with your clients, but maybe extend that to Madison. She's adjusting to a new role, town, and clinic."

"I know." She's right. As flexible as I want to be at work with our clients, I can get stuck in the way things are *supposed* to be in my mind and can limit my mentality in other aspects. I'm inflexibly flexible if that exists.

If I expect Madison to mold to the way things work in Sunshine Falls, then I need to bend to her expectations. It's why I cracked jokes earlier instead of lecturing her.

Putting myself in her shoes, maybe I would've reacted the same way. When an animal is in danger, you don't think clearly to call for help sometimes and just go into problem-solving mode. Whether the idea is smart or not.

We're equals, even if I did tease her about working with farm animals.

15

♥ ♥ ♥

MADISON

I PARK AT WORK earlier than usual with Boots in tow and get out of my car. I couldn't leave him alone for hours since Uncle James and Aunt Susan are already gone. Hopefully he doesn't get into any trouble today.

Yesterday's humiliating situation is still raw, and I hope Ivan doesn't bring it up. I want to show him my ideas for the boarding facility and need him to see me as a professional.

I unlock the front door and walk into the clinic, locking it behind me.

My hand freezes on the lock when a high-pitched cry hits my ears. Everything inside of me ices, my skin prickling.

What in the world?

Boots in his carrier, and he's standing on alert. Another cry echoes through the place. I walk through the hallway, following the sound with careful steps. The farther down the hall I get, I hear Ivan's voice.

Relief floods me, and I search in which room he's in. Maybe he had an early morning call. I swear the man lives to work.

"Ivan?" I open the door to one of our larger treatment rooms and stare at the sight before me. "Um..." My eyes round and my eyebrows draw together.

"Hey." Ivan turns around to face me, plastering on a smile. "This is Llama Mia." He reaches out to pat the llama standing in the middle of the room, but the animal screeches again.

"I'm guessing he doesn't like his name." I arch a brow.

"Right." Ivan steps away.

"What is a llama doing here? Haven't we had enough with coyotes and owls?" I place Boots's carrier on the floor and wave my hands in the air.

"Llamas aren't nearly as defensive as those two animals."

"Where did he come from?" I'm afraid to know the answer seeing how skittish the animal is.

"I found him."

"Excuse me?" I blink and shake my head in case it'll make the words he spoke land differently on my brain.

"I went for a run early this morning and saw him wandering, lost."

"How do you know he was lost and not wild?" I cross my arms.

"Because he had a halter on." Ivan points to it on the table.

"Oh." I drop my arms. Boots purrs from his carrier.

"I guess it's bring your pet to work day." Ivan grins in a way that's too charming for his own good.

"I couldn't leave him alone, but this is different than stealing a llama."

"I didn't steal him. He was lost. I'll keep him here until his owner comes to find him."

149

I shake my head. "Have you lost your mind?" I throw my hands in the air. "We can't keep a llama." I round the animal from a safe distance. He looks cared for, which is a good sign that he hasn't been lost for too long.

"Just until I figure out what farm he escaped from. He'll be safe with us. We're vets."

"What if we get accused of housing an animal that isn't ours? An animal we don't have a license to own." I lift my brows.

"Madison, we're a vet practice, we hold lost pets until they're found all the time. It'll be a few days top."

"How do you even expect it to stay in this room? Llamas are meant to live outdoors." I look around at all the supplies the animal can throw around. This place isn't exactly llama-proof.

Now there's something I never thought I'd have to worry about.

"I'm going to contact the ranchers and farmers I know to ask if they've heard of anyone who lost a llama and research llama farms in the area." He smiles at the llama and pets him on the side.

The llama stares at him unimpressed and a little annoyed. The way his face follows Ivan's movements makes me nervous. He is not happy to be here.

"How'd you even bring him in?"

"Well, I was out for a run, like I told you. Since he had the harness, I was able to hold on to him. Luna brought my car to where I was and I got him into the back seat."

"Stop right there." I lift a hand. "How did this big guy fit in your car?"

"With his head out of the window." Ivan chuckles. "I know it seems crazy but look at how cute he is." He pouts.

I jump when the llama cries out again and steps away from us.

"We should call animal services and have them find the owner," I suggest.

The poor animal is looking startled and angry, which is never a good combination when facing an animal.

"I already did and they're already making calls. Two days, Madison." Ivan holds up two fingers. "Please. I've always wanted to own a llama."

"You have?" I tilt my head, my brows knit together.

"Yeah. Growing up they were my favorite animal. I had a stuffed llama I'd sleep with every night." Ivan presses his lips together. "I don't know why I said that."

I laugh, slapping my leg. "Please tell me you still have that stuffed animal."

He remains silent.

"You do!" My eyes widen. "Oh, my goodness. Dr. Romero, I didn't take you for the kind to cherish a toy from childhood. You should've brought it to work so our friend here could think it's part of his herd."

"Funny, Madison," he says flatly. "Wait, let me get you the Funniest Vet Award."

"I think it's cute." I chuckle. "Is this like your dream, then? Like kids who always wanted to see a mermaid and finally do." My eyes gleam.

"Mermaids don't exist." Ivan crosses his arms. "Great, you're going to hold this against me for the rest of my life." He seems unimpressed.

"Uh." I wave my hand in front of us. "I already have kidnapping an animal to hold against you."

"I didn't kidnap him. I saved him," he says defensively. His body is tense as he looks at the llama.

I laugh at his reaction and shake my head.

He reaches out to pet the llama again, but the animal jerks his head away and backs away.

"They're shy animals," Ivan tells me.

"I know."

"Two days to find the owner?" He looks at me with pleading eyes.

"I'll make you a deal." I lift a brow and grin.

"What?" Ivan sighs.

"I'll give you two days because it's the perfect way to test our boarding facility."

"You've gotta be kidding me." His shoulders drop.

"It's that or lose your childhood dream of owning a llama, even if for a couple of days." I fight back my laughter.

"You're sneaky."

"I'm smart." I shrug. "I have the proposal done and was hoping to show it to you, but this is so much better. Of course, we don't have the area built yet, but we can figure that out."

"Fine." He grits out.

Boots meows loudly, scratching the carrier, and the llama starts running.

"Whoa," Ivan calls out. "It's okay. It's just a little kitty. He's your friend."

Ivan holds his arms out to try to calm the llama down, but he's not having it. He rolls his lips, a low *pfff* sound coming from him as he spits on Ivan.

My eyes pop as I stare at the man before me with llama saliva on his face and shirt, and I toss my head back laughing.

My cackles are loud, and tears build in my eyes.

"This..." My words get swallowed by my laughter.

"Don't say a word," Ivan says tightly.

"If you speak, the saliva will seep into your mouth. Then you could say you've second-hand kissed a llama." I can't stop laughing; my entire body shakes. "I wish...I had a camera." I wipe my eyes and see Ivan grabbing paper towel and cleaning his face.

Ivan scowls, and my laughter grows louder.

"I guess we're even after yesterday," he mumbles.

"Definitely." I nod. This makes me feel so much better about getting stuck in the chicken coop.

"I'm going to wash my face and change."

I wave him off with a wide smile and look at the llama.

"You're hilarious." I point at him.

Boots continues to meow, and I bend down to open the carrier and reach for him. He's probably curious about what's going on. I hold him securely in my arms and show him the room and llama.

"This is a new friend."

The llama tilts his head and looks at Boots with curiosity.

"Do you like him?" I ask him.

The llama makes a humming sound, and I smile. Boots is also looking at him with rapt attention. I walk closer to the large animal to see how he reacts to the kitten. I don't want to be his second spit victim, so I'm being extra careful.

Boots leans forward, rubbing his head against Llama Mia's chin, and I smile. I place Boots on the floor and observe their interaction. He looks tiny next to the llama. They slowly inch toward each other, figuring out if they can trust one another. The llama sits on the floor, and a sense of joy fills me. It's like he wants to be closer to Boots.

After a few minutes, they begin to play together. Boots rubs himself against the llama's fluffy coat and purrs. The llama pets Boots with his snout. Ivan needs to see this.

"I'll be right back," I tell the two and quietly leave the room in search of Ivan.

I go to his office and walk in, halting. His back is to me, and he's shirtless. I once again have the blessing of seeing that defined back as his muscles flex and relax with his movements while he gets a shirt and starts to put it over his head.

Ivan turns around while he finishes tugging his scrub shirt, giving me a peek of his abs. He freezes with wide eyes while I stand at the entrance like a peeping Tom. He hastily brings the shirt down to cover his body, much to my disappointment, and stares at me.

"Uh."

"Oh. Sorry. I was stari—looking at you. I mean, *for* you," I quickly correct.

My face burns, and I avert my eyes from his, hoping he didn't understand my mix up. I was definitely looking at him. Ivan went from handsome to sexy in the span of two seconds.

My heart is racing as I stand frozen in place. My legs feel weak with embarrassment, and I'm afraid they'll give out on me at any minute.

"Is something wrong?" Ivan asks awkwardly.

"No." I shake my head.

"Did you leave the llama alone?" His voice rises.

"Huh? Oh, the llama." I shake my head. "Right. No. Well, technically, yes. I wanted you to see something." I stutter over my words, talking a bit robotically.

"What happened?" Ivan sighs, running a hand down his face.

"Nothing bad. I think you'll like it. Or feel jealous." I smirk, getting my wits about me.

I walk away from his office toward the treatment room with Ivan hot on my heels. When I open the door, I smile. Boots is lying on top of the llama, who's still on the floor.

"You've gotta be kidding me," Ivan mumbles.

When the llama sees us, his ears lift.

"It's like your two arch nemesis are BFFs. I'm sorry that Boots stole your friend." I pat his bicep, wishing I could squeeze his arm a bit and get a real feel of his muscles. My body flushes, so I look forward at the animals instead of the man making me feel things I promised myself I wouldn't.

"I can't believe this." He shakes his head. "I'm going to call some contacts." His shoulders drop, and I smile at him.

"Don't worry, Ivan. We'll try to get the llama to befriend you before he leaves. We can't surrender to a childhood dream so easily." I bite down on my growing smile.

"Just remember you got stuck in a coop, City Girl." He arches a brow, pointing at me.

"And you got spit by a llama, exotic animal whisperer." I shift to face him straight on, not realizing how close we'd be.

"We need to work on your nickname skills." His voice is low, and his eyes burn into mine.

I swallow and nod. The last thing I'm thinking about right now is nicknames. His brown eyes sparkle with hues of gold that are only visible this close. I breathe out, parting my lips.

My brain is releasing warning signs to get me out of this situation, but my heart is dancing in my chest, covering its ears from the alarm bells like a petulant child.

Ivan leans closer, his eyes shifting between mine. He reaches out, touching a strand of hair between his fingers. He rubs it softly as if the texture would be different from his hair.

Tensions zaps between us like electrical currents. My entire body feels hot as I wait for his next move with anticipation. I'm a statue, unable to act out.

"Soft like satin," he says with a gruff voice, releasing my hair.

"Thanks," I whisper.

"I like your freckles."

"Really?" I scrunch up my nose.

"Yeah." He brushes his finger across the bridge of my nose and to the apple of my cheek. "They're like constellations. It was one of the first things I noticed about you at the coffee shop." His words are soft, a blanket against my skin.

Seeing him at the coffee shop feels like a lifetime ago. Like we were different people. And it's the first time either of us brings it up.

"I sometimes wonder what would've happened had I officially met you there before here. Had we talked more than we did before I learned you were James's niece?"

"Would it have made a difference?" I ask because once I knew he was my co-worker, fears of my past would hit me, and I don't know if I can let that go.

"Maybe." He presses his lips together.

My chest rises and falls quickly as my heart beats faster. Ivan leans in, his lips a breadth away. I trap the air in my ribs, waiting and warring with myself. I could give in to this feeling and risk the future, or I can play it safe and stop him right now.

I've got an angel on one shoulder and a devil on the other, both of them making valid points. While I internally argue with both sides of myself, Ivan's lips press against mine, catching me by surprise. It's tentative at first as if he's testing the waters, trying to see if it's safe to move forward.

When I don't fight him, he cups my cheek and kisses me. It's a soft kiss that sparks fireworks throughout my body, making me feel alive. The angel and devil evaporate. Every argument that goes against this silences. The only thing I'm aware of is the humming of my heart and his lips against mine.

I sigh, wrapping an arm around his neck. My soul is exuberant, feeling as if it's wrapped around his. Whatever this is, it's a new feeling. It's like the pieces of my broken heart are fusing together again but in a different shape.

Ivan slows the kiss, inching his head back to look at me. His eyes are intense, and yet he smiles softly.

"Sorry," he whispers.

I shake my head. "Don't be." I move my hand from his neck, smoothing it along his shoulder and chest before dropping it.

"It might not be the best idea since we work together."

"I know," I spit out quickly.

"But"—Ivan continues—"it felt right."

I smile and glance down. Ivan hooks his finger under my chin and lifts my face.

"Don't hide your smile from me." His thumb strokes my cheek.

157

Uncontrollably, my face splits into a wide grin.

"There are those dimples that captivated me from the beginning."

"I thought it was my freckles."

"It's the whole package." His voice is smooth.

I smile like a silly schoolgirl as I stare into his eyes. A loud screech goes off like an alarm and then a crash. We both turn our heads and look inside the treatment room.

At least we had a romantic moment before chaos ensued.

16

♥ ♥ ♥

IVAN

I TURN SO FAST to see what the loud sound was that I almost knock Madison on the floor.

"Sorry." I hold her steady.

"It's okay." She looks into the room and her eyes bug out. "Oh, my goodness."

Different supplies are thrown about, and the llama is sniffing a metal bowl. Boots sits on the top shelf of the built-in furniture, observing from above like an all-mighty presence, but I doubt he's innocent in any of this.

And both of these animals are guilty of ruining the best moment of my life.

My eyes cut to Madison standing beside me, and I smile as she stares around the room with a hand over her mouth. Right now, all I can think about is how sweet it was to kiss her. How much I want to do it again. Madison turns her face to look at me and drops her hand, her eyebrows dipping.

"Why are you smiling? Have you seen this room?" She waves a hand toward the mess, and I nod. "Then? It's not funny, Ivan. We open the clinic in..." She checks her watch. "In fifteen minutes."

My grin widens as she panics. "I'm admiring the view."

"With a smile? It's not something to be happy about."

"No. This view." I reach for her hair again to feel the satiny texture of it.

Madison's shoulders drop and she tilts her head.

"You're cute, and I'm all for you admiring me when we don't have a llama-ster on our hands."

"Llama-ster?" I lift my brows.

"Yeah. Llama disaster."

I chuckle and drop my hand. "Fine. Let's clean this, and I'll tie him up until I can make a few more calls."

We get to work, cleaning up the supplies and washing everything to sterilize it. I'm not planning on using this room today for a big, fluffy reason, but we can't leave it the way it is.

"Here you a—" Kate walks into the room and stops. "What is that?"

I look at her over my shoulder as I finish washing another bowl.

"I mean, I know it's a llama but what's it doing here?" She stares at him with wide eyes.

"He was lost, so I brought him in to find his owner," I explain.

"And fulfill your childhood dream." She giggles.

"She knows!" Madison calls out, pushing her hand through the air as if high-fiving Kate from a distance.

"We all know about Ivan's obsession with Llamas."

I glare at her.

"I mean, love for the animal," she corrects.

"Except the dream of a child was shattered when the llama gave him the cold shoulder and then spat on him," Madison says.

They laugh at my expense while I finish cleaning up.

ABI SABINA

"No! No, no, no. Bad boy," I call out when the llama begins chewing on the paper towel, pulling out the roll.

Kate and Madison's laughter grows as I grab the llama and pull him away, putting the harness back on him. I had removed it to make sure he wasn't injured. Once the harness is secure, I grab a rope and tie him to a bar on the top part of the wall. I still have no idea why that bar is there, but it's serving a great purpose right now.

"By the way, there's no new joke."

"Oh, darn." I tap my pockets, searching for the flashcard. "I left it at home."

"Well, you had an exciting morning," Kate says. "If I was faced with my favorite animal for the first time, I'd forget about everything else." She teases me.

"I can put one up," Madison says.

I look at her for a beat.

"And it's not related to what happened yesterday." She pinches her lips together. "I had an idea the other day and saved it."

"Yeah, that's great. Thanks." After kissing her, I can't really get protective of my jokes. The line between us has blurred.

"What happened yesterday?" Kate asks.

"Nothing," Madison practically yells. "I mean, nothing worth mentioning." She waves her off.

Kate looks at Madison as if she's lost her mind and shrugs. Madison walks out of the room with Kate behind her, leaving me alone with the llama. I walk up to him with raised hands.

"I come in peace. No more spitting, please." He seems to understand and just stares at me. I reach out to pet him and smile when he lets me.

162

"You're a troublemaker but you're cute. I'm sure that's how you escaped your home." I run my hand along his neck and back, smiling to myself. The llama hums, so I take that as a good sign.

Madison enters the room again and crosses her arms. "It's great you're enjoying yourself, but it's time to open the clinic."

"Funny," I say flatly. "I'm going to make some calls before my first appointment. Maybe Roger knows who the llama belongs to or can spread the word for me."

"Sounds good. I made you coffee." She lifts the mug in her hand.

"Really?" I tilt my head, walking toward her and grab the mug. "Thanks."

"You're welcome. I figured you didn't have time for a cup." She bites her lower lip, pulling my eyes toward it.

"About earlier." I lift my gaze to her eyes.

They're round and hopeful yet hold a hint of hesitation. I want to get rid of that uncertainty and leave her open for me.

"Sure, it was unexpected and complicated, but I don't regret it."

She nods silently, reaching for my free hand and squeezing it. "Let's get to work, Dr. Romero."

"I need to check out your joke first." I look back at the room and make sure the llama is okay.

"Come on, Boots." Madison bends and opens her arms. The kitty walks straight to her, and I swear he smirks at me on his way.

I thought he was my buddy, but it seems he's chosen the auburn beauty over me. I can't blame him. I'm enamored with her as well.

163

We head to the staffroom, and I go straight to the cork board to see what joke she came up with.

Why were the ferrets gathered?

For a business meeting.

I chuckle and nod in approval. Madison smiles proudly and takes a bow.

"Madison, your first patient is here. Kate is taking a look now," Rose enters the room to tell her.

"Thanks, I'll be right there." She looks at me with a secret smile before leaving to her appointment.

Once in my office, I call Roger to ask him about this llama. As much as I wish I could keep him, we don't have the space or the time to care for him. Maybe I can make a deal with the owner and go visit from time to time. It'd be the perfect stress-reliever.

♥ ♥ ♥

When I get a short break at work, I go check on the llama. Roger said he'd ask around his circle, and I researched a few llama farms, but none of them are missing one.

I walk into the room and find the llama lying comfortably on the floor, rope undone.

"Uhh..." He looks at me, unbothered, and goes back to resting. At least he's calm, but how in the world did he undo the knot on the rope? I can now testify about a llama's intelligence.

Footsteps echo outside of the room, but I ignore them, figuring it's one of our employees.

"Oh, my goodness, it's true!" I hear Sara's voice and turn around.

"What are you doing here?" I cross my arms.

"I heard you found a llama, and I wanted to come check if it was true. Looks like it is." She walks into the room. "Hey, big guy." She smiles at him.

The llama looks at her with interest before laying his head back down.

"Sara, you can't just show up at my work and walk around the back rooms."

"You're the boss, of course I can." She bends down, reaching her hand out and petting the llama.

"How'd you even find out?" I shake my head.

"Luna told Tía Emma who told Mom. I was at home and overheard the conversation."

"Of course you did." I take a deep breath. "I need to get back to work. Can you leave?" I eye her with my hands on my hips.

"I can stay and take care of him. I need something to do to get my mind off my failure at finding a job." She pouts, batting her eyelashes.

"No."

"Pleeeeease, Ivan. You're the best big brother in the world."

"You're obnoxious." I glare at her.

"No. I'm the best middle sister in the world," she corrects me with an air of confidence.

I snort and nod. I'm going to regret this, but I need to get back to work and don't have time to convince her. She's stubborn as a mule, so it'll take longer than I have to get her to leave, and she knows it.

Her winning smile covers her face, and she sits next to the llama.

"Careful, he spits," I warn her with a smirk, and her eyes widen before she laughs.

"Let me guess how you know."

I grumble and leave the room with a trail of laughter behind me. This place is a zoo today, no pun intended.

"Hey, I'm glad I caught you. Are you busy?" Madison meets me in the hallway.

"I have a patient now."

"Right. Well, can we talk after?"

"During our lunch break," I offer.

"Are you asking me to lunch?" she teases.

"Uh..." I shake my head. "I mean, if you want to." My words come out jumbled.

"I'm joking, Ivan." She lifts her hand to stop me from sticking my foot in my mouth.

That's not exactly what I should say to the woman I kissed a few hours ago. The uncool guy is back, and he can't remember how to talk to the woman he likes. You'd think in my late twenties I'd overcome this stage.

"We can have lunch together."

"You're not smooth." She chuckles. "I wanted to bring up a few things for the clinic, so lunch will be great."

"Perfect. We can eat in my office."

I've been more myself around Madison, so I can't let this insecure part of me take over. Growing up, I was the shy kid in class, always with glasses and reading comic books. Madison makes me feel like a different version of myself. The part of me that's real and honest and uncensored. Maybe it's because she's not from here and didn't know me back then, but it's like I can be myself and not worry about the teasing I endured.

Putting those thoughts away, I get back to work counting down the time until lunch. Hopefully, Sara is gone by then.

After almost getting bit by a dog with an ear infection, scratched by a cat who was against getting her vaccination, and treating a calm bunny, I'm ready to sit down for thirty minutes and eat. Hopefully, without any interruptions.

Before grabbing my lunch, I check on the llama. Sara is still in the room, and she's laughing with Madison.

Great, just what I need. My sister to weasel her way into my personal life.

"What's going on?" I look between them.

"We were just talking about the llama." Sara's eyes shine with mockery.

"Okay..." I say slowly.

"Now I know why you said he spit." Sara guffaws.

I stare at Madison unimpressed.

"Sorry." She holds her hands up. "She took it out of me. She's very good at that." Madison points a finger at my sister.

"I have photographic proof of your incident yesterday," I remind her with a smirk.

"No." Her eyes widen in warning.

"What incident?" Sara looks between us.

"Nothing." Madison spits out.

"Don't you have to leave, Sara?" I look at her.

"Nope. I've got the entire day open. Do you have lunch? I'm hungry."

I close my eyes and sigh, tossing my head back.

"Madison and I have a meeting now. You can grab lunch from Hoagies like I did."

"You ordered lunch and didn't think that your sister would want something? Honestly, Ivan." Sara shakes her head in disappointment.

"I have a running order with them. I didn't know you were coming." I'm not falling for her faux victim card.

"Can I have half of your sub?"

"No, go grab your own. Eat it there. Get some fresh air." I don't trust her here alone with Madison. My high school crush incident is enough proof.

"Are you ready?" I ask Madison.

"Don't ignore me," Sara says behind me.

"Close the door," I shout louder than intended, but I can't have that llama roaming the clinic.

"Got it. Geez." Sara closes the door and stares at me with wide eyes. "You're so uptight." She scrunches up her face.

"If I give you half my sub will you eat quietly and let me do my job?"

"Yup." She beams.

I swear she always gets her way. Madison giggles next to me, and I cut my gaze to hers. I'd like to kiss that smile off her face, but if Sara finds out, it'll be my doom. The entire town will know. My mom will be planning our wedding and picking out names for our kids.

We walk to the staffroom where I give Sara half my sub and my soda, keeping the chips for myself. She sits happily, talking to Harold while he eats. Even the grumpy older man smiles at her comments.

Shaking my head, I walk back to my office where Madison is already sitting on a chair.

"Sorry about Sara."

"No need to apologize. She's hilarious."

"Right," I mumble. "Anyway, what do you want to discuss?" I unwrap my half of the sub from the paper and start eating.

"Do you really have a running order with Hoagies?"

"You want to talk about my lunch choices?" I lift my brows, pausing with my sandwich midway to my mouth.

"No. I want to know how I can get in on that special treatment. Prepping lunch is the worst, and this sandwich is bland in comparison to yours."

"Do you want my sub, too?"

"Don't worry, I'll let you keep it this time." She smiles.

"I'll talk to the owner. Tell me what you like, and he'll add you to the order."

"Thanks."

"You're welcome." I take a bite of my Italian sub.

"Anyway, I got an idea I'd like to run by you. I thought that we could choose one day a week to have a coffee break with the staff, maybe on Wednesdays to overcome that mid-week hump, and set aside fifteen minutes where we don't have any appointments."

"Really?" I ask in surprise. "Miss *We Need to Work, Work, Work* is suggesting we stop for a bit?" I tease her.

Madison crosses her arms and glares at me. "I like structure and following a schedule, but it'd be a nice way for all of us to come together and get to know each other better, as well as take a breather where we don't talk about work."

"I like that idea." I nod, impressed with her suggestion.

"Great. We'll have to check our schedule and see when we can start. Block off from ten-forty-five to eleven on Wednesdays."

"We can talk to Rose and check our schedule for next week. We'll figure out how and when we can start implementing this."

"Thanks." She bites down on her smile. "I also wanted to talk about the boarding services. I have the proposal." She reaches for a folder.

169

"You haven't given up on that?" I purse my lips.

"Nope." She beams. "Remember our deal about the llama."

"For someone who's strict about the amount of time we work, you sure want to add more of a load to our plate." I arch a brow.

"Well, I thought we could ask the vet techs if they'd be interested in being on-call to make a little extra money. The job won't require much but to keep an eye out on the security cameras in case something happens, which is rare. They'd also need to come by on weekends to feed and take them out. Then they can take some time to care for the animals during the day, take them for walks, play with them, etcetera."

She opens the first page of her proposal. I'm impressed by the details she's added, including a graph with revenue, routine for the animals, and necessities we'd need.

"I'll admit this is a well thought out plan, but in order to have someone watch the animals during the day, we'd need someone new. Our techs have their responsibilities assisting us."

"I thought you might say that, so another option is hiring someone for that specific role." She turns the page to a proposed salary for someone on-call.

"That's an extra expense. If the boarding program costs us more, then this profit margin is null," I say.

"It'd be on a must-need basis, so it won't be a constant pay-out. We'd still make plenty. After today, I think I found the perfect person." Madison's smile is too wide for my liking.

"Who?" I tilt my head, afraid of her suggestion.

"Your sister."

"No." I shake my head, crossing my arms over the table. "I already had to give her half my sandwich. I can't have her working here."

"She's looking for a job, and she's been great with the llama today." Madison levels with me. "He didn't even threaten to spit on her." She chuckles.

I glower at her. "Funny."

"Like I said, she won't be here every day, only when we have pets staying here, and depending on how many we have, her hours would be less. She'd come by on the weekends when we're closed and do her job."

I scrub a hand down my face, taking a deep breath. I prefer to keep my professional and personal life separate.

You didn't mind it when you kissed Madison earlier.

I blow out a breath and look at the woman in front of me with a convincing smile. It's safe to say that my work and private life have been blended together since she walked into this office.

"I'll think about it." My sister has been desperate for a job, but she'd ignore my authority. "If so, she'd have to answer to you. She wouldn't take me seriously, and as much as I love her, I can't have her acting like this is a game."

"Deal." She nods.

"I'm still not completely sold on this idea. Let me study this information in more detail."

"That works for me." Her dimples pop with her smile.

I have a feeling I'm going to give in, but I need to look at this with a level head and think about every possible situation, contract clauses to cover ourselves, and think about where we'd even put these animals. It's clear we can't start with all types of animals when our facility isn't prepared for it.

"Are you done?" Sara peeks her head in the office.

I close my eyes and mumble to myself.

"Mom told me to ask you if you want to come have dinner at the house." She holds her phone up. "She's making platanitos maduros and moros with pork chops."

"What are platanitos?" Madison asks, only she pronounces the word *plat-nios*.

Sara chuckles and says, "Pla-ta-ni-tos. They're fired sweet plantains. Moros are black beans and rice cooked together instead of separate. And pork chops are, well, it's already in English. The rest are Cuban dishes."

"I've never heard of them." Madison shrugs.

"You should come! This way you won't have to eat alone." Sara's eyes beam with excitement as if she just came up with the best idea.

"Sara!" I call out.

Madison's eyes widen, and I frown.

"Sorry." It's nothing personal. I'd love to have dinner with her, but not surrounded by my nosy family. If she comes, my mom will invite Tía Emma and her family so everyone can meet Madison.

Sara laughs loudly. "He's just nervous my mom will embarrass him again."

"Not only me. She'll grill Madison more than she already did," I say.

"She totally will." Sara looks at Madison. "But you've also never had food like hers. I won't take no for an answer. Be there at seven. Ivan will give you the address, or better yet, he'll pick you up." She winks and walks away, leaving me alone in this awkward situation.

I look at her, pressing my lips together. "It's not that I don't want you to go."

"I get it." She waves me off. "I guess I can't turn down her invitation?" Her eyebrows knit together.

"Not unless you want her to badger you about why you didn't go and have my mom hate you."

Her face scrunches up.

"I'm joking about my mom," I rush out to say. "I'll pick you up."

I'm already dreading tonight. I was hoping to go home after work, or maybe ask Madison if she wanted to have dinner. But not with an audience consisting of my meddling family.

I hope she's ready to experience the Romero-Amor family dynamic and has a list of answers prepared for my mom's intrusive questions.

17

♥ ♥ ♥

MADISON

I'M NOT SURE HOW I got conned into going to dinner at Ivan's parents' house, but Sara is a sneaky little thing. A part of me wonders if she knows Ivan and I kissed through the clinic security camera or something. Her timing was too coincidental.

A kiss that felt like I was soaring but has since made me feel uncertain and afraid. I know the consequences of falling in love with someone I work with, and they're not in my favor. Ivan doesn't seem like the type of guy who would hurt a fly. The again, Ben seemed like the man of my dreams.

But I lost my job and my home by escaping the mule-butt jerk.

And to follow in Uncle James's footsteps.

The timing to come work at Healing Hands was perfect, even if it was due to heartbreak. My uncle always tells me things happen in a flow we may not understand but are necessary for our soul.

I take a deep breath and shove thoughts of Ben out of my mind before Ivan arrives. I'm already nervous about this dinner. I do not need to my ex-boyfriend's ghost haunting me as well.

My phone rings, and I race to answer it in case it's Ivan. I sigh when my mom's name flashes on the screen and pick up the phone.

"Hey, Mom." I pace the living room.

"Hi, sweetie, how are you? I haven't heard from you today."

Yeah, because I was busy kissing my co-worker and then getting invited to his family's house for dinner.

"It's been a busy day. We rescued a llama."

"A llama? Well, it seems that James's clinic is a lot more entertaining than your old one." She laughs.

"Yup." I sit on the couch to avoid getting sweaty from pacing by the time Ivan gets here. "How are you and Daddy?"

"We're good. We miss you, though."

"Maybe you can come visit once Uncle James is back from his trip."

"I'd love that."

"Great. We can plan it," I say absentmindedly and check the time on my phone. Ivan should've been here already.

"Actually, I need to go, Mom. I'll call you tomorrow." I hop to my feet.

"Is everything okay? You sound agitated."

"It's all great." I look at Boots. "It's that I adopted a kitty. I think I told you, and I need to feed him and take care of a few things." A white lie never hurt anyone.

"What'd you name him? Send me a picture."

"Boots, and I will." I hurry her up with my hand even though she can't see me.

"So cute."

"He is. I'll make sure to send you that photo. We'll talk tomorrow. Bye." I hang up, feeling like I might throw up a little.

How did Ivan and I go from one kiss to having dinner with the parents?

I shake my hands and hop around in place to release this built-up energy. Then, I smooth down my pleated skirt and take a slow breath.

It's just dinner with a nice family so I won't have to eat alone. It's all about the friendly neighbors in a small town. Nothing to do with the man I kissed, who is late. It's already past seven.

My heart races when the doorbell rings. It's the moment of truth. I grab my purse from the armchair with shaky hands and pick up my phone from the coffee table.

Swinging open the door more forcefully than intended, I stare at Ivan. His wavy hair is damp and looks like he styled it using just his fingers instead of a comb. *And he's wearing his glasses.* Those are my kryptonite.

"Hey." He gives me a closed-mouth smile, standing before me looking like the man conjured from my dreams in a light blue button-down shirt with the sleeves rolled up right below the elbows and khaki chinos.

"Hi. You're late."

Ivan's brows shoot up in his forehead, and he chuckles. "Seven for Cubans is really seven-thirty. It's called Cuban time."

"Are you sure?" I tilt my head.

"Positive. I have the genes to prove it. Are you ready to go?" He shifts on his feet, looking at me with amusement.

"Yeah." I lock up and follow him to his car.

When he opens the car door for me, I grin. There's nothing more attractive than a man who's a true gentleman. My eyes trail him as he rounds the car without a word and sits on the driver's seat. I wipe my palms on my skirt and take a deep breath.

"I'm really sorry Sara forced you to this," he says as he pulls out of the driveway.

"It's okay. I'm not going to lie, I'm nervous."

"Don't be. You're not the one they'll be humiliating all night." He glances at me with a grimace. "Warning, don't believe anything they say about me."

I laugh and shake my head. "Oh, no. That's what someone says when they know they're about to be exposed," I tease him.

"This is a nightmare," he mumbles.

"It's okay, exotic animal whisperer. I'll take what they say with a grain of salt."

"Yeah, right." He cuts his eyes to me. "Let's get this over with."

My knee bounces on the drive to his parents' house. They don't live far from my aunt and uncle. The residential area with houses lined one next to the other feels like I'm in a movie. A lot of things about Sunshine Falls feel like a different world.

"Did Roger take the llama?" I ask Ivan.

When I left work, he was waiting for Roger to stop by and pick him up. He offered to keep the animal on his ranch until we find the owner so that he can sleep in the right environment.

"He did. I'm glad we got that sorted because keeping him in the treatment room wasn't right," Ivan says.

"I agree, even if it means giving up your dream," I taunt him.

"It was short-lived, but at least I got to see one up close and personal."

"Oh, you got really personal." I relax into the seat, laughing.

"Do I need to remind you about your chicken reunion, City Girl?"

"Ha. You're such a *yolker*." The pun comes out of me without a second thought.

He lifts his hand for a high five. "Good one." He laughs, and I tap my hand with his.

Ivan turns into a neighborhood and pulls into a driveway where four other cars are parked.

"Uhh... First of all, you said Cuban time and it seems everyone is here. Secondly, *who is here?*"

"I hoped they wouldn't do this," he says to himself.

"Do what, Ivan?"

He turns to look at me with a frown. "I apologize in advance for my family. It seems my aunt, who you already met, and my uncle are also here with Mia and Luna." He forces a smile that does nothing to calm me.

"Oh."

His lips press together. "Yeah."

"Well..." I look at him.

He turns to look at me and lowers his head. "I can turn the car around and tell them I have car trouble." He juts his thumb over his shoulder.

"Right. And what about my car?" I cock my head.

He takes a deep breath, gaze bouncing around the car. Suddenly, he lifts a finger. "Boots peed in it."

"Do you seriously think they'll buy it?"

He shakes his head and snorts. "Not one bit, but it was worth a try. Let's get this over with?" He crinkles his eyebrows and scrunches up his nose.

I take a deep breath and nod. I'm a professional. A successful veterinarian. I'm a doctor, for goodness sake. I can handle a man's family no matter how intrusive they are because if his mom was all up in my business when I went into the bakery, she'll have no limits in her own home.

I'll be ready, though. I already had a taste of her antics.

Determined, I walk to the front door confidently, head held high, following Ivan as he opens and guides us through the house. Whatever his mom cooked smells delicious. The plantains or the beans, or all of it.

Loud chatter is heard from the entrance, and I smile at the sound of camaraderie. When we walk into the kitchen, everyone silences on cue and stares at us. My shoulders curl in as a lot of pairs of eyes look at me with deep curiosity.

So much for being a confident boss babe, Madison.

"You're here!" Clara calls out with open arms and a bright smile, rushing to stand in front of us.

She wraps me in a tight hug, catching me by surprise. My eyes widen, and everyone in the kitchen is smiling at me. I hug her back, not as intensely.

"I'm so happy to see you again." She steps back to smile at me.

"Thank you for having me." I return the smile and look at Ivan.

His lips are pressed together as if he's regretting this decision. That's not a good sign.

"Of course. Come in and meet everyone. When Sara told me you were coming for dinner, I was ecstatic." She pushes me forward to the crowd of people. Thankfully, I know Sara and Ivan's cousin's so that makes this less overwhelming.

"I'm Ana, Ivan's youngest and prettiest sister." The young girl smiles charmingly.

"You look like me, so I'm the prettiest!" Sara calls out in complaint.

I laugh at her comment and say hello.

"This is my husband, Miguel," Clara says. "And you already know my sister Emma. This is her husband Raymond." She goes around mentioning everyone in the family. "You already know Mia and Luna from what I hear."

"I do. Hi." I wave at them.

Luna smiles apologetically, and I have a feeling she and Ivan have similar ideas about this dinner.

"Come sit." Clara pulls out a stool at the peninsula counter.

Ivan says hello to his aunt and cousins, giving them all kisses on the cheek, and shaking his uncle's hand.

If my heart were racing at home before Ivan arrived, it straight out left my body now. I'm living by a miracle.

"Did everyone like the pastelitos? I was right that they'd be better than donuts. I hope you gave Ivan the two I separated for him," Clara says with raised brows.

"Mom," he groans in warning.

"Shush." She says something in Spanish, and I just stare at her.

"Don't mind her. She's reprimanding him for giving her attitude," Sara explains.

I nod slowly, feeling like a painting on full display at a museum. A Van Gogh where everyone is staring at me intently, asking questions about what my meaning is.

"So, how are you enjoying Sunshine Falls?" Clara begins her questioning.

"It's a great town." I smile.

"It's different than Dallas," Emma adds.

"Very." I chuckle.

Mia leans over the counter and looks at me. "How does Ivan behave at work? Is he as uptight there as in real life?"

"My work is real life, Mia," he argues.

"Whatever. I'm talking to Madison." Mia rolls her eyes.

"Um…" I look at him and see his dad clapping his shoulder with a laugh. "He's professional, likes to do his job correctly."

"That's not fun gossip." Mia sighs.

"Do you want something to drink?" Luna asks, breaking the conversation a bit. "We have white wine, red wine, water, Coke, and beer."

"A Coke would be great, thanks."

Luna nods and grabs a can from the fridge, serving it in a glass.

"Thanks," I say when she places it in front of me.

"You're welcome." She leans in. "You can ignore most of what they say," she whispers, saying something similar to what Ivan did in the car.

"What did you make, Mom?" Ivan is at the stove, holding the top of a pot as he peeks inside.

"Don't touch it," she warns. "I made ropa vieja."

I furrow my eyebrows because that doesn't sound like anything Sara mentioned at the clinic.

"It's old clothes," Mia says.

"Oh." I try to school my features, but I must not do a good job because everyone laughs.

"Don't listen to her. It's called old clothes, but it's nothing like it. It's like a…stew," Clara says.

"Oh, okay." I nod.

I am so out of place. Forget being a Van Gogh in a museum. I'm a Van Gogh in a garage sale.

"So tell us, do you have a boyfriend?" Clara asks.

"What?" I cough on my sip of Coke, slapping my chest.

"You scared the girl," Emma accuses.

"It's the direct approach," Clara retorts.

While they argue about their tactics, Ivan groans, dropping his chin to his chest. He looks mortified, and if it weren't me in the other side of this situation, I'd enjoy this. It's probably why Sara and Ana are snickering. If they were in his shoes, I bet they'd have a different reaction.

"I don't have a boyfriend." I go for the straight answer. Maybe if I give them what they want, I'll get over the interview part of this dinner quickly and I can try the food that's making my mouth water.

"Good." Clara smiles, looking at her son.

"I hear Ivan rescued a llama today," Raymond says, likely trying to control his wife and sister-in-law.

"Yeah, but their relationship isn't as strong as Ivan hoped." I laugh.

"The llama spit on him," Sara yells, cackling.

Everyone laughs and starts talking over each other while Ivan scowls, glaring at me and mouthing, *traitor*.

"He loves llamas. You finally got your dream. Remember when you were ten and asked for a real llama as your birthday wish?"

"Mom," Ivan groans.

"He has a stuffed animal. Is it here?" She looks at Ivan.

"Nope, he took it with him when he moved in with Luna," Sara announces.

"So I've heard," I comment, smirking at him.

"He used to take it with him everywhere. When we'd go on vacation, day trips, to camp. He couldn't live without that toy. My sensitive boy." Clara looks at him lovingly.

It makes me miss my mom. It's only been a few weeks since I saw my parents before leaving Dallas, but it feels like an eternity. I can't wait for them to come visit.

"I'm divorcing this family," Ivan calls out.

"Don't joke that way." Clara points at him with narrowed eyes.

"I'm enjoying the hazing Ivan is receiving, but can we continue it at the table? I'm hungry," Ana says.

"Yes." Clara claps her hands and moves around as if she forgot we were here for dinner.

Everyone flurries about, grabbing platters and plating the food on them. People talk over each other, calling out orders. I sit awkwardly, watching them and forgetting my manners.

"Can I help?" I snap out of it.

"No. Go on and sit. You're our guest." Clara looks at me over her shoulder.

"I don't mind." I stand from the stool.

"Absolutely not. Ivan, sit with Madison at the table," she orders.

"Come on." Ivan sighs, pulling out a chair for me at a long dining table that's already set.

He sits beside me and leans in. "I'm sorry. I knew it'd be bad, but wow." He shakes his head.

"It's fine." I wave him off.

"You look like you want to bolt." He arches a brow over the rim of his glasses.

"Oh, I do." I don't deny it. "But it's also fun to observe a big family like this."

Dishes are set on the table—a mix of rice and beans, a red beef stew that looks like the beef's been shredded, and the plantains.

"It smells delicious," I comment.

"Thank you. Now, let's eat." Clara nods, passing me the deep dish with the meat.

I take it, serving myself a bit, and pass it to Luna to my right. Having Luna and Ivan on either side of me feels like a buffer.

"That's all you're going to eat?" Clara narrows her eyes. "Luna, serve her more."

"Oh, no. This is great for now. Thank you. I'll get more after." I smile politely.

"Here. Have moros." She leans over the table and serves me a heaping mound of the rice and beans and then four plantains.

"Thanks." I nod, looking at Ivan.

"Eat what you want."

"I need to eat it all or she'll be offended," I whisper.

"She won't." He shakes his head, but I'm not convinced.

I take a bite of the food and close my eyes. I've never had anything like this before. The meat is tangy and savory with a hint of spice. The flavors pop in my mouth, waking up my tastebuds.

"Wow. This is delicious," I compliment Clara.

She beams proudly.

When I try the rice, the same feeling of fullness hits me. This isn't plain ole rice and beans mixed together. The spices blend and come alive. Cuban food just became my new favorite. Move over tacos, there's a new competitor in town.

Although, this in a taco would be the perfect marriage.

"Do you have siblings?" Emma asks between bites of food, breaking my love affair with this meal.

"She has an older brother," Mia says before I can answer.

"That's nice. Does he live in Dallas?" Emma looks at me.

"No. He moved to Phoenix a few years ago when he got married. His wife is from there," I explain.

"Oh." Emma frowns. "That must be hard."

"It is, but we talk as much as we can." I don't see my brother often, though I wish I did. We talk on the phone, but I can't say we have the relationship Ivan has with his sisters, as obnoxious as he may think they are.

"You don't like the plantains?" Clara asks, eyeing them on my plate.

"I haven't tried them yet. I was keeping them for the end since they're sweet."

Everyone laughs except for Ivan and Luna. I sink down in my seat, wondering what is so funny about what I said.

"That's the beauty of this food. You blend the flavors, mix things that seem unlikely, and create an amazing balance. Go on, try the plantains with the meat." Clara nods encouragingly.

Although Clara was talking about food, her words perfectly describe us. I wonder if we can mix together, our differences blending, to create something greater than what we would be individually.

I follow her guidance and cut a piece of the plantain and fork it with some meat, hoping I like it because cringing in front of everyone wouldn't be a good look. I chew, the sweetness contrasting with the acidity of the stew, and smile.

"Amazing," I say.

They all cheer and start talking in different conversations, interchanging between them. How they can keep track and not get distracted is beyond me. I can barely follow along.

And yet, you can feel the love in the chaos. The joy in the teasing. The strong family bond in the way they come together for a simple meal on a Thursday. They may be nosy, but Ivan's family is the real thing.

18

♥ ♥ ♥

IVAN

"IVAN, WHAT HAPPENED TO the llama?" Mia asks, stealing a platanito from Sara's plate.

"Roger's taking care of him until I find the owner."

"He's a good man," my dad comments.

"He is." I nod and serve myself more ropa vieja.

My mom has outdone herself with the meal, and I have a feeling she put on her A-game to impress Madison. Her soft sighs and smile as she eats tells me she's impressed.

It's been a challenge to keep my distance all night, seeing Madison at my house with my family. It is an odd sensation. I was dreading this because I know how my family is when they get excited about a girl in my life but spending time with Madison is worth it. I wasn't sure how she'd fit in with all of us. If she'd be tense or not understand the humor, but she's different than at work, and all I can think about is kissing her again.

"Madison, are you sure you want to be friends with my brother?" Sara asks with a gleam in her eyes.

"Uh." She turns to look at me. "Yeah?"

"Hacen bonita pareja," my mom tells Tía Emma.

I glare at her, but she laughs, ignoring my reaction.

"What did she say?" Madison leans in, clearly having heard her comment.

"That you're very nice." There's no way I'm going to tell her my mom said we make a good couple.

"So why did you scowl?" Madison crosses her arms.

"I didn't." I shake my head.

"You totally did." Ana smirks.

"No." I clench my teeth, widening my eyes in warning to keep her mouth shut.

"She said you make a good couple," Mia calls out.

The blood drains from my face as I stare at her. Madison's eyebrows knit together.

"She's making stuff up." I wave my hand at my mom.

"Um, thank you." She looks at my mom with pink cheeks.

"So, maybe you wanna be more than friends." Sara waggles her eyebrows.

"Someone kidnap me." I cover my face with my hands and groan when I touch my glasses.

Great. I keep forgetting I have them on, but my contacts have been bothering me more and more lately. Removing my glasses, I clean them with my shirt before I spend all night seeing through fingerprints.

"Don't worry, big bro, we're just helping Madison fit into our family. We all rag on Ivan." Ana shrugs.

"Lucky me," I mumble.

"Pass me the moros, Luna," Tío Raymond says. I'm grateful for his interruption and smile at him. He nods in solidarity and serves himself more food.

"Did you hear that Simon is going to the University of Florida?" My mom asks Tía Emma.

"Teresa is going to miss him." My aunt shakes her head with a frown.

"Teresa is one of their cousins in Florida and Simon is her son," I explain to Madison.

"Thanks. Also, would it be bad form to serve myself some more?" Her round eyes glance up at me with a hint of nerves. She looks beautiful.

"It'd be bad form if you don't." My eyes remain on her face, counting her freckles before taking her in detail by detail.

Someone at the table clears their throats, and we snap out of it, turning to face my family. I force a smile while my dad grins knowingly, and my mom clasps her hands.

"Están enamorados!" my mom calls out.

"What?" Madison's brows furrow.

"Nothing." I give everyone a warning look, and thankfully, my sisters and Mia seem like they're going to keep their mouths shut. Maybe not for long with the grins they're wearing, but I'll take their silence for tonight.

If Madison knows that my mom thinks we're in love, it'll ruin any chance before I even get it.

"Ay, Iván." My mom rolls her eyes, saying my name in Spanish with the emphasis on the A. "I'm just happy to have Madison here. He gets embarrassed easily. I blame the time he was three and had a bathroom accident in preschool. After that, he was always more closed-off and careful around people."

My family laughs, Luna included—that traitor—and Madison tries to fight back her giggle.

"Mom," I growl.

"You were three. It's normal for children to have accidents like that." She looks at Madison. "He was late with potty training, so it was expected."

"Wow." I press my lips together. "We're at the dinner table. Can we drop this conversation?" I wave a hand out.

"We have doggy diapers at the clinic in case you need some." Madison snorts.

"Hilarious," I deadpan.

"It's better than the story when you tried out for the football team and miserably failed." Sara shrugs. "At least in mom's story you were three not sixteen."

"What happened?" Madison asks.

I sigh, knowing it's no use stopping them.

"He thought he had what it takes to make the team. Spent the summer practicing and all," Sara says. "Since he had heard football players take ballet, he signed up for a summer class. That was his first strike. Then, when he went to try-outs, they had him push that cushioned fake person."

"A blocking sled," I correct her, flatly.

"Right, that. Anyway, he couldn't move it." Sara giggles. "He ran as fast as he could to shove that thing like it was a person, and he bounced back instead."

"I'll never live that down." I glance up at the ceiling.

"Nope. You were better at ballet," Sara teases.

High school is a time I'd rather forget about, and that football tryout was a huge mistake. The jocks laughed about it for the last two years. All I wanted was to fit in, and instead I isolated myself even more. Not to mention, word got around about the ballet classes, and people kept calling me ballerina. Small-town charm.

"Ivan is sensitive. It's why he's so great with animals," my mom says with a loving smile.

"I think we've had enough hazing Ivan for tonight." I speak up.

"You're right." Sara nods seriously, as if this were a business meeting. "We need to save some stories for next time." And Madison wants to hire her at the clinic. No way.

"Madison, don't let him fool you. He's still confident when it counts," Mia says with a wink.

My mouth drops, but Luna thankfully comes to my rescue.

"What's your favorite animal to treat?" Luna asks her.

"I love them all. They each offer a different challenge, though I'm getting acquainted with wild animals lately."

"It's the llama's fault, right?" Sara says.

"Actually, it was the coyote and owl before that."

"What? Coyote? Mijo, no me dijiste eso."

"She's mad I didn't tell her about the coyote," I tell Madison before looking at my mom. "It's fine." I shake my head and take a sip of water.

"If you get hurt, I won't have grandchildren anytime soon."

I choke on my water, and it dribbles down my chin. Madison slaps my back as I cough. Grabbing the napkin, I clean my face and clear my throat.

"Well, that's one way to react to having children," Mia says.

"Mom, we've talked about this. I'm still young." Normally, moms badger their daughters for children. Not mine. She is dying for me to get married and have kids.

"Do you want children, Madison?" Tía Emma asks.

"You're kidding." I stare at her.

"Um, one day." Madison purses her lips and shrugs awkwardly.

I don't blame her. My family isn't even trying to hide the fact that they want us to be together. They don't even know her, but in their minds, we're a match made in heaven.

"Don't you think my Ivan would make a great dad? He's wonderful with animals."

"Mom," I say tightly.

"Oh, hush." My mom glowers at me and smiles at Madison, who refuses to look my way.

"I'm sure he will." She nods awkwardly.

"I think it's time for dessert." I stand from the table, collecting plates.

"Sit down and stop being rude." My mom uses a harsh tone, and I sit like a chastised child, lowering my head.

I endure another thirty minutes of conversation, translating to Madison the random words used in Spanish. When my mom announces it's finally time for dessert, I breathe out heavily. I won't forget this dinner soon enough.

"Your family loves you," Madison whispers.

"They do." Despite all the teasing, they're always there for me. I wouldn't trade my family for anything, even if I'm pretending I want to right now.

We have flan for dessert—my mom's specialty—and talk a bit more. Thankfully, the rest of the conversation is less humiliating as my family asks Madison proper questions that have nothing to do with her love life or family aspirations.

"I'm going to make cafecito," my mom says, standing.

"Coffee?" Madison leans in and asks in a whisper.

"Yeah."

"Oh, no thank you," she tells my mom. "Caffeine won't let me sleep at night."

My mom stares at her unblinking while I wait for the argument that I know is coming.

"Nonsense. This is Cuban coffee. You need to try it, and it's only a little bit. Like a shot."

"Really, it's okay." Madison tries to get out of it.

"It's very sweet. It won't do anything. We drink it at night." She waves a hand around the table.

"Pretend to drink it, and I'll have it," I whisper.

"You'll have two?" Her eyes widen.

"I'll sleep like a baby afterward. They've been training us to drink this since we were practically kids."

Her brows lift, and I laugh.

My mom's already moved to the kitchen without waiting for her response. She wouldn't take no for an answer anyways.

After she's mixed the sugar with the coffee, she serves everyone a small cup.

"This isn't so bad. It really is a little bit." Madison lifts the tiny mug and inhales. "Smells good, too." She smiles, taking a sip. "Wow," she says in awe.

"You see." My mom beams.

"It's delicious." Madison nods, taking another drink.

I almost want to warn her, but she'll learn her lesson. Cuban coffee may be sweet, but it is strong.

"Do you want more?" My mom looks at her with bright eyes.

Madison starts nodding, and I place my hand over hers.

"It's strong. Maybe stick to one."

"Right." She nods. "I'm okay, but I'd love to try more another day when it isn't too late." She smiles at my mom, and her words sink in.

My mom's face illuminated with a bright smile. "Ay, she's making plans to see us again." My mom claps excitedly, looking at Tía Emma. "¡Se van a casar!" my mom yells.

I cover my face and slide down in my chair, thankful that Madison doesn't understand Spanish in this moment.

By the time we leave, I'm exhausted and wound tight.

"At least you got this over with." Luna claps my shoulder.

"I know." I expel a deep breath. "Thanks for not giving into the teasing."

"You know I wouldn't."

I nod and give her a side hug before rescuing Madison—and what's left of my pride—from my sisters.

"We gotta go."

We say goodbye to my family, and my mom gives me a tight hug, whispering her approval of Madison as if this were our engagement. I couldn't make this stuff up if I wanted to. My family is unique, that's for sure.

We walk out of the house, and I open the car door for Madison before heading to the driver's seat.

"I'm so sorry," I tell her as soon as we're alone.

"You don't need to apologize, Ivan. Your family is great." She smiles, and it seems genuine but it's kind of dark in here.

"They are great. I love them, but they took this out of proportion. Besides, it was Sara who invited you." As soon as the words leave my mouth, I drop my forehead on the steering wheel.

Way to be smooth, dude.

"I didn't mean it that way." I look over at her.

"I get it." She nods. "Our situation is complicated."

At least she admits there's a situation. I pull out of the driveway and head to her house.

"You're a great guy, Ivan."

"Just what every man wants to hear." I chuckle humorlessly.

"Let me talk," she says slowly. "I had a bad experience dating someone I worked with in Dallas, and I want to avoid that at all costs."

"I'm sorry to hear that." A part of my hope deflates

"I mean, it's not like I go around dating co-workers, even if it seems that way considering I kissed you earlier, and it was a wonderful kiss, and you're great despite our differences. This isn't coming out right," she rambles.

I laugh and squeeze her hand. "Breathe, City Girl."

She takes a deep breath and rubs her thumb over my hand.

"I don't think you go around dating co-workers. I hate that you had a bad experience, but at the same time it feels like I've had a stroke of luck because it brought you here. At least, I'm guessing that might have to do with your move." I glance over at her.

Her response is a nod, worrying her bottom lip.

"This can be tricky to navigate, but after kissing you earlier, I can't lie to myself." I smile, unable to deny the truth.

"I don't think I can either." Her confession is music to my ears.

I lace my fingers with hers and sigh in contentment. If she can say that after everything she just heard about me at dinner, then maybe this could work. So long as we have an understanding that our professional and personal lives are separate and we communicate.

"When I saw you at Ground Love, I thought you were beautiful. Then, James told me you were his niece and all the hope I had of seeing you again dissipated."

"I thought you were pretty handsome." Her voice rings with joy.

"Yeah?" I glance at her.

"I did, and I wasn't in the best place then."

"What happened?" I dare to ask her.

"I broke up with my boyfriend."

"The co-worker."

"Right." She pauses. "Actually, he was my boss." Her voice lowers as she speaks, as if she's ashamed.

"Are you still in a bad place?" I need to know because I don't want to be a rebound, someone to help her get over her ex only to have her move on with someone else.

"No. I'm over him, but it sucks when someone cheats on you."

I blow out a breath and look at her at a stop sign. "You don't deserve that." I lift her hand and kiss the top of it. "You deserve to be cherished and appreciated."

We remain silent as I drive to her house. When I get there, I begrudgingly release her hand. Madison giggles, and it's the most beautiful site in the world. There's been a shift between us. Being on the receiving end of her smiles is the best feeling in the world.

I step out of my car and open the door for her to help her out. She takes my hand without hesitation, and we walk to the front door, facing each other with matching grins.

"I'll see you tomorrow."

"You will," she says. "No llamas, please."

"I've had my fill." I smirk.

"Good." Madison smiles and leans in, pressing her lips to my cheek. I squeeze her hand, pausing her from turning to the door.

"I'm glad you told me what happened. You're beautiful, but besides that, you're smart, confident, and stubborn."

Her brows fly up on her forehead.

"It's a good quality to have at times. Look at how you convinced me to consider the boarding program." I smile. "You're the full package, Madison."

"Thank you." Her eyes soften. "Goodnight, Ivan."

"Goodnight, City Girl."

I walk back to my car, whistling and feeling like a king. Maybe it was a good idea to have her come to dinner with my family. A few hours of teasing led to Madison opening up to me and having an honest conversation.

If there's one thing I'm sure of it's that I'll never make her feel like she's not good enough.

19

♥ ♥ ♥

MADISON

I FEEL LIKE I'M walking on a cloud today. Well, honestly I feel like I'm walking through a fog. Ivan wasn't wrong when he kept me from drinking that second cup of Cuban coffee. It took hours for me to fall asleep once the caffeine kicked in.

And yet, I woke up feeling tired, but refreshed. Seeing Ivan with his family gave me another insight into the man I've started to develop feelings for. I can see him as the more serious older brother. The dedicated son. The funny guy. It makes me like him more.

It also terrifies me.

I never really met Ben's family to get a read on their relationship, which should've been a red flag. We ran into his parents once when we were leaving a restaurant, but all I got was an indifferent hello before Ben pulled me away.

Ivan is different than Ben. While they're both career-driven, he isn't overly-confident like Ben. He's sure of himself at work, but there's a part of him that's not as certain in real life. A part of him that's more vulnerable.

After hearing about some of the teasing he endured in high school, I can understand. I like that he isn't this

200

smooth-talker who uses his charm to get his way. Ivan is honest when he speaks, and that is more attractive than a man who tries to get his way using sleazy tactics.

When Boots purrs, I look down to see him at my feet.

"Hey, little guy." I bend down to pet him.

He rubs against my bent legs and tries to climb me. Laughing, I pick him up and give him a cuddle, which he tries to fight, but when I go to place him down on the floor again, he's using his paws to hold on to me.

"Okay." I shake my head. "You want my lovin'. In you go." I place him in the pocket of my scrub pant and pat his head. Boots purrs softly as I walk to my next appointment, likely enjoying the rocking movement of my steps.

Ivan is at the ranch with Roger and the owner of the llama. Thankfully, we were able to contact him quickly.

Kate meets me in the hallway with a clipboard. "We have a routine checkup for Fluffy's pregnancy."

"Got it. Let's see how that rabbit is doing." I smile at her, and we enter the exam room.

"Hi, Mr. Smith and Sandy." I smile at the dad and daughter duo and then at the rabbit that's expecting her first baby.

Boots peeks out of my pocket, and Sandy giggles.

"Dr. Grover, you have a cat in your pocket."

"I do?" I feign shock and look down. "You're right. This is my new friend, Boots." I pet his head.

"He's cute."

"And he's a good helper," Kate adds.

"He is. How's Fluffy doing?"

"She's good," Sadie says with a beaming smile.

"Great. Are you feeding her the right foods?" I ask her. She's been so responsible about taking care of her pet; she gives me updates each time she comes in.

Mr. Smith is more closed-off. From what I hear, he's a single dad, and all he does is work and take care of Sandy.

"I am." Sandy nods proudly.

"Good. Now, let's check that baby."

"Do you want to help us?" I ask Sandy.

She nods excitedly and pets Fluffy while she waits for Kate to prep the sonogram machine. Fluffy startles when I try to turn her around, and I soothe her.

"It's okay, girl. You're gonna be fine. We just wanna see your baby." Sandy talks to the rabbit, and it melts my heart.

I think my favorite part of being a vet is working with families that have kids. Seeing them with their pets is amazing. They're so intuitive and kind.

"Good job, Sandy." I nod in encouragement.

I reach over to start the sonogram while Sandy holds a stretched out Fluffy. Kate helps to hold her legs when she gets antsy. Before I can begin, though, Boots jumps from my pocket.

"Boots!" I call out in warning.

He stares at me, and I swear he shrugs, before sniffing Fluffy. Then, he lays down over her legs.

"Well..." I look at Mr. Smith. "I guess he wanted to make a new friend." I grin.

He nods, a ghost of a smile appearing.

Getting to work, we're able to do the sonogram successfully. While I talk to Mr. Smith and Sandy about Fluffy's pregnancy, Boots and the rabbit play together. Fluffy hops away and Boots chases her. It's adorable.

202

"Like I said, everything seems great. I'll see you again for our next check-up. Rose can set up your appointment."

I grab Boots and set him back in my pocket so Fluffy will go into her cage and guide Mr. Smith and Sandy to the front desk where Rose is. Ivan is standing nearby, talking to someone I'm not familiar with. He smiles at me when I walk past him, and I can't help the grin that takes over, looking like a crazy teen with a huge crush.

Once I finish with my clients, I head back to my office and see Ivan leaning against the wall in the hallway.

"Was the llama happy to see his owner?" I ask him

He pushes off the wall and walks beside me. "Mojo, and he was. You should've seen him. No spitting or inching away." Ivan shakes his head. "The best part is that Daniel said we could go by and see him whenever we want." His entire face lights up like a little boy.

"I bet you're happy about that. What was it that your mom mentioned yesterday? Your birthday wish about owning a llama?" I tease him.

"You're hilarious," he says flatly and side-eyes me.

"I know."

Boots meows from my pocket, and Ivan looks around before finding him.

"Um, are you a kangaroo now?"

"No. He was feeling needy and he fit." I shrug. "He even helped me calm down Fluffy so I could do her sonogram."

"Really?" His brows lift.

"You should've seen him. He hopped out of the pocket and laid by her legs. The rabbit stayed still. Then, they played together." I pet Boots, and he rubs his face against my palm.

"That's nice." Ivan nods.

"Boots can be our new mascot." I give him my award-winning smile, but Ivan just stares at me. "You know, the face of Healing Hands."

"Like a football team." He shakes his head. "As long as he doesn't make a mess, he can stay around."

"You hear that, Boots? You can stay." I squeeze his face.

"He is cute." Ivan reaches out to pet him, and the cat surrenders, purring happily. "Scratch marks on my back and all."

"You're the one who let him crawl all over you before clipping his nails." I shrug.

"True. Anyway, I was talking to Darlene, the mayor's secretary. Sunshine Falls has its annual festival, and I almost forgot that we always have a booth."

"That sound fun. What's the festival for?" We walk down the hall.

"The town's birthday."

My brows furrow. "Like the day it was established?"

"Yeah, but we literally do a birthday party. It's tradition."

"How old is the town turning?" I can't help but smile.

"A hundred and eighty-five."

"Wow. I guess she's a senior citizen," I joke.

Ivan chuckles. "A few times over. Do you have a moment to talk details? I want to explain what we've done in the past," he asks outside of my office.

"Of course." We walk into my office, and I place Boots on the floor so he can play a bit.

Ivan looks at me for a beat after we sit.

"Are you just gonna stare or talk?" I wave a hand in front of his face.

He breaks contact, looking away, and he *blushes*.
Gah, there's no way to deny that I like him.

"Sorry." He clears his throat. "I got distracted."

I rest my chin on my hand and smile.

"Darlene, right. The festival. We've always had a booth, giving a short demonstration on teaching your dog to sit or turn over. We've also had information about vaccines, ways to adopt pets, and sell some products we have."

"That sounds great. When is the festival?"

"Next Saturday." He presses his lips together.

"And you're telling me now?" I widen my eyes.

"I've been a bit distracted adjusting to my new work situation, and it slipped my mind." He looks at me meaningfully.

"Very true." I smile. "So next Saturday. What do we need to organize? I've got some time this afternoon."

"Want to have lunch and talk about it?"

I smirk and arch a brow. "Are you asking me out, Dr. Romero?"

"I might be." He presses his lips together. "Is that okay?"

"I love that you ask that. It's definitely okay. Can we go to the sub place next door? The one you got me the other day was so good." My eyes widen with hope.

"Of course." He tilts his head and looks at me.

His eyes shine with a softness that make me feel like I'm floating. I don't know if I've ever noticed someone look at me like that.

"Let's go." I grab Boots and squeeze him tightly. "You need to stay here, buddy."

I place him in his kennel, much to his disapproving glare, and grab my bag. Ivan gives me a wink as we walk out of my office.

Butterflies swarm my belly. I don't know what's happening to me, but this man is slashing every attempt to distance myself from a relationship.

"We'll be back after lunch," Ivan tells Rose, who's brows lift in surprise.

I don't blame her. Ivan and I have been a bit like oil and water, but it seems like we're becoming like red velvet cake and cream cheese frosting, my favorite combination.

We walk next door to Hoagies and take a seat. While we wait to order our food, I hum along to a Tim McGraw song.

"Who's your favorite singer?" Ivan asks.

"Kenny Chesney."

"He's great. I love Alan Jackson."

"He's great too. Have you ever seen him in concert? I saw him once at a festival, and he was such a great performer." I lean forward on my elbows.

"I have. He was my first concert when I was a teen. Luna and I went together. It was amazing."

"You two are super close, right?"

"We are. We were raised like siblings. Almost like twins since we're a day apart."

"Wow. I knew you were close in age but didn't realize how much." It must be nice to have a big family like that.

"I know. It's kinda weird to anyone outside of our family."

"No, no. I think it's great. I wish I had a family like yours. My aunts and uncles live out of the state. We aren't really that close. Uncle James is the uncle I'm closest to. Seeing your family together was so fun."

"And embarrassing."

"For you. It was quite entertaining to me. I got to see a different side of Dr. Romero." I laugh.

Ivan rolls his eyes.

"I like what I saw," I whisper.

"Really?" One side of his lips lifts.

I nod, but the waiter interrupts the moment to take our order. Once we do, Ivan leans in closer to me.

"We should talk about the festival."

"That would be smart." I nod, staring into his eyes.

I have a feeling everyone here is watching us closely and trying to spin their own story about what's going on between us.

I'm slowly giving in to my feelings, and it feels right. I just hope they don't betray me.

"We have pamphlets made about the clinic, which we'll have at the table. It's a great way to lure in new clients since many people from out of Sunshine Falls come to the festival as well."

"And what about the training? Is that at a specific time or as people come and ask for it?" I lean back in my seat and grab my phone to take notes.

My heart jumps when a text message from another unknown number appears on my screen, but I ignore it. Ben keeps finding ways to text me. I don't know how many numbers he has since I keep blocking him.

It's a cold reminder of what I went through. My eyes wander to Ivan. I don't want the same fate with him. He's a great guy, and things feel different with him.

"Are you okay?" Ivan's brows furrow.

"Yeah, sorry. I got distracted." Opening my notes, I smile up at him. "We have pamphlets. What else?"

"The training." He shifts his head, eyeing me.

"Right."

"I think it's a good idea to make it at a specific time so it draws people in for something they want."

"Makes sense, but what about those people who can't make it to the festival until the afternoon—or if we do it in the afternoon, they have to leave early?"

Ivan chuckles, shaking his head. "It's clear you've never been to a Sunshine Falls event. People are there from the beginning and stay until the end."

"Really? Even babies?" My brows crinkle in disbelief.

"Yeah. It seems impossible, but people make it happen a few times a year."

"How many events are there in town?" I try to wrap my head around this.

"We have the birthday festival, the Fourth of July festival, the Christmas market and tree lighting, um... I'm forgetting a couple." He lifts his eyes to the ceiling.

"That's a decent amount," I comment while he thinks.

"Yeah. They're fun. It's a way for the community to come together and socialize without the stress of getting to work or home to the kids. I'm missing a few, but you get the point."

"I do. What if we offer two times for the trainings? A morning and afternoon slot."

"I like that idea. We'll be at the booth anyway, so it's not like we'll be there for no reason if people don't show to one." He nods.

"Great." I smile, writing down my ideas. "And we can teach them to sit and roll over as well as to high-five. I think kids would love that."

"I agree." He smiles. "We make a pretty good team despite what we thought in the beginning, huh?"

"We do." I smile shyly and glance down at my phone.

The waiter brings our subs and drinks, and we eat while we continue to talk. We discuss the vaccination information, the products we'll sell, like shampoo, tick treatment, and brushes. It seems they have a solid plan from other years, so it's easy enough to gather the information. Mostly, I want to know how it works so I'm not a hot mess that day trying to figure things out.

"Madison." A familiar voice harshly calls my name, and my heart stops working. It can't be.

I look to my left, and my face pales when I see Ben standing a few feet away.

20

♥ ♥ ♥

IVAN

MY HEAD SNAPS IN the direction of the man who demanded Madison's attention, and I stare at an older guy. Who does he think he is talking to a woman like that? The anger in his voice was evident enough, but seeing his angry scowl puts me on alert.

I stand from the table, but Madison grabs my hand with pleading eyes. Everyone is looking at us as if we're their favorite TV show. Madison stands, gaining control of her emotions, and looks at the man.

"We can talk later."

"I've already tried, and you won't listen to me." He crosses his arms.

I'm guessing this is her ex-boyfriend. The man must be in his early forties, and he exudes confidence and command. And I already hate him. Any man who talks to a woman in a tone that's demanding and angry doesn't deserve her attention.

Madison looks back at me with a frown, her eyes cast down. The last thing I want to do is leave her alone with this guy.

"I'm in a business meeting, Ben. We'll talk when I finish work."

"You shouldn't be working here." The guy doesn't quit it, and I stand, unable to hold back anymore.

"Listen, man, we have work to do. And if Madison doesn't want to talk to you, you need to respect her." I glare at him.

"You're cozying up with this schmuck. That's why you won't answer my calls and messages?" His chuckle is insulting.

Every memory from the mockery I received in high school crashes over me, and I fist my hands. I want to punch this guy. I'm no longer that weak and insecure kid, but I doubt Madison will respect me if I give in to his insults.

"We're co-workers and friends. We're talking about work. Now leave."

"You heard the lady." Peter comes out from the back. "This is a private establishment. If you're not going to eat, I'm going to have to ask you to leave." He crosses his arms and lifts a brow, daring this guy to say something.

He ex-boyfriend narrows his eyes at me and then looks at Madison.

"We'll talk." He walks away, and Madison drops in her seat, keeping her head bowed.

"What was that?"

"That was Ben, my ex-boyfriend."

"And the reason you moved to Sunshine Falls." She's still affected by him, and it crushes me.

I thought we could move forward to have something real, and this jerk shows up as soon as things are starting for us. What I hate the most is the look of sadness on her face and the way she's hiding.

"Are you okay?" I ask quietly.

Madison shakes her head. "Do you mind if we go?"

"Of course." I look at Peter and tilt my head toward the door.

I wrap up our sandwiches and am tempted to hold Madison's hand, but I don't want to draw more attention from people around us. It's enough that the town will be talking about this encounter.

Madison looks shaken up, her arms crossed around her body like a barrier. Her eyes are rimmed in red as if she's trying to hold back her tears with all her might. Seeing her like this ignites a protectiveness I've never felt before.

Once we're in the clinic and by her office, I lift her chin so she looks at me.

"Are you sure you're okay?"

"I'm not," she answers honestly, which I appreciate.

"What can I do?"

"Do you have a body bag?" She attempts to joke. "I'm kidding. No assassin here. I have too much of a conscience."

I smile and squeeze her hand. "I don't like the way that guy talked to you."

"He's been contacting me since I left trying to apologize and get me to return to the clinic. He won't take no for an answer."

"That doesn't comfort me, Maddy. Are you sure he won't hurt you?"

"No. He's just stubborn and persistent." She sighs, rubbing her forehead. "I'm sorry he ruined our lunch."

"Don't apologize for him." I cup her cheek. "He's the jerk that did it. I'm more concerned about you."

"I'm fine. I don't feel anything for him if you're worried about that. But when someone you trusted cheats on you, it slashes your soul. I'm still healing from that." Her lower lip trembles and she tucks it between her teeth, her eyes welling with tears.

My hand on her cheek slides to the back of her neck, and I pull her to me and wrap my arms around her. Holding her like this, even if she's upset about a past relationship, makes me feel complete. Like I've been missing this my entire life.

"You deserve the world. Never doubt that. You're gorgeous and intelligent. I already told you you're the whole package, City Girl. Even if you try to sneak into chicken coops through the wrong door."

She snorts and giggles against my chest. Her arms finally come around my back, and I sigh.

"You're so much better than him." I lift my head and whisper in her ear. Madison shivers and squeezes me tighter.

"Thank you." Her voice is hoarse.

I lean back to stare into her eyes so she sees the honesty shining in them. Grabbing her chin, I smile.

"I mean it." My hand moves to cup her face, and Madison's eyes flutter closed. "He doesn't deserve you."

I press my lips to her forehead, inhaling her sweet shampoo, lavender and vanilla. I think I found my new favorite scent.

"Thank you for being so understanding. I'd hate if he pulled that stunt here in front of clients." She frowns.

"I'd kick him out the way Peter did. You don't do that in someone's business with disregard to their customers or lack of respect to the owner." I shake my head.

"I'm going to have to convince him that I mean it when I say we're through." She sighs, shoulders slumping.

"If you want me to go with you, I will. I'll give you space to talk, but just in case he gets..." I trail off because the thought of this guy even touching her makes my blood boil.

"No." She waves me off. "He's a jerk, but he'd never hurt me. That's one thing I'm sure of."

I hope she's right because if I find out he does, I'll end up in jail, and I love my liberty too much for that to happen.

"I think I'm going to cuddle Boots for a bit. He's my support animal today." She gives me a sad smile.

"If you need anything, I'm across the hall."

"Thanks, Ivan." She squeezes my arm and walks into her office.

I take a deep breath, running a hand through my hair, and go into my office. I don't like Ben one bit. The way he speaks is arrogant. The type who thinks everyone should fall at his feet. If I could make him disappear, I would. Too bad *Harry Potter* spells aren't real. I'd wave my wand, call out the chant, and *poof.* No more Ben.

If Sara were here, I'd let her loose on him. I bet she'd drive him so crazy, he'd leave town and forget all about Madison. I may not have a spell book and magic wand, but I have a persistent sister. They're practically the same thing.

The timing of Ben's arrival sucks. Things seemed to be going in the right direction for Madison and me, especially after dinner with my family.

She fit in with them, her initial shock washing off as she joined in the conversation and teasing. I smile as I remember last night and sit at my desk, reading over the boarding facility proposal until my next client arrives. Anything to distract me from the jerk who ruined our lunch and the woman who may not be ready for a relationship like I thought she was.

♥ ♥ ♥

I get home and change into shorts and a T-shirt and put on my running shoes. After taking Charlie out for a walk so he could go to the bathroom, I stretch before going for a run. I need to expel the energy that's accumulated throughout the afternoon and clear my mind.

The rest of the day was pointless. I wasn't fully present at work, and Madison was worse off. I made sure she knew that I'm available to talk if she needs to after she meets with Ben. She may say she's safe, but I'm still going to worry.

Running is the perfect medicine. I take off, earbuds in my ears as music flows through my phone. Taking steadying breaths, I focus on my even steps as the world around me fades away.

Madison's face when she saw Ben snaps into my thoughts. She was so shocked and upset. Why can't the guy let it go? Especially if he's the one that cheated.

I have a feeling he's the kind of man who thinks everything he does is forgivable, and I'm the *schmuck* that will end up heartbroken. Madison doesn't seem to want to be with him, but is she really ready to be with me? I don't want to be anyone's second place, but we've had moments that have felt real.

"Careful," someone calls out loud enough I hear them through the music.

I lift my gaze to see a woman in my path move to the side, and I stop abruptly, my chest heaving.

"Sorry," I tell the woman walking her dog.

"Just be careful." She nods.

"Of course."

I start jogging again and pay better attention to my surroundings. The last thing I need is to get run over for crossing the road carelessly. I shake off thoughts about this situation and think about paying Mojo a visit. I could use some animal therapy.

When I get back home, my heart is racing, and I stretch my muscles. Charlie runs up to me, licking my calves. I chuckle and pet him before moving to my next stretch.

"You're so intuitive, boy. Thanks for the love." I smile at him.

I sit on the floor, finish off my stretches, and play with Charlie. He brings me his rope toy, keeping a tight bite on it so I can pull it and he wags his whole body fighting me from taking it.

We continue to play for a few minutes before he gets tired and lies down on the floor, sprawled out like an English bulldog carpet. I slide down beside him and rub his back as I stare at the ceiling.

"I don't know what to do, Charlie. I like Madison a lot." He breathes softly beside me, being a silent listener.

"Her ex is a piece of work, but he came before I did. She says she's over him, but I'm not too sure. Besides, he's definitely older than us, supposedly more mature."

Yet he still hurt her in a way you never will.

I take a deep breath, soaking up Charlie's peaceful energy, and close my eyes. When I hear the door open, I remain where I am.

"Uhh..." Luna's confused voice hits my ears. "Are you napping with Charlie?" I open my eyes to find her eyebrows raised.

"You look like a giant from here." I chuckle.

"You look like you need a drink. What's going on?" She drops her purse on one of the dining table chairs and sits on the floor beside me.

Taking a heavy breath, I sit up and tell her everything that happened today. Then, I tell her that Madison and I kissed yesterday.

"I knew it!" she calls out. "You two were definitely high on the chemistry scale last night. She kept glancing at you with a smile, and you were hyperaware of her, too." She points at me.

"Are you serious?"

"Of course I am. She'd look your way when you weren't paying attention as if secretly etching you to her memory."

"You've been reading too many romance novels," I joke because I am not sure what she saw is true.

"I love my romance novels, but I'm right about this." She nods. "So what are you going to do?"

"I'm going to prove to her that I meant it when I said she deserves better. Show her what it feels like to be treated right. I'll never betray her the way he did." Determination fills me as I make a promise to myself not to back down.

She lifts her hands in the air. "That's the Ivan I know."

Charlie stands and walks to her as if just now realizing his owner is home. She pets him while she smiles encouragingly at me.

"I just hope that their conversation ends without any issues and the guy goes back to Dallas."

"Me too. He sounds like a donkey butt."

"He is." I assure her. "Thanks for the chat." I smile at her.

"You know I'm always here for you. Besides, watching you fall for a woman is fun." She smirks.

I roll my eyes and stand. "I'm going to shower."

"You do stink." She covers her nose. "I didn't want to mention anything." She laughs when I glare at her.

"Let's grab dinner afterwards. Want to go to Roy's?" I ask.

"Sounds good to me. I could go for Sasha's tacos."

I walk toward my room, but Luna calls out to me.

"And Ivan." I look over at her with raised brows. "You're worth more than that guy. Madison will see that."

"I hate that people like him still exist in the adult world." I clench my fists.

"They're always going to exist, but true wisdom is knowing how valuable you are and not letting them break through that. This isn't even about Madison. It's about you and believing you're good enough."

"Thanks, Lu." I nod, walking into my room and taking a deep breath.

Society tends to show women as insecure and vulnerable, not realizing that men also experience these emotions. I've worked my whole adolescence to break through those negative feelings and build myself into the person I am.

Ironically, some of the girls that laughed at me in high school have tried to ask me out now as an adult. I may have grown up and matured, but I'll never forget some people won't.

21

♥ ♥ ♥

MADISON

"There's nothing left between us, Ben." I stare at the man I once cared about with frustration.

"That's not true, babe." He reaches for my hand, but I pull it away. "That thing with Marissa was meaningless. It's forgotten." He waves an arrogant hand in the air.

"Maybe to you, but not me. When someone betrays me, they no longer have a place in my life."

He gives me a bored expression, scratching his bearded jaw. "You and I belong together. It's simple. We work well at the clinic—a power couple, if you will." He leans forward, eyes narrowed. "You'll come back to Dallas as if nothing happened."

"I will not." I meet his gaze, no backing down. "I'm happy here. Accept it. Eventually, I was going to move here and take over my uncle's practice. I got an early start thanks to you."

His jaw clenches, and he takes a deep breath, slowly exhaling. "Listen, sweetheart, people make mistakes. I did. I regret it." He turns on the charm I once fell for. How did I never see through the façade?

Rolling my eyes, I tilt my head. "I'm bored of the same conversation."

"Give me a chance." He pouts as if it were cute, but I don't find the appeal in him anymore. "I care about you."

"If you really care, then you'll accept that I'm happy here and let me live my life. This is where I want to be, and you don't have a place here. Please, Ben, just go." I feel my body weaken from exhaustion.

"You'll regret this, and it'll be too late." He eyes throw darts at me before he stands and storms out of Roy's Tavern.

I drop my head in my hands and take a deep breath, willing my heart to slow down. Hopefully, this time he got the hint and leaves me alone. But Ben Watson isn't used to losing anything or anyone.

"Hey."

I glance up and look at Ivan with furrowed brows.

"Um, hi." I hadn't seen him. "Are you following me?" I tilt my head.

"What? No. I just got here to have dinner with Luna and saw you here. You looked upset." He juts his thumb over his shoulder toward a table across the room, and Luna waves.

"Cool."

"Are you okay?" He puts his hands in his pockets and rocks on his heels.

"Yeah." I sigh. "But—"

"Ivan, my boy," Roy roars as he walks around the bar, interrupting me. "Take a seat and I'll get your order."

"Oh, no." Ivan lifts his hand to stop him. "I'm here with Luna. Just saw Madison and thought I'd say hello."

"Oh." Roy nods. "Sure, okay." If I didn't know better, I'd say Roy is disappointed that Ivan isn't here with me, though he saw me a few minutes ago sitting here with Ben.

"I'll give you a few minutes." Roy smiles awkwardly and walks back toward the bar.

Ivan looks at me with a smile. "Come sit with us." He nods his head toward his table.

"I don't want to interrupt your dinner." I wave my hand.

"City Girl, you'll never disturb me. I wanted to ask you to dinner tonight, but then Ben showed up. Come eat with us. Don't stay here alone, allowing your thoughts to torture you." He gives me a lopsided smile, and I exhale deeply.

The way he's so cluelessly attractive makes me like him more.

"Thanks." I smile and stand.

"Don't thank me. I want to spend time with you, so this is for selfish reasons."

"Look at you, being smooth." I tease him, shoving his shoulder.

"I'm being honest." He gives me a meaningful expression. My heart pitter-patters as his eyes shine with emotion. After what I've been through, honesty is an important quality, and Ivan exudes it.

We get to the table, and Luna smiles up at me.

"Hey," she says.

"Hi. Ivan invited me over, but I don't want to intrude."

"No way. We're like the nice version of *Mean Girls.* Everyone can sit with us." She chuckles.

"Thanks." I giggle and feel better being in company, taking a seat.

"You're welcome. How are you? You looked upset." Luna presses her lips together.

"It's just been a rough day." I rub my eyes.

"Because of your ex?" She gives me a sympathetic look.

I cut my gaze to Ivan, and he shrugs apologetically.

"I tell Luna everything. She's like a sister."

"Unlike Sara and Mia, I'm not going to tell anyone about your personal life. I just wanted to make sure you're okay." Her smile is genuine, making me feel more relaxed.

"I am. Thanks. He's in the past, and I think he finally understood that today," I assure them.

"Good." Luna nods.

"I'll feel better when he's out of this town," Ivan murmurs.

I kind of like how he's protective of me.

"You got yourself much better company," Roy says, coming up to our table and not bothering to lower his voice.

"Yeah." I purse my lips.

"That man with you wasn't good news. Ivan here"—he claps his back—"is prime real estate in town."

"Man." Ivan's eyes widen. "What am I? The bachelor everyone wants to play cupid with?" He shakes his head.

"You're one of the best guys in town." Roy's belly shakes with laughter. "I only speak the truth."

"I guess *one* of the best guys is the best compliment I'll get." Ivan looks at him.

"Gotta be fair to the rest of the good guys. Just staying partial." He winks and grabs a small notepad. "What can I get ya?"

"I'll have a glass of Chardonnay and the tacos al pastor," Luna says.

I lift two fingers. "Make that two glasses of wine and a cheeseburger."

"A beer and tacos for me."

"Sounds good. I'll bring your drinks in a sec." Roy walks away from our table.

Ivan sits back in his chair, looking intently at me. I bite down my smile and stare into his eyes, mesmerized. My heart starts to race, wanting nothing more than to feel his hug again, his kiss.

I've always had a habit of going for guys that are like Ben. Unreliable, walking red flags. Ivan is the total opposite, and it feels great. Luna clears her throat, and I snap out of it.

"Were you here with Ben?" Ivan asks.

"I thought this would be a good place to talk to him since Roy and his wife know me, and I didn't want to meet him at home." It felt like the right decision when I told Ben I'd meet him to talk.

"I'm glad you decided that," Ivan says.

"Yeah," Luna adds.

"It's done." I smile. "Let's change subjects."

"Did you like dinner last night?" Luna asks.

"I did. I had never tried Cuban food, but it was delicious." My mouth waters just thinking about it.

"I'm glad. I also heard Mojo the Llama went back home. Ivan's disappointed he lost his friend," she teases.

"I really thought llamas would be friendlier to me. He didn't like me." Ivan shakes his head with a frown.

"It takes a bit for people to warm up to you," I tell him.

"I'm delightful." He crosses his arms.

I chuckle, feeling myself relax for the first time since I saw Ben this afternoon. No matter how we started, Ivan makes me feel at ease. And Luna is someone I could be good friends with.

Maybe moving to Sunshine Falls was exactly what I needed. Not as a form of escape but because it's where I'm meant to be to grow in this next chapter of my life. It's a pretty amazing town to learn about myself, my career, and life.

♥♥♥

"Dr. Grover," a woman says frantically. "I don't have an appointment, but my little Caramel has something strange on his skin.

I look at my client with confusion. She was here with Caramel last week, and his checkup was great.

I look around the waiting room, and the clients waiting are all Ivan's. Sighing, I nod.

"I have a few minutes to take a look."

Mrs. Anders grabs the cat and follows me through to an exam room.

"My son was playing with him and felt a lump on his stomach. I thought he was exaggerating since we were here the other day, but it's true. My Caramel has a small lump to the left of his stomach. I thought it was a tick at first, but it didn't feel like it." She frowns, waving her hand around as she speaks.

"Let me take a look." I smile to try to calm her.

Caramel hisses and tries to run away, but Mrs. Anders holds him firmly, his belly up. I move my hands around to examine him, not sensing anything off. Moving more to the left, I feel what she's talking about. Separating his long hair, a nipple comes to view.

"Mrs. Anders." I look up at the woman, trying to bite down my smile.

"What is it? Is it cancerous?" Her eyes are round.

"Breathe easy," I assure her. "It's a nipple."

"Really?" Her face scrunches up. "But he's a male."

"And male animals also have them." I nod slowly. "Just like humans."

It dawns on her and her face grows bright red. "Oh, my goodness."

I chuckle and pat Caramel, getting him a treat.

"This is so humiliating. I'm sorry for freaking out, Dr. Grover. Of course. Animals have teats." She shakes her head. "I guess you can tell anatomy was not my best subject in school," she jokes.

I laugh and wave her off. "It's what we're here for. Caramel is healthy."

"Thanks again."

"You're welcome."

Once she leaves, I let my laughter flow. My professional façade was begging to slip.

"What happened?" Ivan sneaks his head in.

"Nothing." I swallow down my chuckles.

"No, no. Tell me. I want to laugh, too." He walks in, wearing his scrubs.

It's my favorite outfit on him. The sleeves let me admire his biceps, and he loves to wear the jogger scrub pants, which are my weakness.

"Mrs. Anders came with Caramel, fearful he had a lump on his stomach."

"Is he okay?" Ivan's eyes widen.

"Oh, yeah. A little lesson in anatomy goes a long way when I told her it was a nipple. She got so flustered and embarrassed."

Ivan laughs, shaking his head. "Poor woman."

"It worked out."

He lifts his hand. "So wait..." His eyes narrow intently. "Did you take a walk-in without hesitating?" A slow smile creeps up his face.

"Yes." I cross my arms. "I didn't have any patients, so I took her in."

"Well, well, Dr. Grover." He steps closer to me. "I have to say, I like this development."

"I'm still firm in my belief that they have to wait if we have appointments." I arch a brow.

"That's okay." He nods.

His smile is crooked and inviting, making me want to kiss him again. Standing inches from each other, a huge grin takes over my face. Ivan makes me feel different. Like structure and routine aren't as important as I thought they were. Like time can flow freely.

"Uh, we have a situation." Kate peeks her head in, breaking the moment.

I jump back, looking guilty. "What happened?" I blink toward her.

She presses her lips together, and we hear a loud voice.

"The Matthews are accusing us of trying to kill their dog."

"What?" Ivan yells.

"That's impossible." My eyes widen.

We rush out of the room and head to the reception area. When the Matthews see us, they turn their angry glare our way.

"You." Mrs. Matthews points at Ivan. "You animal killer."

"I don't understand, Mrs. Matthews. Can we talk about this privately?" He shakes his head, face white like a ghost.

"Oh, no. I want everyone to hear how you treat innocent animals."

He lifts his hands, completely shocked.

"What's going on?" I step in.

"This clinic prescribes vitamins without reading the dangers in them. You told us to give Max that oil, and we did. He's been throwing up since," Mr. Matthews explains.

"That oil shouldn't have that side effect. Why don't I take a look?" Ivan stares at them with furrowed brows.

"Absolutely not." Mrs. Matthew tightens her arms around Max. "We're going to another clinic. They'll know how to treat animals the right way."

"Wait." I lift my hand. "It could be an allergic reaction. What area of his body did you apply the oil?"

"We mixed it into his water."

Ivan closes his eyes and sighs.

"Mr. and Mrs. Matthews, the oil is to rub on his coat so his skin soaks it. It's topical use, not oral." He shakes his head as he explains slowly. "Do you remember I told you to put it on the areas affected by the fungus?"

I stare at the couple and breathe out. Sometimes this job is frustrating when we have situations like this.

"No." Mrs. Matthews shakes her head.

"Yes. We went over it. I explained where to apply the oil, how often, and for how long."

Mr. Matthews glares at his wife now. "You told me he said to put it in his water."

"I thought it could be added in his water and it'd work faster." She looks at Ivan. "You never specified it was bad to ingest."

"But I told you *how* to use it. Never did I mention giving it to him in water. Please let me examine Max."

Sometimes, I wonder how some people have pets when they don't read information on how to properly care for them. Clearly, Mrs. Matthews is stubborn when she refuses to hand Max over. Her husband grabs the dog from her and walks with Ivan to an exam room, leaving her huffing and puffing, still blaming us instead of accepting that she messed up. Thankfully, Max should be okay.

The dose of clueless clients today has been plenty. Unfortunately, I still have a few more hours of work, and it seems today is a full moon, or Mercury is in retrograde, or the forces are against us.

By the time we close the clinic for the weekend, I'm exhausted.

"Was today a strange day, or is this normal for Sunshine Falls?" I look at Ivan as we both lean against the hallway wall.

"Today was possessed by something. I don't know what was up with people. A client accused us of stealing because his consultation cost a hundred dollars—which was the price Rose gave him *before* booking." Ivan rubs a hand down his face.

I laugh because there's not much to do.

"By the way, I've been reading up on the boarding proposal, and it's solid." He rolls his head against the wall to look at me.

"Yeah?" My eyes light up.

He nods and yawns. "Sorry," he says. "Let's get through the festival next week, and we can talk about it. I have a few ideas to make the transition easier."

"Great." I perk up.

"Now, do you have plans for dinner?" He pushes off the wall and walks toward me.

"Are you asking me out, Dr. Romero?"

"I sure am." He leans his hand against the wall beside my head and leans in close. "I want to spend some time with you, get to know you better outside of these walls." His voice flits across my skin like a caress.

"I'd like that." I look up at him, seeing the dark shades of brown in his eyes. They sparkle with pride, his lips right there.

"Good." He nods, bending his head.

His lips brush against mine in a soft kiss, and I melt against the wall. I don't know what it is about this man that makes me feel alive. It makes me feel like I could battle dragons and ride unicorns. Like if Taylor Swift would write a love song about us.

"What the..." Ivan jumps back, abruptly breaking the moment.

"What happened?"

He turns around, and I bend over in laughter. Boots is hanging off his back, claws out.

"I have a chaperone," Ivan complains.

"Oh, my goodness." I slap my knee, laughing. "He's protecting me," I say on a gasp.

"From what? I'm a nice guy!" He calls out. "Boots, you liked me once."

"Until he became my loyal protector." I walk toward him. "Stop moving around so I can grab him."

"The little jerk has his nails in my skin again."

I laugh louder, snorting, and Ivan stares at me, guffawing.

"You're adorable," he says. "But get this cat off me, please."

I grab Boots, chastising him. He pushes his head into my hand like an angel who didn't just attack Ivan.

"Right, play the nice cat card now," Ivan mumbles. "How's my back?" He lifts his shirt to show me his skin, and I swallow.

"Scratched," I squeak.

"Any chance you want to help me here?" He looks over his shoulder.

"Come on." I drag him into a room and grab the hydrogen peroxide and cotton balls. "I'm going to start charging you for medical treatment."

"I can pay up with kisses," he retorts.

"Hmmm...I'll consider it."

I rub the cotton over the scratches, and Ivan tenses. I softly clean them out, though they are pretty superficial.

"It's not too bad," I tell him.

"Good." His muscles flex as he shifts. "That tickles." He chuckles.

I smile and run my finger along his skin, following the lines of definition. Ivan's breath catches, and I take my time admiring him. Once I'm done, I lean forward and place a kiss on the center of his back. He shivers and drops his shirt, turning around to face me.

"Thank you." His eyes bore into mine, and he reaches out to cup my face.

"You're welcome." My voice is soft and hazy.

Ivan closes the gap. "I need to make up for that disaster." His lips touch mine, and a rainbow of emotions explode inside of me. It's like I reached the pot of gold.

Ivan feels like a treasure. He's kind and humble, caring and sweet. He's nothing like the guys I've met in the past. It must be true that there's a difference between city guys and small-town men. Or maybe it's just Ivan that breaks the mold.

Whatever it is, I never want to stop feeling this way.

Boots purrs by my feet, and Ivan tenses. I chuckle and lean back to watch him. He glares down at the cat, who looks up at us with round, innocent eyes.

"Go out with me tonight," Ivan says with a hint of authority. "Leave Boots at home, though."

I giggle and nod. After the fiasco with Ben yesterday, I should stick to myself, but it's clear that Ivan is someone I don't want to put distance between.

"Great." His beams.

"I have one request." I lift my finger.

"What's that?" He arches a brow.

"You wear your glasses."

His brows furrow and he goes to adjust them until he realizes he isn't wearing them today.

"Do you like my glasses?" He tilts his head, his lips twitch with humor.

"I love them. You look...handsome with them on."

"Were you going to say sexy, hot?" He grins.

"All of the above." I shrug.

"Your wish is my command, City Girl." He brushes his lips on my forehead. "I'll pick you up for our first official date."

"I can't wait." My words ring with honesty.

"Me either. Let's close up and leave. The sooner we do, the faster I get to see you again."

"Being smooth again, Dr. Romero," I tease.

"You bring it out of me." He winks.

"I very much approve."

"Usually, I'm better with animals than humans, but something about you makes me feel comfortable being myself."

I crinkle my brows as his words sink in.

"You should always be yourself." I squeeze his hand. "Who cares what others think? If you're constantly trying to hide your truth, you'll never be happy. And I very much like the person you are."

Ivan nods, looking at me with a soft gaze that makes my heart gallop freely. Whether my heart warns me or not, I can't help but fall for him.

22

♥ ♥ ♥

IVAN

I KNOCK ON MADISON'S door, adjusting my glasses on the bridge of my nose. My smile widens when I remember her request. Who knew my glasses were a hit with women?

The door opens, and Madison smiles at me.

"Hey."

"Hi." I take her in, wearing a skirt with small flowers on it.

The material looks soft and flowy, and my sister's would probably know the right name for it. I'm just admiring her beauty. It doesn't matter if she wears silk, cotton, or linen. Madison is gorgeous either way.

Her white top is tucked into the skirt, and her long auburn hair cascades down her shoulders.

"You look beautiful," I finally say.

"Thank you. I see you took my advice." She locks up the door.

"Ah, yes. I couldn't let you down." I reach for her hand and kiss her cheek. Her perfume fills my senses with a sweet, floral aroma.

I'm nervous about this date. It's the first one I've had in a long time. Any guy would be embarrassed to admit that. Dating isn't a normal occurrence for me,

234

and I'm pretty sure Madison figured it out by my mom's excitement that a woman went to dinner at the house. My priority for years has been work.

Guiding Madison to my car, I open the door for her. The smile she aims my way makes me feel like I'm on top of the world. I would've never dated anyone at all if it meant I'd end up right here in this moment.

"Where are we going?" Madison asks once I'm in the car.

"Have you ever been to a drive-in?" I smile over at her, pulling out of the driveway.

"No." Her eyes widen. "Are you serious?" she asks excitedly.

"Yup. I saw they're playing the new superhero movie and thought it'd be fun, so I snagged us some tickets."

"I love the idea."

"I noticed your keychain at work has the logo of the franchise, so I hoped you'd want to watch it." It was fate to see that the drive-in was playing it. I bought the tickets quickly before they sold out since there were only a few left.

"You're observant."

"I like you, so I pay attention."

"I didn't know Sunshine Falls even had a drive-in. It's so exciting." She shifts her body to look at me.

"It's in the outskirts and serves a few different towns."

"So cool." She leans back on the seat.

Despite my eyes being on the road, I'm hyperaware of her movements, her voice, her sighs. My entire being is attuned to Madison, and it's been like that since I met her. We may have our differences when it comes to work, but that makes me like her more. She doesn't give in and surrender to the way we've always done things at the clinic. She challenges me, our job, and knows when to admit defeat or ask for help.

Fifteen minutes later, I pull into the drive-in, and Madison gasps.

"This is so cool." She leans forward on the dash.

Cars are already in place, claiming the spots up front. I follow the path and park a few rows back from the screen. I can finally turn to look at her, and I'm met with a wide smile and bright eyes.

"So you like the idea?"

"I love it. It feels like we're back in time but with modern cars." She laughs.

"I'm glad, but if we were back in time we might have a chaperone. It'd probably be one of my sisters, so I'm glad we don't because they'd ruin this for me." I joke.

"I think I've seen the extent of their meddling, and I'm still here." She reaches for my hand.

"In high school, they told my crush that I liked her, and I had to be lab partners with her. Awkward is putting it kindly."

Madison chuckles, her face lit with happiness. "It doesn't surprise me from what I've seen."

I shake my head and squeeze her hand. "I'm glad this worked in my favor."

"It did, though I doubt it was that bad. I'm sure the girls were happy to have your attention."

"Um, you heard the same stories as me at dinner the other night, right?" My brows pull together. "The ballet classes kind of killed my game." I shake my head. "Actually, I don't have game."

Madison giggles, unbuckling her seatbelt and leaning close. "I'm glad that you don't. You're honest, whether it means telling someone their shoes are ugly or that you love their haircut."

I stare at her with a soft smile.

"Besides, games are for players, and I'm not in the market for a player." She shrugs and leans back, putting space between us.

"Well, I couldn't even tackle a fake person in football tryouts so pretty sure I'm not a player." I joke.

"But how was your balance in ballet?" She teases with a gleam in her eyes.

"Impeccable," I admit.

Madison falls back on her seat, laughing. "I would've loved to see that."

"Your laugh is my favorite," I say.

She looks over at me, giggling. "You're being sweet."

"So? Isn't that the point of a date?"

"It is." She nods, sighing and looking out of the windshield. "Uhh... Ivan?" Her voice drops in confusion.

"Yeah?"

"Didn't you say they were playing the superhero movie?" Her brows furrow as she looks back at me.

"I did." I nod slowly.

"Then why does the screen have the *E.T.* movie poster projected?"

"What?" My eyes snap to the screen, and sure enough, it's showing the big moon with E.T. flying on the bike.

My palms sweat as I look from Madison to the screen with wide eyes. This can't be happening.

"It's okay," Madison says, attempting to calm me. "I love this movie and haven't seen it in ages."

"Uh, huh." I nod.

"Ivan, honestly." She smiles, but my reason for panic has nothing to do with the wrong movie.

"I'm going to buy food at the concession." It's an escape to ask the attendant what movie they're playing.

"Are you okay?" She looks at me with narrowed eyes, trying to get a read on me.

"I'm great." My response is way too eager, not convincing her at all when her eyebrows fly up on her forehead.

"You're not. I don't care. This date is perfect, even if we saw commercials all night."

I look at her and take a deep breath, calming my racing heart. Ever since I was a boy, I've been terrified of this movie.

"I promise I'm okay," I tell her. "What would you like to eat?" I open the app that has the menu, and read out the options.

"Ohhhh. A brisket dog, please." She licks her lips, and I chuckle.

"Just one? It looks like you want stock of it?" I tease her.

"One is enough." She glares playfully, and I add the number two in the square next to the item to order one for myself, too.

"Want to share chili cheese fries?"

"Is the sky blue?" Her eyes widen.

"Right now it's like a black color." Although, the sky here is full of stars, which makes this date even more romantic. I'm patting myself on the back.

Except for the fact that you're terrified of the movie they're going to play.

Right. I need to get this squared away.

"Jerk." She shoves my shoulder. "I'd love to."

"Teasing you is fun." I wink. "How about drinks?"

"A Coke for me, please." I add two as well to the order and open my car door.

"I'll be right back then."

"Want me to help you bring everything?"

"It's okay. They'll put it all in a bag and give me cupholders for the drinks." No way I want her to overhear me asking about the movie.

I rush toward the concession, feeling like I'm living a nightmare. I get to the stand and wait in line until it's my turn. When the attendant takes my order, I ask her what movie is playing.

"*E.T.* is tonight's showing." She points to the screen with raised brows as if I were dense.

"Right, but I thought it was the Thor movie."

"That's tomorrow night's showing."

"What? No. I saw the website and it didn't say anything about *E.T.*," I argue although she's telling me the facts.

"You must've gotten confused with the movie poster, but tonight's showing is that." She shrugs. "Would you like anything else?"

My pride back after Madison sees my reaction.

"Sno-Caps." I order some chocolate for dessert.

"We'll call your name when your food is ready."

I nod and stand to the side, letting others place their order. Grabbing my phone, I send a text to my family group chat.

> Me: SOS. This is not a drill. E.T. is playing at the drive-in.

> Luna: Oh no.

239

Me: Oh yes

Sara: You're at the drive-in?

Mia: With who?

I squeeze my eyes shut and run a hand down my face. I panicked and forgot Sara and Mia know nothing about my date. I'm never going to hear the end of this.

Me: No I'm not. I was thinking of going to the movies but it's E.T.

Sara: Nuh uh. You're there now or you wouldn't freak out. Who are you with? OMG! Are you on a date with Madison?!

Sara: Mom is going to love this. She was saying what a great couple you 2 make.

Me: Sara...

Mia: He's totally with her.

Luna: Girls, for once, keep this to yourselves.

Me: Thanks Lu.

Sara: I'm sooooo excited!!!

Me: Why didn't I stop and think before writing in this chat?

Mia: Because your subconscious wanted to tell us the news. Congrats, cuz.

Sara: You hate E.T.

Mia: He doesn't just hate it. He's scared of it.

Sara: Didn't you see the movie playing before buying tickets?

Me: I got mixed up with tomorrow's movie.

Mia: So tell her the truth.

Me: Right. And seem like a loser?

Luna: You are not a loser.

Sara: Don't talk that way. She's lucky to go out with you.

Sometimes, Sara is sweet. This is one of those times. "Ivan!" the attendant calls out.

Me: Gotta go. Wish me luck.

THE NICE GUY

Sara: Don't get abducted by E.T.

So much for her kindness.

I grab our food and drinks and head back to the car while taking deep breaths and plastering on a smile. I place the drinks on the roof to open the door. Madison reaches out for the bag, and I hand it to her so I can grab the drinks and sit.

"So there was a mix up. I read the wrong movie, and tonight's showing is, in fact, *E.T.*" I frown. "Sorry."

"I already told you I don't care. You're too uptight. Relax."

"Sorry."

"And stop apologizing." Her voice is stern.

"Yes, ma'am." I smile, hoping I can sit through this movie.

I'm a man now. I doubt a fictional alien that scared me as a boy will affect me as an adult. I hope so at least.

We start eating and talking while we wait for the move to start, and it's the distraction I need.

"Have you always lived here?" Madison asks and takes a bite of her brisket dog.

"Yeah. I stayed local for college so I could work at the clinic."

"Impressive. You really love working there, right?"

"So much that I became partner and endured this stubborn red head." I roll my eyes, fighting back a smile.

"Working with me is a delight." She sticks her tongue out.

"It is," I say honestly, taking a chili cheese fry.

"I didn't know what to expect when I first moved here. Sunshine Falls was such a foreign idea, even if I had visited Uncle James and Aunt Susan in the past. It was usually quick trips and I hadn't been back in years." She takes a bite of her food.

"I never saw you around."

"Most of my time was spent at their house or visiting the surrounding area." She shrugs. "We must've just missed each other."

"Probably." I nod, finishing off my brisket dog.

"Oh! The movie is starting." She shimmies and raises the volume on the radio station.

I take a deep breath, hoping to keep my food down. Nothing is worse than throwing up on a first date.

As the movie begins, I pretend I'm watching and shove more chili fries in my mouth. Madison stares at the screen with rapt attention, thankfully missing my stressed out reaction. I wish I remembered the plot in more detail to be prepared for certain scenes, but any scene with the alien is enough to freak me out.

Her eyes cut to mine minutes later, and her brows furrow.

"Okay, that's enough. You need to relax." She looks at my fisted hand. "So it isn't the movie you planned, but I don't care. I want to spend time with you. I already told you this isn't a big deal. Believe me." Her eyes widen.

I take a deep breath and shake my head. I'm ruining this date with my fear, which is worse than admitting the truth.

"It's not that." I press my lips together.

"Then what is it?"

I take a deep breath and stare up at the roof before looking at her round eyes.

"I've been terrified of E.T. ever since I saw the movie the first time." I wait for her to laugh.

"Terrified?" Her brows lift and she chuckles. "Okay, I wasn't expecting that." She tries to fight back her laugh.

"Go on and laugh," I say monotonously.

"No." She shakes her head. "Sorry." She smiles, covering it with her hand. "I think it's cute."

"Right. It's adorable that a grown man is afraid of a movie."

"If you need to hold my hand, you can," she teases.

I take a deep breath and glare at her. Madison laughs and leans forward, kissing my cheek. The simple action jolts me awake, almost making me forget about the looming alien.

"I'm joking, but you really can hold my hand." She reaches it out. I take her hand, stroking my finger along her skin. "And don't be embarrassed. We all have our weaknesses." She giggles.

I grumble in response and look at the screen, determined to overcome this. When E.T. appears, I jump and knock the chili cheese fries from the center console onto my lap.

"Oh, sheep." I release Madison's hand and lift the container. My pants are stained with chili.

"Are you okay?" Her lips tuck into her mouth as if trying to hide her laughter.

"Peachy," I deadpan, grabbing the fries from my pants and placing them back in the container to throw out.

Laughter bubbles out of her, and she covers her mouth.

"It looks like I had a reverse poop accident in my pants."

Madison throws her head back, laughing.

"I'm sorry," she says through her cackles. "It's just...it does kinda look like poo." She snorts.

I close my eyes. "Just the way I planned this date to go."

"Here." She hands me some napkins, and I do my best to clean up the excess chili on my pants before tossing the waddled papers in the container.

"I'm going to smell like a giant bowl of chili."

"I do like chili," Madison jokes.

My fingers sneak under my glasses, and I rub my eyes. "I can't believe I did that."

"It makes for a memorable date." She giggles. "And if it makes you feel better, I still like you."

"I'm blaming the creepy alien."

"He's fake," Madison says, soothingly.

"Right. Those long, bony fingers are freaky," I comment.

She holds out the box of Sno-Caps. "Here. Eat something sweet."

I pour some in my palm and try to ignore the wet splat on my pants. As the movie progresses, Madison grabs my hand and strokes her thumb over it. It's calming and helps me focus on something else. I chuckle at a scene, and Madison smiles over at me.

"Not that bad, huh?"

I shake my head and look over at her. She's beautiful in the dim car, the lights from the screen illuminating her face. I lift our hands and kiss the top of hers. She shivers, keeping her eyes trained on mine.

The fact that she didn't make fun of me, instead teased me good-naturedly, and held my hand speaks volumes. I've got the best woman by my side.

Take that, high school jocks.

As the movie finishes, I sigh in relief.

"You did it." She dances in her seat, lifting my arm.

"Thanks to you." I lean forward, pecking her lips.

Madison's face brightens. "I'll gladly take the credit." She blows on her nails and buffs them on her shoulder.

"We should get going," I say when we're one of the last cars in the lot. "I've got another thing planned." I wink.

"More than spilling chili and your fear of aliens?" She grins.

"Something better. Something that will hopefully make you forget about that." I nod.

I drive away from the drive-in, heading to a darker road.

"How do you say alien in Spanish?" Madison asks.

"Extraterrestre," I answer.

"Like extraterrestrial. That makes sense." She bounces in her seat a bit. "How about movie?"

"Película." I smile her way.

"You should teach me Spanish so I can understand what your family says when they get into a conversation."

I chuckle because they do tend to switch over when they get passionate about a topic, or at the very least speak Spanglish.

"We'll work on that."

"How do you say handsome?"

"Guapo."

"You are guapo."

I chuckle at her compliment and reach out for her hand.

"Thanks. The whole sentence would be, Tú eres guapo."

"Tú eres guapo. I sound terrible." She drops back on the seat.

"You'll get the hang of it." I love that she's interested in learning about my family's culture.

"Eres preciosa," I tell her, squeezing her hand.

"Precious?" She guesses.

"Beautiful." I smirk over at her.

She bites down her smile and bows her head.

"Don't hide your smile from me."

I pull into an open field not far from town that has an uninterrupted view of the sky.

"You don't get this in the city." I glance over at her as I park the car.

"Wow." She leans forward to look out of the window. "How do you say stars?"

"Estrellas. Come on." I open my door and round the car to meet her by the passenger side. She takes my hand when I reach out, and I tug her to me, wrapping my other arm around her. Not even stained pants will stop me from holding her close.

I hum and sway to a random beat, sighing when she rests her head on my shoulder. My world feels right. I'm living a moment in time that was meant for us. Who knew we'd end up here?

"The estrellas shine so brightly," Madison whispers. "They're gorgeous."

I look down at her, and she lifts her head. Cupping the side of her face, my eyes stare into hers.

"You're the brightest star I see. Nothing compares to your beauty." I pull her closer, resting my head beside hers. "Mi Estrella," I whisper.

She shivers in my arms, sighing softly. I'm falling for this woman, and I pray that we can make this work.

23

♥ ♥ ♥

MADISON

BETWEEN SEEING PATIENTS AND preparing for the town Birthday Festival, the past week has flown by. Any other town would call this Founder's Day, but not this place. I love that they don't conform to what others do.

Everyone has been buzzing with excitement all week. Every conversation revolves around the plans for the festival, what they're excited for—apparently there's an amazing display of fireworks—and where they're meeting each other. It's contagious, and I've had an extra pep in my step as well.

Except my pep isn't only due to the festival but the man who is stealing my heart. Our date on Friday was amazing. I especially loved Ivan's nervousness about the movie but prided myself in helping him through his fear.

I love that he doesn't pretend to be this tough guy when he isn't. Ivan is strong, confident, and sexy without being in your face about it.

Next time we should see a horror film so he can soothe me. I'd very much like to feel his arms around me. Maybe in a movie theater because the center console of a car doesn't make cuddling easy. And apparently with Ivan, I'm a cuddler. At least, I want to. We just haven't had the chance.

I never really cared about that with Ben. It's a stark comparison, and maybe it's because he wasn't big on snuggling or being too affectionate thinking back on it now. But he always used compliments and told me how beautiful I was. I liked being on the receiving end of his attention, even if it meant keeping our relationship a secret.

Ben blamed it on our work environment. Now, I know it was to maintain his single status to the public.

I shake my head, tossing out any thoughts about the man that holds no importance in my life anymore.

Boots comes up to me, reading me like a book. He always knows when I need an extra dose of love. Picking him up, I hug him and sway my body.

"Ready to go to the festival?" Boots has unofficially become the clinic's mascot, much to Ivan's feigned chagrin. Deep down, he loves the little guy.

Boots purrs and rubs his head against the underside of my chin. Sometimes I feel like he's half-dog with his behavior.

"Good because we need to get there on time to set up, or Ivan will accuse me of losing my punctuality." Boots just blinks up at me unbothered and jumps from my arms.

Ah, there's the cat part of him reappearing.

Instead of putting Boots in the carrier, I clip a leash to his collar and head out of the house. After fighting me to go in the carrier a few times last week, I decided to try the leash. He loves it.

It's a beautiful day to be outdoors. Having things within walking distance is my favorite thing about living in a small town. It allows me to connect to nature more and provides a sense of freedom—as if I'm living in a different time. Except everyone walks with smartphones in their hands.

People wave and say hello as I pass them, some laughing at the fact that Boots is on a leash. The streets are decorated with banners, balloons, and signs celebrating Sunshine Falls. It's like the town is personified, the people's best friend. Laughter echoes in the air, and kids run around as they play. It's early in the morning, and there are already people out and about with coffee cups and pastries, roaming as small businesses set up their tables.

I find Ivan by ours, talking to a man about his age. They laugh, and the view of Ivan tossing his head back makes my heart squeeze. This man makes my belly somersault. With my eyes trained on Ivan, I pick up my pace and run into someone.

"Oh, sorry." I look up at the woman.

She gives me an unimpressed look and smooths her dress, rolling her eyes when Boots catches her eye. "Careful where you're walking."

Oooookay, then. Not everyone in Sunshine Falls is sunshiney. Go figure.

"Right. I apologize." I nod and walk away, paying attention to my surroundings instead of Ivan until I reach our table.

"Hey." I look between the two guys.

"Hey, you're late." Ivan looks at me with a teasing gleam in his eyes.

"Blame Boots." I tug the leash and look at the other man. "I'm Madison." I smile at him.

"I've heard a lot about you. I'm Ezra." He gives me a knowing smile that makes me blush. I look at Ivan with raised brows, but he ignores the question in my eyes.

"Ezra is my best friend," Ivan says.

"Really?" My brows furrow. "Does Luna know you've replaced her?"

Ivan chuckles and shakes his head. "Ezra and I have been best friends since we were kids, but he moved away the summer before seventh grade."

"And you've remained friends all this time?" I lift my brows, impressed.

Ivan claps Ezra's shoulder. "We sure did." He smiles proudly.

"That's amazing. It's nice to meet you," I tell Ezra.

"Likewise. I can't believe I came in time for the festival." He looks around, slipping his hands into his pockets.

"A great coincidence. I'll be busy here, but we close our booth at four, and then we can hang out." Ivan smiles.

"Don't worry about me. I'm going to roam around, see if anyone remembers me. It's kind of fun having anonymity here."

"Has it been a while since you've visited?" I ask him.

"It's been years. I think the last time I came was right before starting high school."

"Wow." My brows lift.

"I know." He chuckles. "It's strange and yet really nice to be back home."

"I bet."

"Anyway, y'all set up. I'll see you later."

"Sounds good," Ivan says while I wave.

I unhook Boot's leash, petting him. He's learned to stay near me, so there are no worries about him running away. I grab the pamphlets Ivan brought and set them on the table that's already covered in a white tablecloth.

"I haven't said a proper hello." Ivan's deep voice hits my back.

I turn around and grin at him, leaning my hands on the table behind me. His fingers brush along my cheek.

"Good morning." I bite down my smile.

He looks handsome in a fitted white Polo shirt tucked into beige chino pants. His skin glistens against the shirt, the white contrasting against his tan skin. His hair is mussed in waves and he's wearing those darn glasses that make me weak in the knees.

"Are you done admiring me?" he teases.

I roll my eyes. "I wasn't admiring you. I was...making sure you were dressed casual yet professional."

Ivan laughs deeply and leans close.

"You don't need to feel embarrassed. I was definitely taking you in." There's a husk to his voice. "I like the sundress." He smiles.

"Thanks. It has pockets." I put my hands in them and hold out the skirt to prove my point. Ivan chuckles and shakes his head.

"Pockets or no pockets, you look beautiful." He winks, and I sigh happily. "Let's set up before people start stopping by."

I nod, snapping out of the spell he puts me under, and get to work. Once we're set up with all the information necessary, a jar of treats, and Ivan's Joke of the Day, we're ready for people to visit us.

"Oh, you two are adorable together." A woman says with a bright smile. She doesn't even have a pet. "I heard you're dating. What a great story to tell your kids. Meeting at work."

Ivan and I stare at each other with wide eyes.

"Um, Mrs. Dario, we're working." Ivan tries to get her to stop.

"Right, right." She winks as if she were keeping our secret.

"They do make a cute couple," another woman says, coming up to us.

Ivan sighs, scrubbing a hand down his face while I try to hold back my laughter because I cannot believe these women.

"Leave my boy alone." Clara walks up to us. "Don't embarrass him, Stella," she tells Mrs. Dario.

"I'm not, but I had to come see what you were telling us."

"Mom," Ivan says in exasperation.

She ignores him and smiles at me. "Madison, mija. How are you?" She rounds the table, embracing me in a tight hug.

I bite down my smile as I look at Ivan, hugging Clara back.

"Can you stop telling your friends gossip about us?" Ivan asks when she pulls away.

"It's not gossip." She glares at him.

"It is." He nods. "Can my life be private for a little while?" He closes his eyes.

"Oh, fine." She kisses his cheek, rubbing off the pink stain of lipstick she left there, and I laugh. It's such a mom move.

Ivan groans and sends her and her friends away. When they leave, he looks at me with his mouth in a tight line.

"I can't seem like a professional when my mom is wiping lipstick off my face."

Laughing, I grip his arm. "I think it's cute."

Throughout the morning, different clients come and see us, some wanting to teach their pet new tricks. Thankfully, mostly are dogs.

"Dr. Grover, I want Brownie to learn a trick." A little girl holds up her hamster cage.

"Oh." I smile. "Hi, Katie. I think we can do that." I cut my eyes to Ivan, who shrugs.

I've never trained a hamster before, but there's a first time for everything. From what I've read, they're not too difficult to train. I grab a small piece of carrot, but Katie stops me.

"Brownie doesn't like carrots. I have sunflower seeds for her." She hands me one.

"Thanks." I smile at her. "Now, it's important to feel like you're in charge and not let her steal from you. If you allow her to, then she's never going to listen."

Katie nods with rapt attention, and I place the cage on top of the table, opening the top.

"Place your hand above her head like this." I hold the seed over Brownie's head. "Stand," I command.

The hamster stands to reach for the seed. I give it to her and praise her.

"Wow. That's cool. Can you make her jump?" Katie's wide eyes look at me.

I nod, grabbing another sunflower seed and holding it higher above Brownie's head so she has to extend to jump to reach it. As Brownie stares at the seed, stretching higher to get it, she's about ready to hop. Boots jumps on the table, looking at what has our attention, and hisses.

"Boots!" I call out as my naughty cat leaps onto the cage with a screech. Brownie squeaks while my cat tries to get him with his claws. Chaos erupts around us.

"No!" Katie calls out.

"Stop," I yell, reaching for Boots, but he runs away, knocking down the cage and the jar of treats.

The stacked papers on the table are a mess. Katie cries, and I try to assure her we'll find Brownie, who ran away terrified. I can't blame her, I'd be scared if something twice my size came after me.

Ivan mumbles a curse and looks under the table, picking up the empty cage. I bend down, looking all around.

"I'm going to kill that cat." He looks at me under the table.

"Not kill. I will put him in a kennel as soon as I find him." I trust Boots will return, but right now my client's pet is more important.

I crawl around the floor, not caring if my dress gets dirty. Thankfully it's knee-length or I'd be flashing people on top of losing a pet.

"Brownie," I call out softly. "You're safe, girl." Where in the world did she go? Why couldn't it be a sloth that moves like molasses? No, it has to be a hamster that's a fast animal.

Katie's mom hugs her while her dad helps us search.

"I'm so sorry." I look at them with round eyes and a frown. "As soon as I catch Boots, he's in big trouble."

Her mom shakes her head, whispering comforting words to Katie. A crowd has gathered around our table to see what is going on, but this isn't the attention I want on us.

"I'm going to spread the word so people are careful where they step," Ivan says, jogging away.

I look behind the tree near our table but don't see her. She's nowhere to be found. Panic starts to set in with the more time that passes.

"Hey, Ivan told me what happened." Luna walks over to me with Charlie.

I frown and nod, desperate to find the hamster. It's not like it's a horse you can spot anywhere. Brownie is small and could burrow in the ground to hide.

"I'll help you look." She ties Charlie to the tree and joins the few volunteers that have offered to search for the scared hamster.

"Dr. Grover, where's Brownie?" Katie sobs, her breath shaky.

"We're looking for her. I promise." I smile sympathetically and guiltily. "I'm so sorry." I apologize for the millionth time.

I didn't expect Boots to go crazy-hunter on the hamster. Cartoons show the antagonistic relationship cats and rodents have, but it's like the universe wanted to demonstrate it to us in real time view. I rather not live out a *Tom and Jerry* situation.

Charlie barks, wagging his tail.

"Sit," Luna commands, but he ignores her, getting more agitated.

We continue to look for Brownie, moving further away from the table because I'm sure that at this point the hamster has driven off to the sunset. I can picture her in a small red convertible, waving goodbye as she races away from the place that almost gave her a heart attack.

Oh, no. Hopefully, she didn't get so scared she croaked.

Charlie barks louder, and Luna sighs.

"Fine," she calls out, walking to him and mumbling how stubborn he is.

I bend in front of Katie and grab her hands, squeezing her fingers.

"I won't stop looking until I find her. I know how much you love Brownie." I attempt a smile as I stare at her tear-soaked eyes, but my heart breaks.

Katie nods silently, sniffing.

"Madison!" Luna hollers. "Over here." I race to her, almost tripping as I stand from the position I'm in.

Luna is carrying Brownie, and Charlie looks up at her, shaking in excitement.

"Katie!" I look over at her.

Her eyes widen with happiness and relief as she runs to us. Luna hands her the hamster, and Charlie tugs on his leash to get closer.

"Charlie here found her. I think he likes her." Luna pets her dog.

My shoulders slump, tension rolling off me. This is not the way I wanted to start the festival. Or any day, really.

Katie's mom tucks Brownie safely into her cage and thanks us. I'm not sure why since my cat almost ruined her daughter's happiness.

Ivan returns a few minutes later while I thank everyone for their help and talk to Luna. It seems the entire town came to see what happened, which makes my skin crawl because it is not a good look for the clinic.

"We found Brownie. Actually, Charlie did." I smile at him, but he's shaking with anger. "Uh, are you okay?"

"We need to talk," he says tightly.

"I'm, uh, gonna go." Luna points away from us and unties Charlie, high-tailing it out of here.

"Look, I'm really sorry. I didn't think Boots would react that way. Oh, Boots! He hasn't returned. Did you see him?" I was so nervous about finding Brownie, I blocked Boots from my mind. What kind of cat mom does that make me?

"I haven't, but I'm sure we'll find him. Something else has come up." Ivan grabs me and tugs me away from people and holds up a letter that's crinkled in his hands.

"What is that?" I look between the paper and his face.

"Read it."

I grab the letter and skim the contents, my blood icing when I read it's a complaint stating I've practiced on wild animals without the proper certification. I re-read the letter from the Board of Veterinary Medical Examiners, shaking my head.

"Where did you get this?" I ask him.

"Rose saw it this morning in the mailbox when she went into the clinic to organize a few things for the festival. She had forgotten to give it to us."

"This can't be right." I stare at him.

"We're under investigation."

"This isn't true." I lift the letter.

"You and I know that, but someone filed a complaint against you." Ivan runs a hand down his face.

"Today is going from bad to worse." I blink back tears. "Uncle James will be back in a week. He can't find out about this."

"I know. The speech he gave us at Roy's when you got here keeps ringing in my head. He's so proud of us. He trusts us blindly to keep this business blooming." He shakes his head.

"We need to prove this isn't true." I widen my eyes.

"I'm going to talk to our lawyer when I get a chance, but he's with his family so I don't want to interrupt his day off."

I nod and look down at the letter, tears building in my eyes. I can't let Uncle James down, especially for a lie like this.

"Who could've done it?" I look up at Ivan.

He shakes his head. "No idea. Our clients like us, and none have complained in person. Trust me, if someone in Sunshine Falls doesn't like something, they'll voice it before taking these types of actions." He points to the letter.

"I thought so." A gray cloud has hung over me, pressing down on my mood. I'm like Eeyore.

I was so excited for today's festival, and now it's ruined. Between Brownie, Boots, who's still lost, and now this, the festival feels more like a nightmare than a celebration.

"What do we do?" I look at the destroyed table and feel like giving up, closing up shop, and going home.

"Pretend everything is great and do our job. We know this complaint has no foundation. We need to trust the system will prove that in the end." Ivan lifts his head and squeezes my fingers.

I wish I was as hopeful as him, but it seems like every time I start to fit in here, something happens to set me back a few steps in my adjustment.

Starting with Ben not leaving me alone.

Ben.

My head snaps up. No.

I grab my phone and send him a message.

Me: Tell me you didn't.

Ben: Didn't what?

Me: File a complaint against us.

Ben: I have no idea what you're talking about. Did someone do that?

Ben: I'm sorry to hear it, but if you need a job, your old one is available.

Me: That won't work with me.

Ben: I'm just letting you know that I'm here for you.

Me: By destroying my career and then claiming to help me? If I find out this was you...

Ben: I only want to be with you, babe.

I pocket my phone, not trusting anything he says. My gut tells me he's involved. His ploy to get me back by burning down someone else won't work. If he knew me at all, he'd know that's not the way to win my heart.

24

♥ ♥ ♥

MADISON

WHAT SHOULD BE AN amazing day blows. Ivan and I have been tense at the table, trying our best to be present with the people that stop by, but after Brownie ran away and the complaint letter, it's clear that neither of us are truly focused on our jobs.

Not to mention the guilt eating at me. If it weren't for me, Ben would have never done this. While I know we have everything at the clinic in good standing, it's a terrible situation. If word gets around, people may believe the complaint is true, and it'll jeopardize our business regardless. Word of mouth isn't always positive marketing.

And then there's Ivan. What will he think when he finds out my suspicions about Ben?

"What's got you looking like your puppy died?" Ezra asks standing before Ivan.

"Nothing." He smiles. "Just tired."

I press my lips together, not wanting to give anything away.

"Are you almost done here?" Ezra asks.

"Yeah. We'll clean up in thirty minutes, and we can hang out." Ivan stacks the few papers we have left. It's a nervous action because they were already perfectly placed.

"Great. I think I saw Luna from far. Does she have a dog?"

"Yeah, an English bulldog."

"Yup, that was her. Man, I haven't seen her since we were eleven or so. How is she?" Ezra smiles.

"She's great. She manages the bookstore in town."

"Really?" His brows lift in curiosity.

"Do you like to read?" I ask him based on his reaction.

"I do."

Ezra stays by our table until we finish. He tells me about living in Austin, his career as a chef, and what it was like growing up in a small town. It's a nice distraction from the mess that awaits us come Monday morning when we're back at the clinic.

It's nice getting to know him, and it makes the last thirty minutes pass by quickly. When it's time to clean up, he helps us put the pamphlets, treats, and other products we didn't sell in boxes. Ivan and I carry them to his car when we're done while Ezra talks to a woman who was friends with his parents.

"Let's enjoy ourselves today and figure out the rest later," Ivan whispers when I'm placing a box with supplies in his trunk.

I turn around to look at him with a frown.

"I know. I'm going to take Boots home." I step forward.

Ivan holds my arm and looks at me with a smile.

"Want me to drive you so it's faster?"

"No, stay and hang out with Ezra."

"Are you sure?"

I nod, squeezing his arm. "Thanks, though."

"You're coming back, right?"

"I think so."

His eyebrows pull together and he tilts his head. "I know you're upset about this. I am, too, but all we can do is enjoy the festival. We haven't done anything wrong."

"You're right." I shake off this mood because if I don't, Ben wins.

He will not ruin this for me because he doesn't know how to lose or own up to his mistakes.

"I'll be back." I lean forward and kiss his cheek.

"Good." He grins. "I'll be here."

We walk back to the table, and I grab Boots's leash, walking home to drop him off. I'm quick to walk home, feed Boots, and leave him in my room. Taking Ivan's advice, I brush off the complaint and focus on today. It's the only true moment that exists. I'd hate to not enjoy my first Sunshine Falls festival with Ivan.

As I'm walking back to the festival, I run into Luna with Charlie while he does his business. She's looking down at her phone.

"Hey," I say when I reach her.

"Hi. I came out this way so Charlie could do his thing and it wasn't in front of everyone. What are you doing here?" She cleans up after Charlie using a small poop scooper and plastic bag.

"I took Boots home and am going to meet Ivan."

"Oh." She scrunches up her nose.

"Uhh...why the face? He's your cousin." I lift my brows.

"He's with that guy, Ezra." She scowls. Her hand fists around Charlie's leash.

"His best friend, yeah." I nod. "I met him earlier."

Luna rolls her eyes and tugs on Charlie's leash when he tries to move farther away, walking to a garbage bag to throw the bag away.

"I take it you don't like him." I cross my arms, wondering what about Ezra is so bad. He seemed like a nice enough guy.

"He used to call me Lunatic when we were in school. It annoyed the heck out of me." She shakes her head.

"Really? I'm sure it was just immature boy stuff. He was nice earlier," I say as we start walking back toward the festival.

Luna shrugs noncommittally with a huff, and I chuckle. We find Ivan and Ezra talking to a couple of guys. Ivan chuckles, seeming more relaxed. My heart settles as I watch him. At least he took his own advice and is enjoying the afternoon. When he pushes his glasses up the bridge of his nose, I smile to myself. He really is handsome.

"Luna, you remember Ezra, right?" Ivan says when we reach them.

I guess she avoided them to the point that she hadn't even said hello.

"Yeah." She nods.

"Hey, Luna. It's been so long. How are you? Ivan was telling me you work at the bookstore." Ezra smiles at her.

"Hi, yeah, I do." She nods awkwardly.

I fight back a smile and look at Ivan. He comes around to my side and holds my hand. Everything feels right in this moment. The simple action brings me so much peace, as if Ivan were a lifeline to the center of my heart.

"Did Boots stay okay?" He turns to look at me, and I love that he cares.

"Yeah. I think he was tired. You know, with all the excitement of chasing a hamster." I lean into his arm.

Ivan laughs, shaking his head. "I thought we were done for."

I nod, giggling until I remember the letter. Ivan tenses beside me.

"Are you okay?" I glance up at him.

"Yeah, I guess it was wrong choice of words. I should be asking you that, though. You're edgy."

"Can you blame me?" I whisper.

"No, but I want you to enjoy this. We'll be okay." He lifts our laced hands and kisses the inside of my wrist, causing a swarm of goosebumps to break out on my skin.

I nod, swallowing back my suspicions for another day and losing myself in the way he makes me feel.

"Ay, mijo!" A loud and excited shriek sounds behind us.

"Oh, no." Ivan closes his eyes and turns us around slowly.

Clara points at us. "Emma, look how adorable they are. Aren't Ivan and Madison perfect together?" She clasps her hands and looks at us with bright eyes.

"Mom." Ivan runs a hand down his face.

"How dare you lie to me about being together." She slaps his arm. "You didn't say anything when I was by your booth. Instead accusing me of being chismosa."

"You were being a gossip," he says. "Look at what you told your friends without knowing the facts," he defends, but she just slaps his shoulder again.

I chuckle beside him as Ivan tries to protect himself from his mom's hands.

People have gathered nearby, looking at us with curiosity. I ignore them and look at Ivan's mom and aunt as they give us wide, kind of creepy, grins.

"You're causing a scene," Ivan says tightly.

His mom starts saying something in Spanish, swatting her hand around. It looks like she's angry, but then she laughs loudly and pulls me in for a hug. Caught by surprise, I look at Ivan with wide eyes. His lips are pressed into a straight line.

"I was telling him that he shouldn't be embarrassed of people knowing you're together. I think it's wonderful, and you make a beautiful couple. I might even have grandchildren soon." She laughs again, and I cough out at the last part.

Clara releases me, and I avoid Ivan's eyes because his mom thinks we're going to get married and have a baby when we've only gone on one date and my ex-boyfriend is now trying to ruin our career and livelihood.

Wonderful.

When Sara and Ana join us, Ivan groans.

"What's going on?" Ana asks.

"Your brother and Madison." Clara waves her hand toward us.

"Yes, they are standing in front of us." Ana nods slowly, sarcasm filling her voice that I have to chuckle.

"They're dating!" she exclaims.

"Really?" Ana tilts her head and looks at us. "It works." She shrugs, indifferently, and turns to her mom. "I'm going to hang out with Stacy and Bianca."

"And you say I can't keep a secret." Sara smiles triumphantly.

"You knew?" Clara stares at her with wide angry eyes.

"Oops. I think Mia's calling me. Gotta go!" She races away, causing me to laugh at her antics.

"Can we discuss this later, like without an audience," Ivan pleads.

It's adorable how he hates being the center of attention when he's the only guy in his family and lives in a small town.

"Who is that?" Emma asks, signaling to Ezra, who is watching us with a wide smile.

"I'm Ezra, Mrs. Alvarez. Ivan's best friend." He walks toward us.

"Ezra?" Clara's eyes widen. "Come here." She opens her arms to hug him. "I didn't see you there. I was a bit distracted."

He laughs, hugging Ivan's mom. "Don't blame you."

Emma looks at Luna curiously. I don't miss the way Luna glares at her. I smile at her with raised eyebrows, but she rolls her eyes and shakes her head. After spending a little bit of time with their family, my guess is that her mom thinks Ezra is handsome enough for her daughter.

They're matchmaking mommas, and it's hilarious to watch because they definitely have no filter. However, if it were me on the receiving end of it, I wouldn't be laughing.

"How long are you in town for, Ezra?" Emma asks.

"Just a week."

"Oh." She frowns. "Well, hopefully you won't be a stranger anymore." She smiles kindly.

Luna rolls her eyes and shifts away from her mom, likely a move to get out of her view so she doesn't say anything that would compromise her.

After settling down the conversation and Ivan promising he'll go to his parents' house for a late lunch tomorrow, we roam around the festival. Different clients say hello with warm smiles. I hope they remain as supportive if word gets out about this fake accusation.

"Are you hungry?" Ivan breaks my thoughts.

"Not yet." I spot a table with jewelry and other accessories. "Oh, let me see that a sec."

"Go on." Ivan chuckles.

"I'll go with you," Luna says, handing Charlie's leash over to Ivan. I'm impressed how patient the dog has been, enjoying the festival and being playful with people who stop to pet him.

"Look how cute this is." I grab a necklace with a small star on it. Smiling to myself, I think back to dancing under the stars with Ivan last week.

"That's adorable."

"Hi, ladies," a woman says from the other side of the table.

"Hey, Trish, you have such cute stuff." Luna smiles at the woman.

"Thanks. We got new pieces in for the festival. It was hard to not display them at the store before today." She giggles.

"I bet. Trish, this is Madison."

"It's nice to meet you," I say. "Your jewelry is beautiful."

"Thank you. Are you enjoying the festival? It's your first in Sunshine Falls, right?"

"It is." I can't help but laugh. "I feel like everyone's watching me."

"You'll get used to it." She waves me off with a smile.

I buy the necklace after talking to Trish for a bit. Then, I go in search of Ivan. He's standing with a crowd of kids, some of them I recognize as clients at the clinic.

"Play with us." One of the boys looks at him with a toothy grin, holding a soccer ball against his waist.

"Sure." Ivan nods, and Luna grabs Charlie from him.

"Um, is that a good idea?" I tease.

He raises his eyebrow, looking at me with a lopsided smile.

"Football may not be my sport, but fútbol is."

"That's the same sport." I stare at him.

"Soccer. I can kick a ball."

"I'd like to see this." I smirk, standing back.

"So much for my support system," he says dryly.

"I'm only joking. I can't wait to see you play soccer."

Luna and I stand back while the boys kick the ball. Ivan makes a big show of failing to steal it from them until he grabs it and kicks hard across the field.

"Wow," one of the boys says in awe.

Impressed, I follow the ball, but instead of going toward the goal it leans right and hits a tree branch. I can't help but laugh at his missed aim.

"The bird!" the goalie calls out.

"What?" Ivan asks, jogging toward him.

"You killed the bird." The boy points an accusing finger at him.

Luna and I walk toward the tree, and sure enough, there's a small, injured bird on the ground. Ivan's eyes are wide as he kneels beside the little guy or gal, trying to revive him. He touches its chest, looking at me with panicked eyes. I help him, figuring two vets against one bird will be in our favor.

"Come on, birdie. Don't do this to me in front of these kids. Get up and fly," Ivan whispers.

"Really?" I stare at him with raised brows.

"Do CPR!" A boy calls out.

"That's not..." Ivan shakes his head.

"Yeah. That's what they do on TV. Give it CPR, Dr. Romero. It'll come back to life," a second boy says.

The rest of the boys start to chant, "CPR, CPR."

"I can't believe this," Ivan mumbles while I hold back my laughter.

"I guess you have no choice. We know it doesn't work that way, but if this bird dies and you didn't give it CPR, those kids are going to blame you."

Ivan grunts, takes a deep breath, and raises a hand.

"Okay, okay." He looks at the boys over his shoulder. "But you need to be quiet so it doesn't get stressed."

He holds the bird's beak and looks at me.

"This is ridiculous."

"Do it for the kids." I bite down my smile.

"I can't believe this. Kissing a bird. Here goes nothing." He bends down and barely breathes into the bird's mouth, and then taps a finger down on its chest.

He repeats the action, and the boys stand in a circle around us. Luna covers her mouth, her shoulders visibly shaking with laughter. I swallow down my own cackles threatening to burst out of me.

"Keep going, Dr. Romero. I think it's coming back to life," the boy who started this whole thing says.

Ivan glares at him, but I elbow him. Whether we're in or out of the office, we need to be kind to our clients no matter how embarrassing a situation is.

Or hilarious for those of us watching.

He goes in for another mouth-to-mouth breath, and the bird's eyes widen. It clutches on to Ivan's top lip, biting him.

"Whoa!" Ivan's scream is muffled, and he sits back, trying to grab the bird, now flapping its wings while attacking his enemy. Everyone laughs at the scene, as if it were a prepared skit.

"Oh, my goodness." I cover my mouth and stare at the scene before me. Talk about attack of the birds.

"Help," he mumbles awkwardly, swatting his hands in front of it in an attempt to get the bird to release him.

I try to help but can't stop laughing long enough to keep my hands still. The bird flies away angrily, and Ivan sits there with a swollen lip. Thankfully, he didn't get cut.

He sputters, wiping his tongue.

"I think I ate feathers. So much for support, huh?" he says, touching his lip and grimacing.

"I'm sorry, but it was hilarious." I giggle, extending a hand to help him up. "Are you okay?"

"I don't know." He shakes his head. "I need to get this checked out."

"I'll help you." I look at Luna. "We'll be back."

She nods silently, wiping under her eyes and still laughing. I take an unamused Ivan toward Healing Hands since we aren't far from the clinic. We enter, and I grab some ice, handing it to him.

"You can now say you've kissed a bird before." My voice cracks with a chuckle.

"Madison," Ivan growls.

"Right, right." I lift my hands in peace. "Let me see."

Holding his chin, I take a look at his lip and then at the underside of it. It's completely swollen, and I carefully rub a cotton ball with hydrogen peroxide inside and outside his lip to disinfect any cuts that may not be visible at the moment.

"I feel like you've gotten the most use of the hydrogen peroxide lately. I hadn't pegged you for someone who is accident prone." I stare at him with raised brows.

"I'm usually not." His voice is even and a bit muffled due to the swelling.

"Right." I nod incredulously and place the ice back on his lip. "Keep this here."

"It's bad."

"But you made those kids happy." I smile.

"I can't believe I kicked the bird." He shakes his head.

"We need to work on your aim."

He rolls his eyes and wraps his free arm around my waist, catching me by surprise.

"My aim is just fine when it comes to you." He leans in to kiss me, and I place a hand on his chest, keeping a straight face.

"Are you going to kiss me with bird breath?" My brows lift.

Ivan's face falls, and I giggle.

"Kidding, exotic animal whisperer."

"Already told you that you need a new nickname. This one is a mouthful," he counters.

"Bird savior?"

"I do have the battle wound to prove it."

"Very true." I laugh and lean in a bit, softly kissing his lips. "So it feels better."

"Your kisses always make me feel better, whether I'm injured or not." He tightens his hold around my waist.

My smile breaks free. "You're cute, even with a bird attached to you."

Ivan smiles, though it looks like he got plastic surgery and his smile is lost beneath inflated skin.

"Are you okay?" I hold the side of his face.

"I will be, but I need painkillers. I'm trying to be strong in front of you, but man does this hurt like heck."

"You don't need to hide what you're feeling from me." I shake my head. "Acting tough isn't going to win me over. I like that you're vulnerable and sensitive, smart and kind. Any other guy would've told those kids that CPR didn't work that way and disappointed them."

"I should've," he says.

"But you're not any other guy. You're amazing, and I like everything about you, even with a puffed up lip and bird's breath."

He reaches his hand out to me, lacing our fingers. "I like everything about you, too."

I smile, kiss his cheek, and pray that's still true come Monday morning when we discuss the complaint.

"Let me grab you some ibuprofen." I move to the side and reach into a cabinet for some medicine. I hand him two so it'll help with the pain and swelling and get him some water.

Ivan cringes as he drinks, but he can swallow the pills without any real problems.

While he ices his lip, I look around the clinic, hoping that we can quickly disarm the lie and I can keep my job at Healing Hands.

25

♥ ♥ ♥

MADISON

I SIP MY COFFEE and stare off while Boots eats his breakfast. Yesterday was an exciting day, and my body and mind are feeling it today. I want to veg out, watch TV, and not think about anything for twenty-four hours. My mind just needs to get the memo because it's on overdrive.

I've never received a complaint at work before, not informally from a client or formally from the board.

It's caused an array of emotions from being unprepared for this move to failing at everything I do. I've always been confident. Is this an after effect of being cheated on? Not feeling good enough?

You always hear the stories, read about them, but when it happens to you, it's strange.

I shake away those thoughts because I know it's my mind trying to bring me down. What Ben did is on him, not me. I just have to repeat that like a mantra until it soaks in my soul. Channel my inner Taylor Swift and *shake it off*.

That's exactly what I need. Listen to some Taylor Swift and dance out these emotions. I open my music app and play her music, singing off-key. So much for doing nothing, but this is way better than being stuck with a whirlwind of thoughts.

Taylor always heals the soul, heart, and mind. When all else fails, turn on her music and dance it out.

Boots stares at me with fear in his eyes, but I grab him and dance with him in my arms. He meows in complaint and tries to jump away from my strong hold. I lift in him in the air, which causes him to hiss.

"Okay, fine." I place him on the floor. "Party pooper." I stick my tongue out and he moves away from me, sliding one of his golf ball toys with his paw.

When "Tim McGraw"—my favorite Taylor song—comes on I go all out, practically howling like an injured animal. Thankfully, being a singer was never something I strived for because that would've been my downfall.

My singing is for myself, in my safe place and away from any ears. It's the same with my dancing.

I bounce around, only pausing to serve myself some more coffee and take a sip. "Love Story" plays, and I spread my arms wide, singing as if I'm at a concert.

The music stops abruptly mid-verse, and I stare at my phone. Ringing has replaced the music, and Ivan's name flashes on the screen. I take a deep breath and answer the call.

"Hello?"

"Hey, are you done with your concert or did you pick up a coyote?" Ivan's voice rings with amusement, and my heart stops.

"What?" I swallow thickly, looking around the kitchen though I know he's not in here.

"I've been knocking on the door and ringing the doorbell, but your singing has apparently drowned my attempt to get you to open the door."

"You're kidding, right?" Humiliation fills my body, my face burning.

"I am not." He snickers.

"How did you even hear me?" My face heats.

"I think the entire neighborhood could." Ivan laughs, unable to hold back any longer.

"Kill me," I mumble. "So, you're outside?" I look down at my clothes, my heart pounding.

"Yeah, can you open for me?"

"I need to change. Wait outside a few minutes." There is no way I'm going to open the door when I'm wearing my most loved (read: overused) pajamas. They have holes and the fabric is so thin it might be see-through at this point.

"Sure, but keep singing to keep me entertained," he jokes.

"Ugh. I'm hanging up now. And maybe I'll only talk to you through the door so I won't have to face you."

Ivan guffaws, and I hang up on him, racing to my room to change. Most of my clothes are dirty. I really need to do laundry. That was part of my plan for today. Plans that are apparently about to change.

Grabbing a T-shirt dress, I throw it on, wrap my hair in a bun, and slip my feet into flip-flops. I take a deep breath, embarrassed to face Ivan after he heard my singing. Hopefully, it was a muted version of what I really sound like and he heard Taylor more than me.

I rush to the door and swing it open. Ivan is leaning against the porch column, one hand in his pocket and a foot crossed over the other. I caught him midway brushing his fingers through his hair.

He smiles, eyes shining with mischief as his brows lift slowly above the frame of his glasses.

"I didn't think I'd get a concert today. Shall I enter and you continue?"

"No one should've heard that."

My face burns, and I just know my cheeks and neck match my hair color. Ivan chuckles and pushes off the column, walking toward me. His fingers skim my cheek.

"I'm not no one. No need to be embarrassed, City Girl."

"I like the nickname you used on our date better. Mi Estrella." I shift on my feet, looking at him.

"Yeah?"

I nod.

"Me, too. It's a better reflection of what you are in my life." He winks.

My body tingles with delight at his words.

Ivan picks up a bag by the door and stands straight.

"What's that?" I ask.

"Breakfast. I thought we could discuss the complaint and go over a game plan since we'll be busy tomorrow with clients." He presses his lips together, and that pressure in my chest builds.

The pit of my stomach bottoms out as I nod and step into the house. Not sure I'll be able to eat, but I need to face this and tell him who I believe is behind this. I'd rather do it in private than at work with our employees around.

"Would you like some coffee?" I turn to look at him when we're in the kitchen.

"That'd be great, thanks."

I fix him a cup and hand the mug to him. Boots finally comes out of hiding and rubs against Ivan's leg.

"You remembered you liked me, huh? Or are you choosing me now that you've heard your owner's singing?" He jabs, petting Boots.

"Funny," I deadpan.

Ivan wears a goofy grin, and I can't help but match his smile. My heart soars when I'm around him.

"What did you bring?" My gaze lands on the bag.

"An assortment of pastries from the bakery." He pulls out a box and opens it.

My mouth waters as I see his mom's pastelitos.

"Can I have that one?" I point at a guava and cheese one before reaching for plates. I tried it when I took them to the clinic, and it was like an explosion of deliciousness on my tongue.

"You can have whatever you want, Mi Estrella."

A wave of butterflies rushes in my belly. I love hearing him use that nickname. It's unique to us and a memory that will always be special.

"What?" Ivan asks.

"Huh?" I lift my brows, shaking my head.

"You're staring at me with some weird expression. Do I have something on my face?"

"No! I got distracted. So pastries. Yummy." I'm rambling. "Let's sit at the table." I take the plates with me along with my coffee mug while Ivan grabs his mug and the box.

Ivan chuckles and serves me the pastelito while he grabs a muffin. I take a bite, moaning at the flaky deliciousness. The dough is crispy and the filling is sweet and tart at the same time, balancing it all out.

"So good," I say, covering my mouth with my hand.

"I'm glad you like it." He chuckles, taking a bite of his muffin and washing it down with some coffee.

"I know this isn't what we want to do today, but we should look over the information they sent us with a clear head and no distractions." He pulls out the letter from his bag and opens it.

"We have twenty-one days to respond with all the necessary documents and reports they're asking for, but I want to send everything over as soon as possible," Ivan says, looking at me.

"I agree." I nod. "We have the proof to discredit this."

"I keep trying to think who could've done this." He runs a hand down his face. "Usually our clients talk to us directly. It's not like we had wild animals roaming around or in contact with other animals that clients could be concerned about illnesses."

I chew on my lip, looking at him as I come up with the right words.

"My dream of having a llama backfired on us." He shakes his head.

"It didn't." He can't feel guilty for this. "I think I know who it was," I blurt out and brace myself for the consequences.

Ben is manipulating this situation and using a scare tactic because of me, not because Ivan is a good person who wants animals to be well and treated.

"What? Who?" His eyebrows pull together tightly.

"I think it was Ben. I don't have proof, but it's the only logical explanation. He's bent on me going back to him and to the clinic. He showed up the day we had the llama, and knowing the way he can charm anyone, he might've gotten information about the clinic from an employee without it seeming like it's strange."

"Ben?" he says slowly. "That jerk." His hand curls tightly around the mug.

"I'm so sorry, Ivan. It's my fault. Had I not come here, this wouldn't have happened." I take a slow breath. "Clearly, his aim is to get me out of the clinic."

"Don't take the credit for that guy's scheming. Do you have any proof?"

"No. I texted him but he's too smart to admit anything in writing." I open my messages and slide my phone toward him.

Ivan reads the messages with a scowl.

"This guy's a piece of work. I don't know what you ever saw in him."

I flinch at his harsh tone.

"He wasn't like this when we were together." Why am I defending Ben? No, I'm defending my choices. I fell for the sweet-talker.

Ivan's eyes snap up to mine. He shakes his head, remaining silent.

"I need to talk to Steve so he can confirm I called him as soon as we saw the coyote." He jots down a note to call him tomorrow.

"Good idea."

"We need to send copies of our licenses and certifications," he says. "Let's get everything in order even if we know that there's no foundation to this threat."

I nod, grabbing a notepad and pencil. I write down the tasks we'll have to complete this week.

"We should talk to our lawyer," I tell him.

"I already called him and asked for a meeting, but he can't see us until Wednesday."

"Our first coffee break." I frown. "I shouldn't have moved here." I shake my head.

"Hey." Ivan holds my hand. "This isn't on you. I wish we had proof this guy did that, but ultimately it doesn't matter if we're being investigated. How did he even get this processed so quickly?"

I hadn't thought about the timeline. I think back to what I know about Ben.

"Wait." My eyes widen. "I think he has a family member that works for the board."

"You're kidding." Ivan snorts humorlessly. "Thankfully, I have some training on wild animals from college. It isn't a certification, but hopefully it'll favor us. They can't pin it on you, like the complaint says, if I'm the one treating the animals."

I nod, finishing my pastry though my excitement about it has diminished. My head's a mess, and I barely focus on our work or what Ivan talks about. All I want is to grab Ben and give him a dose of his medicine. Unfortunately, I'm not wired for revenge.

"Maybe I should step back from the clinic."

Ivan's eyes narrow. "Why? You want to give him the upper hand? Or make him think he won?" He shakes his head.

"I want to fix this. If his goal is for me to return to Dallas, then I can pretend to and have him drop the accusation."

"And when he realizes you lied, he'll do it again and again. I know guys like him. They're the high school jocks of the world. They aren't used to losing." He runs his hand through his hair, mussing the waves.

"You read him correctly." Ben will make this a regular thing.

"Guys like him made my life miserable growing up, but I won't lose you because of him." He holds my hand again, and I smile sadly.

I'm the one who doesn't want to lose him because of Ben's donkey butt ways.

Ivan's ringing phone interrupts the conversation. "Sorry, I gotta get this."

He picks up the call and smiles apologetically.

"Hey, Sara."

I sit back and let him have his conversation while re-reading the requirements the board is asking for. It's ridiculous to have to even go through this, but I'll follow protocol to prove I'm innocent.

"Yeah, yeah. I'll grab ice on the way," Ivan says, rolling his eyes.

I silently laugh to myself while he finishes the conversation.

"Sorry about that," he says once he's hung up. "Sara is wordy. I almost forgot about lunch at my parents' house. I gotta go. We can finish talking about this tomorrow."

"Yeah, don't worry." I stand, grabbing the plates and mugs, and take them to the sink.

"I'll talk to you later." Ivan grabs the letter.

"Do you mind if I keep that so I can keep working on some stuff?" I ask.

"Yeah, sure. Take it to work tomorrow."

"Of course." I feel stilted and robotic around him, as if my guilt is conflicting with the easiness we've had recently, and I hate it.

"Bye." Ivan smiles, but the lines around his eyes and forehead scream of stress.

"Enjoy your lunch." I hold on to the open door.

"Thanks."

He walks down the porch steps and waves before sitting in his car. He didn't even kiss me.

And you didn't kiss him either.

Shaking those negative thoughts, I head back inside and tell myself that Ivan and I are fine. This doesn't affect our relationship, especially after he said that he wasn't going to lose me because of it.

It's still not a good idea to date a co-worker. It's like I didn't learn my lesson the first time around, and now I'm falling for my partner.

Ivan is nothing like Ben, though. He's actually one of the good ones.

26

♥ ♥ ♥

IVAN

MADISON WALKS INTO MY office while holding out a paper. "Hey, here's a copy of my veterinary license." She pauses, looking at me. "Is everything okay?" Her brows furrow.

I thought I had schooled my face, but it seems she reads me better than I thought. I nod, grabbing the paper she's extending.

"Right, and I sing just like Taylor Swift." She sits on a chair, and I chuckle.

"I love your sarcasm." I shake my head. "It seems clients have found out about the complaint. They don't know what it's for exactly, but I've had to answer questions all morning about their pets being safe and cared for."

Madison frowns, slumping back in her seat. "I haven't heard anything."

"That's good, then. Hopefully, my responses will douse the rumors. I really don't want to publicize this."

"No." The words come out rushed and harsh. "Sorry." She sighs.

"I get it. Don't worry." I smile at her. "Steve is going to send the necessary documents and a letter stating he was called immediately when we got the coyote in here.

288

And the llama ended up being someone's pet, not a wild animal."

We've barely had a moment to talk today, and it's nice to sit with her, even if talking about this stressful situation.

"Perfect." She purses her lips.

I take in the worry in her face and wish I could make it disappear. Her eyebrows are permanently crinkled, and her bright eyes are dim. This is a trial in our careers. We're not the first or last vets to get a complaint, but I wish it was an honest one instead of a manipulative tactic by her ex.

That guy really is something. He's the type that doesn't hear the word no often, and when he does he throws a fit. A part of me is afraid she'll give in just to save James's business. I'll refuse to let her do that, though.

"By the way, I told Aaron that if he had an opening before Wednesday to let us know." I update her on when we might meet with our lawyer.

"Good." Madison nods. "Hopefully he can squeeze us in, so we can send this over and have things moving along. I feel like the longer we wait, the more this pressure piles on us."

"I agree. Do you want coffee? I need to get away from this office for a few minutes." I stand, stretching my arms.

Madison remains seated, eyes focused straight ahead. I glance around and then down, noticing that my shirt lifted a bit when I raised my arms. I lift my brows and clear my throat. Madison looks up at me with a pink blush on her cheeks. Smirking, I round my desk and extend my hand.

"You can stare at me all you want, Mi Estrella."

289

Her lips press into a straight line as her blush deepens, and she grabs my hand to stand.

"Don't get shy on me now." I wink, kissing her forehead.

She relaxes, taking a soft breath. When her arms wrap around my back, I hold her close and cup her cheek.

"We're gonna be okay." I lean down and brush my lips with hers.

This complaint is weighing on both of us, but I'm glad we've got each other to lean on. This woman has conquered my heart, and as much as I tried to fight falling for someone I work with, I was up against the impossible. She's everything I've always wanted in a woman.

When I was younger, I'd think Madison was way out of my league. But now I know that there are no leagues and games. There are just people who come together in a way that is just meant to be.

We walk to the staffroom in silence, and I open the door for her to enter. It's empty, and we both get around to making our coffee.

"I liked today's joke," she says, looking at the card.

"Thanks. I wasn't feeling too inspired, but it came to me."

"It's appropriate for the situation." She snorts.

I laugh at her and add creamer to my coffee.

"Llama Mia seems like something a llama would tell a vet. Or maybe that's just in our brains since humans like puns so much. Whatever the reason, it's funny," Madison rambles.

"Thanks." I shake my head in amusement, drinking my coffee.

"They're dat—" Kate stops speaking, staring at us with wide eyes as she and Tom come into the room. "The date. What's today's date?" She looks at Tom.

I cross my arms and stare at them, careful not to spill my coffee. She thinks she's being slick. Madison's brows lift as she looks at me and then our employees.

"It's the sixth, I think," Tom says, playing along.

"Nice try." I shake my head. "Yes, Madison and I are dating, but our personal life will not interfere with how we run Healing Hands, and it certainly will not affect your jobs. I expect privacy and respect."

"Of course." Kate nods.

"I know it's unconventional and you might worry about our work environment since James and I never had a situation like this."

Madison chuckles into her coffee mug, and Tom covers his laugh with a cough.

"Wait, this isn't coming out right. It's a new situation, but our priority is Healing Hands." So much for my professional and authoritative speech.

"I'm glad you don't find my uncle attractive," Madison says, unable to hold back her laughter.

Kate and Tom laugh as well.

"I give up." I throw a hand in the air.

"Don't. We love your awkwardness," Madison says.

I roll my eyes and rinse my cup once my coffee finishes. "Time to work." I clap my hands.

Madison chuckles behind me as we leave the staffroom. It's a nice change from her mood this weekend. I'd make a fool of myself every day if I heard her laugh like this. It would be my life goal to make Madison happy if she'd let me.

"I'm glad I could provide some humor on this Monday."

"I needed that. Thank you." She leans in and quickly drops a kiss on my cheek, making me feel like a king. I almost puff out my chest like a proud rooster.

"You're welcome. I need to get to my next patient."

She nods, smiling, and walks into her office while I head to the exam room. Harold is waiting for me outside the exam room with his signature frown.

"Evelyn is worried about Spots's black gums." His voice is flat and uninterested. I have no idea why he still works here when he always seems miserable.

"Thanks." I open the door to find Boots sitting on top of Spots, who doesn't have spots but more so a white mark down her chest. The Portuguese water dog is walking around the room giving Boots a horseback ride. Or would it be a dogback ride?

"Isn't this hilarious!" Evelyn, my client, says, recording the scene before her.

"Uh... It's something." I shake my head, chuckling. Working with animals is never a dull moment.

Harold simply huffs.

"Spots was so nervous, but this cat has really helped calm her down."

"I'm glad to hear that." Maybe Madison is right, and Boots can be our mascot.

He jumps off the dog and looks at me skeptically. Spots goes after him, wanting to play.

"It seems Spots is doing well." I look at Evelyn. "You're concerned about his gums, though."

"I am. His gums are black, and I read that could be a sign of heart or lung issues. I can't lose Spots." Her eyes water.

"Black gums can be a sign of disease, but some dogs naturally have black gums. Portuguese Water Dogs are one of those breeds. I'll examine him to be on the safe side."

"Thank you, Dr. Romero."

I walk to Spots, and pet him, but Boots meows. I look at the cat a moment before turning my attention on Spots. Boots hisses and jumps on Spots.

"Hey, boy, it's okay. I'm just going to make sure your new friend is healthy." I swear this cat is possessive of his friends and hates me being close to them. So much for being the first one to help him when they brought him in.

Boots reaches out to scratch me when I try to get close to Spots again, and Evelyn gasps.

"Oh, my. I think he's protecting Spots." She shakes her head.

"It seems that way, yes." I nod, taking a deep breath.

"I'll grab him." Harold steps in and reaches for Boots, who happily allows Harold carry him.

"You've gotta be kidding me," I mumble, getting closer to Spots.

Boots leaps out of Harold's grip and stands between the dog and me.

Evelyn giggles, stepping in to hold Spots, which Boots doesn't get offended by. So I'm the problem. I'm going to make that cat love me if it's the last thing I do. I glare at him in determination and do my job, assessing Spots with Evelyn's help in keeping Boots happy.

During my lunch break, it's going to be him and me alone, though. I'll give him all the treats until he loves me back.

When I finish, I walk Evelyn and Spots to the front desk. She's much happier now that I've confirmed that Spots is healthy and his dark gums are a normal trait for his breed. When we reach the waiting room, Kate is cleaning up the floor, and Rose is holding back her laughter by covering her mouth.

"What's going on?" I look at her.

"A dog vomited," she responds with humor in her voice. "Sorry." She turns around her laughter. What in the world is so funny about a dog puking?

"I'm so sorry." A woman calls out, face red like a tomato.

I look at Evelyn with a smile. "Thank you, and we'll see you for Spots's annual checkup in a few months."

Once she leaves, I give Kate my attention.

"Do you need help?"

"No, no. Kate's got it." The young woman shakes her head furiously.

"I'm okay, Dr. Romero." Kate looks up at me with wide eyes.

"You sure? I can—"

"No!" the woman yells.

Taken aback by her reaction, I nod and step away. That's when a pink underwear catches my eye. It is mixed with the puke on the floor. I don't need to see any of my client's unmentionables.

"Right. I'm gonna..." I point behind me, starting to walk before I turn around and bump into Rose, who has gotten herself under control, and make her drop the cleaning spray. The sound scares the dog, who starts barking and running in circles, on the vomit, making this unnecessarily messier than it is.

Kate stares up at me with a glare, her uniform dirty, and I grimace.

"I'll give you a raise," I blurt out and run out of there.

Lesson learned. When a client tells you they don't want your help, it might be because their pet threw up a pair of their underwear and they don't want you to see.

Madison's eyes widen when she sees me rushing down the hallway.

"What—?"

I lift my hand, cutting her off. "Don't ask."

"Um, okay. Have you seen Boots?" She swishes her head, looking around.

"Yeah, he was riding on one of my patients."

"Excuse me?" She shakes her head and blinks her eyes.

"Like a horse. He has a thing for riding dogs. I bet if he spoke, he'd say 'Run, peasant,' and lift a paw."

Madison continues to blink at me with a concerned expression. I don't blame her. I'm concerned for myself at the moment.

"Sorry, I saw a client's underwear."

Her eyes widen.

"I really need to work on my delivery today. Her dog puked the underwear. I'm gonna go back to work."

"Wait. Is the dog okay?" Her eyes bug.

"Yup." I nod quickly, pursing my lips. "Kate's on it. The client practically kicked me out."

"I'm confused."

"Me, too." I laugh, unable to hold it back anymore. "The dog ate a pair of her underwear and threw it up. The woman's embarrassed."

"Oh." Madison bites down on her lips.

"Uh, huh. Anyway, I'm going to look for Boots and make him love me."

She opens her mouth to speak but then closes it. "You know what, I'm not going to ask."

"That's best." I nod.

When I find Boots, I take him to my office and grab a ping-pong ball. I sit on the floor with him, tossing it and prompting him to grab the ball. He tilts his head, judging me. I bet he's thinking, *I'm not a dog you human fool."*

I should've grabbed a ball of yarn, but unfortunately I don't own a *Mary Poppins* bag. I juggle the ball in my hand, thinking of another way to get Boots to like me. If I fill him up with treats, I'll have an incident similar to the one in the waiting room, and I don't feel like cleaning up a mess like that.

Boots walks to me, hopping to try to take the ball from my hands. I lift my brows and pause. I was going about this all wrong. He needs to be enticed by what I have, so he'll want to play with me.

I juggle it again, laughing when he goes crazy hopping around trying to steal it. He walks back and gets in position to pounce. I throw the ball faster between my hands and wait for him. When he comes at me, I throw it in the air, catching him off-guard.

We play like this for a while until I give in and let him win. When he grabs the ball, he looks at me with arrogance, and then plays soccer with it by kicking it across the floor with his paws. I bet he wouldn't hit any birds.

Boots comes to my lap, dropping the ball between my crossed legs.

"You wanna play?" I smile at him.

He pushes the ball toward me with his nose. I grab it, juggling again, and he goes crazy. Smiling to myself, I lean against the wall and continue to play with him until he climbs on my lap and curls his body. I pet him softly, feeling like I at least accomplished one thing successfully.

Hopefully, settling this complaint is a lot easier than juggling things around until they trust that we're doing our job correctly.

27

♥ ♥ ♥

MADISON

I walk into the staffroom excited about our first Wednesday coffee break as a team. I was afraid we'd have to postpone it another week, but Aaron can't meet with us until the afternoon.

"Bean me up, Tom," Kate says, holding out her mug to him.

I laugh at her expression and take a seat at the rectangular table, waiting for my turn to make my coffee. Ivan is talking to Rose on the other side of the room, and I assume it's about the complaint. She's the only employee who knows since she received the letter.

My phone buzzes in my pocket, and I fish it out to see who it's from. Uncle James and Aunt Susan haven't had a lot of phone service, so talking to them has been difficult, and I spoke to my parents this morning so it shouldn't be them.

Ben: Hi, I wanted to see how you're doing. Have you resolved the issue with the complaint?

I roll my eyes at his message and breathe in patience. Anyone who reads this message would guess he's sincere, but I'm still not convinced it wasn't him. All the signs point to him except the piece of information where he found out about the other wild animals like the coyote.

Or he didn't and his timing with the llama was just right for him to hang on to something.

Me: Yup, I'm great. It's all resolved.

Ben: Really? So quickly?

Me: Of course. It was a false alarm.

Ben: The clinic had a llama without the proper requirements.

Ding, ding, ding. And that is how you catch a liar.

Me: Llama?

Ben: Yeah, isn't the complaint about treating wild animals without the certification necessary.

Me: I never told you what the complaint was about.

Typing bubbles appear and disappear without a response. I'm fuming that he'd go this far to try to get me back as if he didn't know me at all. My heart pounds as my fingers type out a message.

Me: I know your moral compass isn't the best but I overlooked it in the past because I cared about you and was too big of a fool to stand up to you. Drop the false complaint, and I'll keep your dirty secrets to myself. Don't test me, Ben. I have proof of negligence and covering your behind with clients so they wouldn't sue.

I drop my phone on the table, causing a loud crash. Everyone looks at me with raised eyebrows, and I scrunch up my face.

"Sorry."

Ivan stares at me as if communicating something but I can't read his mind, so I shrug. If Ben is smart, he'll retract his attempt to bring us down and step away, letting me live my life. I hate that it has to come to threats, but he's not going to get away with manipulating me. I wasted enough time thinking he loved me. I'm not his trophy.

When the coffee maker becomes available, I stand to brew a cup. Ivan walks toward me with narrowed eyes.

"What happened?" he whispers.

"I'll tell you later, but I think I may have resolved our issue." I look at the rest of the team out of the corner of my eye, silently communicating with him.

"How?"

"Later," I say, smiling. I'm so happy I could grab his face and kiss him. Ivan tilts his head as if trying to read my mind, and I giggle.

"So, are y'all gonna be like our parents now?" Kate asks, and Ivan coughs deeply.

"You scared him," Tom says, laughing.

"What?" I turn to look at her.

"You know, like when couples adopt the younger people in their group and act like parents? Because you're dating."

"Kate," Ivan growls. "What did I tell you the other day?"

"Right, privacy. It was just a question. It's not like I asked how many times you've kissed."

"Oh, my goodness." I turn around, my cheeks burning red.

"Can we start this?" Harold asks, unimpressed.

"Yes." I face them again and nod. "My idea for our weekly coffee breaks is to get to know each other better and decompress—so no conversations about work." I smile at them.

"Or about your relationship." Kate chuckles when Ivan glares at her. "I'm only kidding, but it's too fun not to mess with Ivan. After all, I had to pick up dog puke with an underwear." She arches a brow.

"And I appreciate that." Ivan nods.

"You mentioned a raise." She smirks.

"No work talk," I remind them and look at Harold. He's the only one I haven't had a real conversation with. "Harold, what's your favorite animal?"

The grumpy old man frowns.

"Harold loves sloths," Tom says. "He watches videos of them on his phone during his lunch break."

"Tom, I can answer for myself."

"Well, on with it then." Tom claps his hands, clearly teasing the old man.

"Sloths," Harold says.

"That's great." I nod, eyeing Ivan. He simply shrugs as if he's also been unsuccessful in bonding with the man.

"Have you seen the video of that kid who was zip-lining and crashed into a sloth that was on the line?" Rose asks. "I think they had to wait like thirty minutes for the sloth to move away."

"It was fifteen minutes," Harold corrects her.

"So you saw it?" I grin.

"Yeah," he says gruffly but the ghost of a smile appears on his lips. That's a win in my book.

"Do you prefer living in Sunshine Falls or Dallas?" Kate looks at me.

"Sunshine Falls is winning me over. It's different than a city, and a much-appreciated change. Sometimes unexpected decisions turn out great."

"I agree," Rose says. "I met my husband that way."

"That's amazing. How long have you been married?" I ask her.

"Fifteen years now. He still tolerates me wanting to drive thirty miles to Target, and I tolerate him taking over the TV during football season. It's a win-win."

I laugh along with her and then ask, "Is Target really thirty miles away?"

"Yup, but so worth the trip. It's in Buttenville, and there are some other great shops and restaurants in the area worth a day trip."

"Wait." I lift my hand. "Did you say Butt-and-ville?" I blink at her.

They all laugh, Harold included, and nod in unison.

"Butt-EN-ville." Kate pronounces slowly. "And yes, they're always the butt of the joke around this area." She laughs loudly, snorting.

"Some people argue that it's actually a long U sound, but it wouldn't be spelled with a double T then." Tom shrugs when we all stare at him. "My mom's a kinder teacher, and she's all about phonics."

"That somehow makes more sense." I tease him.

Our first coffee break is turning out to be a huge success, and I'm so happy about it. I can't wait to have these few minutes of downtime each week and grow a stronger relationship with them. Ivan was right when he told me we're a community here.

The door chime rings, and Rose stands.

"Well, this is the end of our break," she says.

"Thank you all for taking a chance on this idea." I smile genuinely.

"It's a great idea, Madison." Kate nods and rinses her cup.

We all get back to work, and Ivan grabs my arm to stop me outside my office while Tom is in with my patient.

"What happened earlier?"

"Ben basically confessed to framing us." I reach for my phone, and Ivan's brows furrow.

"I doubt that." He snorts sarcastically.

"You doubt incorrectly."

"What?"

303

"I don't know. That didn't make sense but read this." I hand him my phone with the messages open, and his eyes scan it.

"That..." He clenches his jaw.

"He'll retract it," I assure him.

"I don't even want to know what he's done with his patients, but I'm so glad you were smarter than him." He grins. "I was afraid you'd leave just to save our business."

"I considered it," I confess. "But I'm in this for the long haul. And I don't just mean Healing Hands. Us, too." I step close and smile when his arms come around my waist.

"I like the sound of that." Ivan smirks. "I'd hate to tell James we ruined his dream of us working together after that proud speech he gave us."

"There was no way I'd let that happen." I shake my head.

"And as for us, I'd hate even more losing you, and that's a lot coming from someone who lives for his career."

I bite my lip and smile at him. "I'd hate that, too." I lean forward and kiss his cheek.

"I think we need more than that." He holds me tightly and bends me over, kissing me like in a movie scene.

I gasp in surprise and then melt into him, knowing he's got me. After a toe-curling kiss that leaves me breathless, Ivan steps back with a wide smile. A wave of emotions takes over as I look at him. He's everything I never knew I needed.

"Somewhere between arguing and working together, I fell for you," I confess.

"I love you, Madison." His eyes soften and kisses my forehead.

"I love—"

"Madison." Tom calls outs, interrupting the moment. "Oh, sorry." He grimaces and turns away from us.

I close my eyes, cursing his timing. Ivan laughs and taps my lower back.

"Go on and do your job, Dr. Grover. I can't have a partner who slacks around."

"You wish." I jab his chest and smile. "I'll see you later."

"You bet you will." His face is illuminated with joy.

The feeling is mutual. I could float in the air, walk on clouds, live with the Care Bears in their sky paradise. If I were a Care Bear, I'd be named, *Fool In Love*, and I wouldn't want it any other way.

♥ ♥ ♥

"Since you have twenty-one days to respond, let's see if Ben does withdraw his accusation first before getting into this messy part of the process." Aaron looks at us with a confident nod.

"Are you sure he will?" Ivan looks at me.

"I'm positive. He wouldn't risk his pride."

Ivan's jaw tightens. "As if the woman he supposedly cares about is worth less than his pride. Arrogant son of a gun."

I hold his arm and squeeze softly. He takes a deep breath, shoulders sagging. Then, I look at Aaron.

"Are you sure this is the best option? Should we cover ourselves anyway?"

"You haven't done anything wrong." He smirks.

"That's true."

"Besides, it's not like you're hoarding wild animals and endangering anyone. Honestly, his complaint has no basis, and the board would likely drop it as soon as they review the information."

"Ben knew that, too." I shake my head. "I bet his plan was that we'd get so stressed and fearful, that I'd decide to step back in order to save my uncle's business."

"I've seen it done in all aspects of life. It's a manipulation tactic more than a real threat." Aaron frowns. "I'm sorry you had to go through that."

I nod, smiling at him.

"Okay, so we'll wait to see if we receive any news, and if we haven't heard back in a week, we'll plan to send over our proof," Ivan says, tapping the table at Aaron's office.

"Exactly." Aaron nods.

"Thank you." I look at Aaron.

"You're welcome. It'll all end in a scare."

We stand from the table, and I feel so much lighter after talking to Aaron, and he confirmed what I already believed. Ben's got nothing on us that would be real substantial proof to ruin our reputation.

And he knows that.

He lost. For the first time since I found out he cheated on me, I feel like I can breathe easily.

We walk out of the office into the warm afternoon, and Ivan grabs my hand. I look over at him with a smile.

"If we were in a movie, I'd need to do a grand gesture to win you back," he says, tugging me closer.

"But you never lost me." I place my hand on his chest. "Besides, I prefer small gestures. They're the underrated gestures in life."

"I agree." His eyes stare into mine before he leans in and kisses me.

"Ohhh! This is adorable!" A loud squeal interrupts us.

"Dear God, no," Ivan mumbles.

I step back and look to my left, seeing Sara and Mia standing before us, clutching their hands.

"Aren't they perfect together?" Sara looks at Mia.

"Yes! And we didn't have to intervene so his crush knew he liked her. Ivan is growing up and taking charge of his life. Good job, primo." Mia pats his shoulder.

I laugh at his expense. "This is what we get for kissing out in the street."

"Very true." He arches a brow. "But I couldn't help myself."

My grin is wide and silly and full of happiness.

"Well, we'll let you get to it." Mia waves at us, and they leave.

"It's like they pop up out of nowhere." He sighs, grabbing my hand and lacing our fingers.

"They seem to have a gift for that." I giggle.

"For real." He squeezes my hand. I don't think I'll ever get tired of such a simple touch.

"Do you have any plans now?" His eyes skim along my face.

"Nope."

"Good, good." He nods. "What if we have dinner?"

"Are you asking me out?" My smile grows.

"I'm not doing a very good job if you have to ask me that."

"I love your awkward ways of asking me out." I lean forward until we're a breadth apart. "I'd go anywhere with you."

"I love you." His husky voice washes over me.

"I love you, too." I'm finally able to say what I wanted to earlier.

Ivan closes the gap and kisses me again to seal our confessions, not caring we're out on the street. I don't either. This man won my heart in a slow-building fire that allowed me to appreciate all of him.

I'm proof that there's hope in changes. The sun always shines after a storm. But especially, that if you stand up for yourself, you open the doors to amazing things.

No one should allow others to hurt them and stay. No one should put themselves down to please another person who so quickly and disrespectfully disregards them. Honest love exists, and I unexpectedly found it.

28

♥ ♥ ♥

IVAN

"WE'VE GOT MAIL." MADISON walks toward me, swaying her hips with a wide smile. She waves an envelope in her hand.

I couldn't care less about mail if I have her in front of me. This past week went by smoother, though we've both been anxious to see if Ben really did withdraw his complaint.

I lean against my desk before my hands land on her hips, and I pluck the letter from her hand and tuck it into my pocket.

"First, I'd like a kiss." I waggle my eyebrows.

"You're impossible." She giggles, resting her hand on my chest and leaning forward.

I close the gap, pressing my lips to hers in a deep kiss. She sways in my arms, and I pat myself on the back for getting that reaction from her.

I've always loved my job, but now I love it more because Madison is here with me. I had my doubts about working with her. Our differences in running this business were pretty great, but we've managed to meet in the middle and compromise.

And after polling clients this last week, we have a pretty vast interest in expanding to a boarding facility.

"I hadn't had a chance to see you this morning." I hold her close to me, never imagining I'd find this. That someone could feel so right.

Madison is that missing link in my life. The piece I thought was an impossibility for me. Yet I've got her in my arms, smiling at me as if I'm the king of the universe.

"You were busy with a patient. How did the dental surgery go?"

"The dog was so loopy after I finished that he kept running into the wall." I chuckle.

"Poor guy." She covers her mouth.

"Yeah. The owner finally grabbed him and got drooled on since he had no control of his mouth."

"Oh my." She giggles. "Anyway..." She steps away from me and lifts her brows. "Are you going to read the letter you stole from me?"

"I took it so I could kiss you. I'd much rather do that." I smirk, grabbing the wrinkled envelope from my pocket. "Whatever news we receive, it could wait until I said hello to my beautiful girlfriend."

"You're going to make me blush."

"I love making you blush." Madison wears her emotions on her face. She can't hide her reactions.

I cut open the envelopes with my fingers and shake out the letter. Madison moves to my side to read it along with me. We're both silent as we read, and then Madison punches the air.

"I knew it!" She turns to me with a wide smile and jumps around.

"You did this." I hug her, spinning her around. Relief fills me that Ben retracted the complaint the way Madison predicted.

"I only did the right thing." She shakes her head.

I hold the side of her face, stroking my thumb along her skin. She's my present and my future. I'm going to marry this woman one day.

Someone clears their throat a few feet away, and we both turn our heads in unison. I drop my hand from her face, and Madison steps back when we see Sara staring at us with a smirk.

Thankfully, she remains quiet though her face speaks enough.

"Hey, sorry. Were you waiting long?" Madison asks her.

"Nope. I just got here, and Rose told me you were in Ivan's office. I'm quite curious what this meeting is about." My sister looks between us.

When it comes to compromising, Madison won out the idea of hiring Sara for the boarding program. I'm happy to help my sister out since she hasn't found a job, but I need it to be clear that she can't act like this is our house.

"Let's meet in my office." Madison waves her hand out toward the open door.

Sara walks into her office, and Madison follows behind her. She looks at me over her shoulder and nods, confident enough for the both of us when it comes to this plan.

I enter the office after them and close the door, taking a seat.

"We're expanding the clinic and working on offering boarding services for clients when they go out of town."

"That's great," Sara says. "What does that have to do with me, though?" Her eyes widen as she stares at me, but it's Madison who speaks.

"We'd like to offer you a job."

"What?" She jumps from her chair. "Do I get to play with puppies all day?"

"I told you this was a bad idea," I tell Madison.

"Not quite." Madison remains professional. "It would be part-time and on a necessary basis since we won't have animals here all the time, but you would be in charge of checking their paperwork, feeding schedule, taking them out, and cleaning up after them. You'd be a pet sitter in simple terms." Madison crosses her hands and looks at Sara.

"Wow."

"We need to prepare the space, so we're looking at starting in a month. Is this something you'd be interested in?"

"It could be." My sister glances at me out of the corner of her eye and her lips curl in a smile. "Work with Ivan? It's like I won the lottery."

"You'd be treated as an employee, Sara." I glare at her.

"But I can still annoy you." Her eyes shine with mischief.

"You will have to follow our rules and respect us despite having ties to both of us." Madison arches a brow with a no-nonsense look that I love.

I chuckle and nod.

"I didn't mention before. When we have animals under our watch, you'll have connection to our cameras to keep an eye out in case there's an emergency and then contact us. It's not something we expect to happen but need to be careful."

Sara nods, sitting forward on her seat and listening to the rest of the details. When we finish, we walk with Sara toward the front desk to get her employee paperwork.

Sara looks at me and says, "Who's the hunk carrying the bunny?"

Madison laughs, and I shake my head.

"That's Mr. Smith, one of our clients," Madison responds.

"Phew, he is one hot man." Sara fans herself.

I widen my eyes and clear my throat. Mr. Smith looks at Sara unamused. No doubt he heard her. My sister isn't exactly quiet. It's a family trait.

Sara smiles at the man, and he scowls.

"He might be pretty, but he's not so nice," she whispers, taken aback by his reaction.

"Sara," I warn tightly.

I better not regret this decision. Nothing is worse than having to fire your own sister.

She smiles and squeezes my arm. "I'm joking but thank you. I appreciate this."

"You're welcome, sis." I give her a side hug. "I gotta get back to work. Madison will give you the rest of the info."

"Sounds great."

♥ ♥ ♥

"Hello, my people." James walks into the clinic almost at closing time wearing shorts and a short-sleeve button down shirt with a floral print on it. His face is red from the sun.

I don't think I've ever seen him dressed like this before. It matches his personality, though. I could see him bartending on a Caribbean island.

After a storm postponed their flight, Madison told me they finally arrived last night. She also mentioned she was going to talk to him about our relationship.

I swallow and smile at him. Our relationship will be different now, and it's a bit intimidating.

"James, how was your trip?"

"Great. I heard your time here was wonderful, too." He winks, and I cough.

He says hello to the few clients waiting to be seen and to Rose. Kate and Harold walk out in that moment and greet him.

"I like this new style, James," Kate says, laughing. "Are you wearing Crocs?"

"Why didn't anyone tell me about these shoes before? They're the most comfortable thing I've ever slipped my feet into," James says.

I laugh, glad he's happy.

He turns to look at me. "Ivan, are you free now? I'd like to talk."

Everyone's eyebrows lift, and I swallow thickly, nodding. No doubt clients and employees all know that this conversation has to do with my relationship with Madison. The town's been talking about it nonstop. I blame my mom, even if she promised that she's kept it to herself. When she gets excited, she doesn't even realize what she's saying until it's out of her mouth.

"Good." He claps his hands. "Let's go."

James and I walk in silence to my office. This is worse than talking to her father because I've admired this man for years. If he doesn't accept our relationship or he finds it conflicting, it'd mess with me.

As soon as we're in my office, he wraps his arms around me, catching me by surprise. With how my family is, a hug shouldn't be a big deal, but James and I have never hugged before.

"Welcome to the family, son."

My brows shoot up, and James laughs.

"Madison told me about the two of you. I have to say I'm happy about it. You're a great man, and I know you'll respect and love my niece."

"I do," I say confidently.

James takes a seat, and I grab the chair beside him instead of behind my desk.

"I'm not sure if you know this, but Susan worked here for a couple of years when I first opened."

"Really? She's not a vet."

"No." He chuckles. "She can't stomach a lot of medical things, but she was the office manager."

"I had no idea."

"I'm going to give you some tips on keeping the love alive when you work together." His grin widens.

Oh, no. I'm not sure I want love advice from my old boss slash girlfriend's uncle. James takes my silence as a green light and begins talking.

"Never take work home with you. When you're together building your relationship, leave the office and your clients behind. Don't talk about it."

This isn't so bad. That's actually good advice.

I nod, encouraging him to continue.

"If you disagree at work, remember it's just a part of you... not your entire relationship. You're professionals here, but what you have is separate from this. It's hard to do that when couples work together."

"I can imagine."

"Yeah, Susan and I learned that the hard way, but we made it work. Even if sometimes she wanted to smash something across my head." He chuckles. "Don't let the stress of work seep into your personal life. Always kiss and make up."

I groan at him talking about us kissing but appreciate his advice.

"Thank you, James."

"You're welcome. After everything she's gone through, she's lucky to have found you."

"I'm lucky, too. She's amazing."

"I know. That goes without saying." He smirks.

I shake my head, laughing. The door swings open, interrupting us, and Madison stands by the door with wide eyes.

"Sorry. I hadn't realized you were talking. I'm gonna..." She points behind her.

"Nonsense. Come in, sweetie. We were talking about you."

"That's what I was afraid of," she mumbles.

I laugh quietly and grab a chair for her.

"I was giving Ivan advice for working together like I did to you yesterday."

Madison frowns. I furrow my brows and look at her. James's advice has actually been constructive.

"Don't forget to always put your relationship first. This place isn't everything in life." He waves his hand around my office.

Madison sinks lower in her chair, as if what James is saying is terrible.

"Most importantly, always make up when you argue." He winks slowly. "It's the best part about fighting."

"Right. Of course. Thank you, James." I glance at Madison, who's shaking her head.

"Anyway, I'm glad everything is good here. Is there anything you want to tell me before I go?"

"Nope." We both shake our heads.

"I'm glad. Healing Hands is in good hands. *Ha!* That's the point. Your hands... Never mind." He shakes his head, not continuing his own joke.

James leaves and Madison sighs.

"That was embarrassing."

"He gave me good advice." We both stand.

"I hope none of it was too personal because last night was awkward at home."

I laugh and get closer to her.

"No, except for that last bit." My hands land on her hips, and I kiss her forehead.

"Good." She sighs and wraps her arms around my neck, relaxing into me.

She yawns, and quickly covers her mouth. Chuckling, I pull her to me.

"Tired?" I lift my brows.

"Yeah. Uncle James and Aunt Susan kept me up late telling me all their stories about Aruba and showing me pictures. It looks like a beautiful place."

"And here I thought I'd be able to take my girlfriend out tonight." I squeeze her hips.

"I'd go anywhere with you, tired or not." She tilts her head, smiling at me.

"I like the sound of that." My lips curl up in a smile.

I have no idea how I got so lucky to meet this woman. The fact that she loves me is a bonus. Maybe my mom's prayers about me finding a nice girl worked. Or maybe fate was waiting for our paths to cross. It must be why we first met at the coffee shop instead of here.

Whatever the reason...however destiny worked its magic...I'm happy it happened. I'm proof that the nice guy doesn't always finish last.

♥ ♥ ♥

Sara's story is coming next, and she has her eyes set on a grumpy single dad. When she becomes his daughter's babysitter, sparks fly. You can pre-order The Single Dad, coming later this year.

Scan the code below to purchase Abi's books or download them on Kindle Unlimited.

Connect with me through my Abi's Sweet Reads email where I share all the bookish news, behind-the-scenes, and book recommendations. Scan the code on the next page to sign-up and receive a free novella, *The Set Up*.

THANK YOU!

♥ ♥ ♥

First and foremost, thank YOU, dear reader, for picking up The Nice Guy and reading my book. Kicking off a new series is always nerve-wracking, but I've been so excited about sharing these characters. You've been the push I needed to put it out in the world with your outpouring of love. I'm so grateful for you.

It takes a village to publish a book, and I owe a ton of gratitude to an amazing group of people! To Daniele for beta reading and answering all my questions, especially contacting her sister back and forth with all my vet questions. Thank you to Mary Elizabeth for giving me invaluable feedback and making this story even stronger and better. Thank you to my editor Victoria for making this this story was the best version. Melody, your design skill astound me. You perfectly captured Ivan and Madison to create a stunning cover.

ARC readers and bookstagrammers, you are amazing. I continue to be in awe of this community and how you show up and support authors and their stories as well as each other. I love being a part of this community!

Savannah, I can't thank you enough for all you've done to support me from the start. I appreciate you more than you know.

For my family, who encourages me daily to follow this dream. Thank you.

ABOUT
ABI SABINA
♥ ♥ ♥

ABI SABINA WRITES SWEET closed door romance full of swoon, sass, and humor. She traded in the big city life for small town living when she moved to Spain.

She hasn't wrangled herself a country boy yet, but she writes books based on charming heroes and small town charm. (And she throws in the city setting every so often.)

She loves coffee, country music, and the mountains. Her goal is to write stories that make you feel, smile, and cheer on love.

Printed in Great Britain
by Amazon